Unleaving

SIÂN COLLINS

Gomer

for Bruce

First published in 2019 by Gomer Press,
Llandysul, Ceredigion SA44 4JL

ISBN 978 1 78562 308 0

A CIP record for this title is available from the British Library.

This book is published with the financial support of
The Books Council of Wales.

Printed and bound in Wales at
Gomer Press, Llandysul, Ceredigion
www.gomer.co.uk

ACKNOWLEDGEMENTS

The staff at Gomer for being willing to take a punt on me; my wonderful family, for unfailingly cheering me on; Bruce, Kate, Matt, Clemmie, Kath, Susie and Lynda for reading drafts and putting me straight; the Arvon Foundation whose residential course gave me the self-belief to begin the novel; the jolly band of talented writers at Wrights Emporium; my dear friends and fellow 'bookies' Monica, Lynne, Jessica, Lesley, Ella and Gwyneth. I owe the greatest debt of gratitude to my editor and 'fellow traveller', Rebecca John. Her wisdom, shrewd critical judgement and constant encouragement have been invaluable.

Last, but never least, I am grateful for the landscapes and communities which inspired this novel – the beautiful Dyffryn Tywi, place of my heart, and the Drakensberg mountain region of KwaZulu Natal, which I first encountered in my twenties and have never forgotten.

SPRING AND FALL

to a young child

Margaret, are you grieving
Over Goldengrove unleaving?
Leaves like the things of man, you
With your fresh thoughts care for, can you?
Ah! as the heart grows older
It will come to such sights colder
By and by, nor spare a sigh
Though worlds of wanwood leafmeal lie;
And yet you will weep and know why.
Now no matter, child, the name:
Sorrow's springs are the same,
Nor mouth had, no nor mind, expressed
What heart heard of, ghost guessed:
It is the blight man was born for,
It is Margaret you mourn for.

Gerard Manley Hopkins (1844-89)

CHAPTER 1

Margaret

The dead bird stirred in the breeze blowing cold through the open cowshed door. Its head lolled sideways at the end of the long neck, the sharp yellow beak still agape. A bright hunter's eye, stilled to dullness. Margaret stood on tiptoe to take a closer look, gritting her teeth against the stabbing pain in her left ankle. She examined the small dark stain on the breast where the bullet had pierced the bird's soft feathers.

'Poor thing! Why's it strung up like that?'

Wil paused in his sweeping of the cowshed floor and regarded the dangling bird. The answer was obvious, wasn't it? Look around you, girl, work it out for yourself. He shrugged his shoulders and returned to his work. Margaret put out a tentative finger to stroke the soft, cold creature and noted its strong-boned wings jutting at ugly angles from the body, the sharp V of the tail feathers stiffened by death.

Mr Hughes, passing through the shed with a barrowload of dung, glanced briefly at the dead bird. 'Vermin, that's all they are, Miss. Scavengers. We hang 'em up there for a warning.'

'Warning of what?' Margaret persisted. She hated mysteries. But Mr Hughes was already gone, heading to the midden in the corner of the yard to deposit the load. A cow shifted restlessly in the gloom at the far end of the shed and kicked against the wooden side of the stall which separated it from the others waiting to be milked. Who would you want to warn? She frowned at her feet, irritated by the puzzle. Faint splashes of bird blood beaded in the muddy straw, red smears on brown. One of the tail feathers was lying on the ground. She picked it up and held it to the light. Delicate filaments of red tipping the grey.

'Look, Wil.' She held the feather out to him. 'It's beautiful isn't it?' He took it from her, turning it slowly in his hand. His fingers were long and slim, not stubby like hers. Strong too. Less than an hour ago she'd been sprawled on the muddy riverbank, her leg trapped in a tangle of broken branches and alder leaves. He had scooped her up and half carried her back to the farm. Served her right, he said, for ignoring his warning not to climb so high, the tree wouldn't hold her weight. For once, though, he hadn't mocked her for being clumsy.

He was still examining the tail feather, his thick dark eyebrows knotted in that funny way when he was thinking hard about something.

'Dad strings them up like that to keep the other birds away. It scares them.'

So that was it. Like heads on pikes, she thought, remembering her history lessons.

'All the farmers round here say they're pests, worse than foxes. You should see what a mess they make of the sheep, lambs especially. Eyes pecked out, guts ripped, blood everywhere.'

Margaret shivered, feeling the suffering of the lambs. It wasn't fair, the poor creatures had only just begun their lives.

Wil considered the hanging bird. 'You're right, he is quite a beauty. *Y barcud,* that's what we call him in Welsh. The red kite.' She relaxed, knowing he understood her feelings for the bird, and saw he was looking at her – the dark bright eyes, the familiar lopsided smile.

'You should keep his feather for good luck.' His voice was softer than usual, less matter of fact. He placed the feather gently in her open palm. 'At the rate we're shooting them, there won't be any kites left soon. Someone needs to remember them.'

Later that day, in her room, Margaret wrapped the kite's tail feather carefully in tissue paper and placed it in the top drawer of the dressing table along with her other treasures. She thought about the bird still spinning on the end of its noose, pictured the downy breast feathers falling to the ground like dead leaves, smothering the bloodstains.

Downstairs in the hall Betsan was ringing the bell for dinner and here she was, still in her dirty outdoor clothes; they would be waiting for her with long faces and the usual tut-tutting. She closed the drawer and hobbled over to the wardrobe to extract a rumpled navy skirt and blouse from the heap of clothes at the bottom. She was wearing some of David's old things today and the trousers were far too long. The bottoms were all torn and muddy from the riverbank and when she lifted her right arm she saw there was a big rip in the side of his flannel shirt. Not that he'd notice the damage when he was next home on leave, such a swank he was these days in his officer's uniform. She made a bundle of the clothes and thrust them underneath a chair. Mair would surely find them there tomorrow morning when she cleaned the room and there'd be another scolding. She dressed quickly and pulled out a pair of smarter shoes from underneath the bed, struggling to ease her swollen ankle inside the stiff leather. The sound of footsteps running up the stairs, stopping outside her room.

'Miss Margaret, you must come down now please. They are wanting you in the dining room.'

So much fuss her parents made about being on time, not keeping people waiting; she would tell them how hard it was to get dressed with a sore ankle. Betsan's quick breaths on the other side of the door. 'You have to hurry, miss. They are waiting for you.' Her voice didn't sound right, the words coming out all of a rush.

Margaret glanced at herself in the wardrobe mirror as she tried to pull a comb through her tangled hair, teasing out the bits of alder leaf and bark still lodged in it from her fall. There were mud spots on her face; she spat on her fingers and rubbed them away, then twisted her hair into a rough plait. That would have to do, Betsan's voice was scaring her. She opened the bedroom door and went out on to the landing. In the hallway below she heard the maid's quick footsteps receding towards the kitchen. Slowly, painfully, leaning on the wooden banister rail to take the weight off her foot, she made her way down the long curve of the stairs.

The dining room door was open and she could hear the low steady tick of the grandfather clock in the corner nearest the window. She halted on the threshold. Mother was sitting at the table with her back to the door, her head buried in her arms; her shoulders shook slightly, the only discernible movement in that still room. Father was in his usual chair at the head of the table. His hands were clasped tightly in front of him, his head was bowed and his eyes were shut. Could he be praying? In all her thirteen years she'd never seen him do that; in church he always sat ramrod straight and grim-faced in the family pew, refusing to kneel for the prayers. She hovered awkwardly at the doorway, a visitor intruding on a private scene. Then she remembered Betsan's urgent summons and stepped into the room. The air smelled keenly of daffodils, spring-bright and joyous in the tall vase on the dark mahogany sideboard. Father raised his head. His eyes were blank, as if she were invisible; then he blinked, became his normal self again.

'There you are, Margaret. Close the door if you would.'

Her mother stirred, adjusting her bony shoulders to their habitual stiffness under the high collared cream blouse. Her small hand reached round to the nape of her neck, felt for the neat coil of fair hair, delicate fingers threading the wayward strands.

'Sit down here, my dear.' Margaret made her way slowly to the chair beside him. He seemed not to notice she was hobbling even though she put on quite a show of pain.

A small piece of paper rested on the table between them. She read the telegram's geometry – the neat black lines, the brief handwritten message below the busy Post Office crest – and felt a sharp pain in her chest like the twist of a blade. These days the village talk was telegrams: the twins at Ty'r Efail, Tomos and Daniel Jenkins, killed in Ypres last month; Mair's cousin Dylan Davies just before Christmas; the Evans boy from Maesybont, blown to pieces by a mine somewhere in Flanders. All of them knew her brother.

Margaret felt her father's cold hand clutch her own; she dared not move her fingers inside the freezing grip. A muffled, gulping cry and the sound of Mother's chair scraping across the parquet. Then she was stumbling towards the door, wrenching it open. They listened to the urgent tap-tapping of her little boots, fading away as she crossed the hallway. Margaret half rose from the table to follow but Father was holding on to her hand; his face was a ghastly white, the deep lines in his forehead and cheeks like ink strokes. The illness was back, how had she not seen the signs earlier? The same haunted look as last autumn when they thought he might die.

'Let her alone for a while, she'll be better soon. It's been a terrible shock.'

His chest was making those wheezy sounds again. He released her hand and delved into his pocket for a handkerchief. She waited for the spasm – the painful, racking coughs – to subside.

Her father pushed back his chair and got to his feet, mustering the usual briskness.

'I'm riding over to see the Thomases at Dan y Bryn. Young

13

Hywel was killed the same day; he was in David's regiment.'
He patted her shoulder as he passed. 'Be brave for your mother,
there's a good girl.'

The clock beat out each slow, hollow second.

When she emerged from the dining room, Betsan was
hovering in the hallway. Her normally cheerful round face
was reddened and blotchy.

'There's some hot soup and bread for you in the kitchen,
miss, if you was feeling hungry. Mrs Lewis says she don't want
nothing.'

She was hungry, ravenous in fact. It had been an eventful
day. Such a shame she hadn't seen the otter cubs in the
river bend. She went through the servants' passage to the
kitchen. The room was warm with cooking and the smell of
Mrs Hughes's crusty brown bread. This news about David,
it was just a piece of paper, not real like falling from a tree
and hurting your leg. She devoured the chicken broth, wolfed
down cheese and a slice of *bara brith*, generously smeared
with butter. Betsan came in and out of the kitchen, busy with
laundry chores and tight lipped. She wanted to tell her about
the fall from the alder, enlist her sympathy, but now wasn't
the time.

Margaret limped upstairs to her room and fished out the
bundle of clothes from beneath the chair. She took off her
formal clothes, the too tight shoes, and pulled on the muddy
trousers and the torn shirt. She was shivering, her skin
puckered with goosebumps. In the bottom of the chest of
drawers was David's green fishing jersey, another borrowing.
She pulled it quickly over her head and it came down to her
knees, comforting as a warm blanket, smelling of bracken
and the pipe he used to smoke out of doors when nobody
was watching. She left her room, quietly crossed the landing,
and went down the back stairs. In the boot room David's old

walking boots were in their usual place on the rack, alongside the outdoor shoes, galoshes and wellingtons. She crouched on the stone flags, kneading the boots' stiff leather laces until they opened wide enough for her feet.

Bad luck, Mags, you'll never be a dancer with those clod-hoppers of yours! She smiled. He must be in the cupboard where they kept the fishing rods and tackle. He was moving around in there, knocking into things, deliberately giving the game away as usual; she would pretend she hadn't heard him. The boots were a tight fit; she winced as she fastened the laces across her left foot. The pain would disappear if she ran fast, took the short cut down through the wood to the lake. That way she might reach the summerhouse before him.

Even the trees of Coed Mawr were weeping. Bare branches like pinched bones, a few skeletal leaves, winter's leftovers. Icy tear drops, frozen mid fall. A thin white mist of cold hung wraith-like over the lake and a tangle of half-submerged leaves dragged the surface of the water. Such heavy stillness. Only the rustlings of small animals seeking shelter and the anxious thudding of her heart. She hugged David's jumper tightly around her, the rough wool scratching her neck. His trousers were already soaked through from her plunge down the steep bank to the lakeside and her ankle was throbbing badly. She noticed the backs of her hands were streaked with blood from rose thorns and clutching bramble.

She leaned against the summerhouse door, the wood under her hands soft and sticky with damp. The door gave way easily and she stumbled inside. One of the window panels had collapsed and her boots crunched over shards of glass and jagged splinters. In the dim spring light ivy tendrils snaked their way through holes in the walls; her old nursery chair lay upturned in a dusty corner, dead leaves humped in a brown drift beneath the little writing table. The whole place smelled fusty, unloved, long abandoned.

She picked her way across the room to where the tattered copy of *The Jungle Book* lay among the debris of summers past – scrunched up paper, bits of string, old sweet wrappers. She knelt down and picked it up, blew the dust and cobwebs off the faded brown cover. Some of the pages were stuck together, limp and mottled with mould, and the ink had run. Carefully, gently, she prised open each sticky page until she came to their story. It was still intact, thank goodness, the fingers of damp hadn't spread that far. David's funny cartoon of the two of them was palely visible in the left-hand margin. He was Nag the cobra, sleek and dangerous; she the plain little mongoose, Rikki Tikki, with hair like a bottle brush, *'eaten up from nose to tail with curiosity'*. She closed her eyes and summoned up the old battle chant, the delicious shiver of dread before their chasing game began:

> *Eye to Eye and head to head*
> *This shall end when one is dead;*
> *Turn for turn and twist for twist –*
> *Hah! The hooded Death has missed!*

He was six years older, just nineteen and swift as a hare, how dare he let death catch him. No one warned her this could happen to him. She ripped the page into tiny fragments and hurled the book into the corner of the room, to land amongst the shrivelled corpses of flies in their cobweb shrouds.

Voices were calling her name, distantly, somewhere up beyond the trees. She got stiffly to her feet and went outside. The light was dimming, the afternoon turning so quickly to the darkness. Anxious birds called across the lake.

'Margaret! Where are you? Please answer…'

A sudden crashing through undergrowth, a squawk of

birds scattering in fright. Gwennie burst out of the bushes and hurled herself at Margaret, a crush of happy Labrador, all stinky breath and muddy paws. Beloved dog. She buried her face in the animal's soft fur.

'It's alright. I'm with Gwennie. We're coming home!'

CHAPTER 2

Wil

He was packing the grocery order in the village stores when he heard the news from Doris Jones the post office.

'*Ydyw e'n wir*? Is it true then, Wil bach? The Lewis family all moving out?'

Emrys Davies the Gof had been in earlier to collect the letters for Mrs Harris, Pentrebach, she said. He'd heard it from John Owen up at the Lodge who'd heard it from Betsan Evans herself.

'They say the Colonel's put the Hall up for sale and they're going to Africa. Taking everything with them they are – furniture, china, the lot!'

Wil tried to concentrate on filling the box, his hands fumbling with the slippery packages of tea, sugar, candles, soap. He could feel Doris's eyes on him, she wanted an answer. It couldn't be true; he would have heard about it by now, word got around very fast on the estate. No one had said anything at home. The paraffin stove beside the counter sputtered and whispered in the waiting silence.

'*Dere*, Wil boy, you must know something about this. Emrys says they'll be selling off the land separate from the Hall if they can't find someone to buy the whole place. There's lots of people round here worried sick about losing their jobs. What's your dad going to do?'

Wil crammed in the last of the packages, heaved the box into his arms and muttered an apology.

'*Sori*, Mrs Jones, *rhaid i mi fynd*. I've got to go, Mam's in a hurry for these.'

The shop bell clanged behind him as he staggered outside with the heavy box and headed for the opposite side of the road where Dan was stamping his hooves in the cart traces, impatient to be away from his long wait in the cold. Wil lowered the grocery box into the back of the cart alongside the heavy bags of flour from the mill. He felt a touch on his shoulder.

Nansi Davies was standing right behind him, her thin arms hugging her chest. He took in the threadbare elbows of her brown cardigan, the faded overall fastened around her narrow waist with a piece of string, the scuffed shoes, the dishevelled auburn hair. She glared at him with narrowed, fretful eyes. That look was making him uncomfortable. Had he done something to annoy her? She could be tricky, Nans, you had to watch your step with her.

'You're a liar William Hughes, keeping secrets from me. You knew they were selling Bryntowy.'

Mawredd! Even she was accusing him now. She had a hasty tongue on her, always jumping to the wrong conclusions, but he would never hide this news from her.

'That's my chances gone, isn't it? Mrs Lewis told Betsan I could have a position up at the Hall after Easter, train as a parlour maid when she gets married. Then we'd have a bit of money coming home at last. You should have told me!'

She wiped at her face with the grubby sleeve of her cardigan. He wondered what to do if she cried, he was no good with that sort of thing.

'You know it would be a life-saver, Wil, to have a job up there, with the little ones at school and Mam on her own. There's no work round here now the men are back from France taking all the jobs. Nobody cares about us.'

She brushed past him to the horse and made a show of turning her back, burying her curly head in Dan's thick mane.

There was nothing he could say. Nansi's life was difficult, everyone knew that. She was one of seven, a year or two younger than him. The oldest in her family now, since her brother was killed at Mametz Wood in '16. If the Lewises were selling up then all the local people would suffer, no question about it.

'Look, Nans, I don't know anything about this, you have to believe me. It's probably only gossip; you know how it is round here. It was the same thing two years ago, remember? Everybody said Colonel Lewis was selling up and then he changed his mind. He's been in a bad way ever since David died. Wait until we know for sure, then you can decide what to do.'

Nansi's head was still pressed against Dan's neck. Wil reached out his arm and patted her shoulder gently. Her thin bones beneath the woollen material felt fragile as bird's wings.

'Look, I've got to go, take this stuff to Mam. She's on kitchen duty at the Hall tonight. *Welai ti*. I'll see you around.'

The girl loosened her grip on the horse and turned to face him. She flashed him a bitter look.

'Is that all you can say? Why don't you ask Miss Margaret la-di-da what's happening? You see plenty of her don't you? They say she's always hanging round the farm, like she's got nothing better to do than chase after you.'

Diawl erioed, he'd lost patience with her now. Back to her usual taunts she was, needling them into his skin.

'That's enough, Nans. I thought you were better than this, listening to stupid gossip. You're as bad as the rest of them.'

He climbed swiftly into the driver's seat, took up the reins and clicked the horse on. He knew she was still standing in the road, probably with that same hostile look on her face, and he felt briefly sorry for her. But if the news were true there would be sorrows enough for his own family. Three generations they'd been tenants at Bryntowy, he'd always expected to take over from Dad when he got too old, now there was no certainty about anything.

The cart turned into the farm track and bumped its way across the ruts towards Hendre farm. He glanced up through the wooded hillside to the grey roofs of the Hall just visible above the trees. Strange to imagine the place without Margaret; he'd always taken it for granted the two of them would be here for ever.

Margaret

It was nearly dusk when she came over the brow of the hill. She stopped for a moment to catch her breath from the long pull up from the bridge at Pant Glas. Down in the valley a scattering of lights, bright pinpricks in the gloaming. The air was still winter cold, but she could smell the new sharpness of the turning season: early daffodils in the hedges, pale primroses, leaf sap.

Below her the river Towy snaked its wide course towards the estuary at far-off Llanstephan and beside it brooded the ruins of Dryslwyn castle, a watchful sentinel over the waters. In the late afternoon light she could just make out the craggy outline of Dinefwr castle on its wooded bluff guarding the eastern side of the valley. This was her favourite view. Or was that only because she was leaving?

She shivered, feeling the air cold on her skin after the exertions of the hill climb. She'd lost track of time sitting in Miss Roberts's cluttered front room talking about books. There was *Jane Eyre* to read next and then Mrs Gaskill's *North and South* ('You'll like the heroine, she's another strong-willed Margaret'). If only everyone could be like Miss Elen Roberts.

By now Mother would be in one of her frets – the tea's cold again, Betsan's broken another plate in the china room, nobody appreciates my efforts to organise the packing of this huge house. I need you here, Margaret, not wasting your time with the village school mistress. She should be focusing her energies on her pupils' education, not filling your head with nonsense about rights for women –

Margaret reached into the bicycle basket and rummaged under the parcel of books for her old blue felt hat and woollen gloves. Jamming the hat tightly over her ears to keep out the cold, she set off again. At least there were no more hills now, just a gentle pedal along familiar twisting lanes to the lodge gates. Time to gather her thoughts before she faced the packing cases, the disapproving looks. As she turned in at the gates the village trap was approaching along the drive so she waited at the side of the road for it to pass. Mr Jenkins tipped his cap to her as the empty trap rattled past, the pony's breaths white in the frosty air. Another visitor perhaps, someone else taking a look at the estate before it went to auction next month. There'd been one or two enquirers since Christmas, tweedy old men with prim, long-faced wives, but no real interest. Since the war, Father said, nobody could afford to buy large country estates, especially if they were in 'the bloody back of beyond'. He was so irritable these days, quick-tempered or else morose and silent, his study door shut firmly against any intrusion.

She remounted her bicycle and pedalled slowly along the avenue. The lowering western sun at her back inked her long shadow across the lumpy gravel and lit up the house's tall front windows. The pale limbs of the beeches arched above her head, a few brown remnants of last summer's leaves still clinging to the branches; from a clump of rhododendron a lone song thrush was summoning the evening.

She was tired of so much heartache. Losing Bryntowy, all the precious places: the secret corners of dusty attic rooms;

the little graveyard in the wood where the family pets were buried. But you couldn't keep on living with death, it leached the joy out of everything. Her parents were miserable, greying figures shut off from each other by grief and illness. She'd been glad to escape to boarding school, even if it was across the border. When eventually her father told her that the bank had foreclosed on them and they would have to sell up, she saw a look of relief on his face. Her parents had a plan: they were leaving the country altogether, moving to South Africa, to a farm he'd inherited from some distant relative. A 'godsend' he called it, a way out. Margaret had no words. Wales was her home; she would not conceive of any other.

At the end of the drive a familiar tail was thumping the flagstones in front of the great stone porch. She propped the bicycle against the wall, took out the parcel of books and bent to stroke Gwennie, who was struggling stiffly to her feet. 'Good girl, time to go inside.' She's old before her time, Margaret thought, perhaps she knows she's not coming with us. Another heartache.

A murmur of voices in the drawing room to the right of the hallway. The door was open and she saw the fire had been lit and the lamps turned up; for a moment in the spring evening light this formal, high ceilinged room transfigured into a place of warmth and rich colour. But as she walked into the room the magic dissolved. The heavy mahogany furniture, stern-faced family portraits and the dark-clothed figures of her parents standing stiffly near the occasional table emerged into sharp focus.

Their visitor was standing in front of the fireplace, stretching his hands towards the thin flames; he turned as she came in. He looked about David's age, or the age he would have been now, tall and lean with sparse sandy hair and a faint moustache like a pencil mark above a rather fleshy mouth. His face was freckled and weather-beaten, as though he had spent a lot of time outside under a fierce sun.

'Shut the door, Margaret, you're letting in the cold.' Mother's voice sounded rather strained, more abrupt than usual.

'And send Gwennie off to the kitchen, won't you. That dog stinks more and more every time I see her.'

Margaret looked at her father in surprise. Even in his worst black moods he always had time for Gwennie; she would sit patiently next to his chair while he seethed and grumbled, her steady presence seeming to calm him. But this afternoon he looked ill at ease, hunched into himself, restless fingers drumming the back of the chair in front of him. His cough had worsened; when he breathed she could hear the crackle of phlegm inside his thin chest. She ushered the dog out of the room, waving her towards the back of the hall.

'Go on girl, find Betsan. Supper time.' Obediently, Gwennie shuffled off towards the kitchen, her old worn claws clicking across the polished wood.

The drawing room seemed unnaturally silent when she returned, as though she had interrupted some private conversation, her parents and the stranger posed like actors on a stage. The delicate ormolu clock on the mantelpiece was a faint heartbeat in the background. Her father fumbled in his pocket for a handkerchief to stifle another bout of coughing and the other man came to life.

'Miss Lewis. I've been looking forward to meeting you.'

He held out his hand, smiling, a dazzle of white teeth. A swift appraising look. Disconcerted, she stumbled on the loose edge of the rug as she moved towards him and pitched forward. He seized both her hands to steady her and held on to them, rather too tightly. His eyes were the palest, coldest blue. All the men she knew, including Wil from Hendre, had brown eyes. She pulled her hands free of the man's grasp and looked questioningly across the room at her mother.

'This is Mr Percival Flynn, Margaret, from South Africa, related to us on your father's side. A second cousin twice removed, I believe, or is it third, Arthur?'

Her father had moved to the sofa and was trying to still his trembling fingers. He gave no sign he had heard the question. Her mother gave a little sigh of annoyance.

'Well, a relation in any case. I can never remember what people are, once one gets beyond the first tier of family.' She raised a hand impatiently and waved away the thought.

The visitor looked a little nonplussed, but his face maintained the polite smile.

'I agree, Mrs Lewis. These relationships can be very complicated, especially for those of us who live in the colonies. We're never quite sure how we should behave back in the old country. My mother was always trying to teach me the family tree. We had one framed in our porch at home but I could never sit still long enough to learn all the names. Her name was Margaret too; you have a look of her, Miss Lewis, if you don't mind my saying so.'

His accent was unfamiliar, the vowel sounds abrupt, unpleasantly clipped. When he spoke his lips barely moved. Well, it didn't much matter what she made of him, Margaret thought, he was only distantly related to them, probably on some tour of Europe and making a dutiful detour to West Wales. He wouldn't be staying.

She was longing to sit down after her long bicycle ride but Mother was still standing by the table and it would be rude to sit before she did. Percival Flynn shifted his balance and she saw his hand move uncertainly to his throat and pluck at his tie as if to loosen it. The grey tweed suit looked tight and uncomfortable; he must be used to wearing lighter clothes in Africa. She conjured a picture of him in loosely flowing robes atop a loping camel and smiled to herself at the absurdity. This man was no Lawrence of Arabia. He glanced inquiringly at her mother.

'Perhaps I should explain the reason for my visit, Mrs Lewis? To your daughter I mean.'

Her mother gave Flynn a terse nod and sat down beside her father on the sofa. Percival Flynn seemed to take this as his cue to sit down too and Margaret lowered herself gratefully onto the nearest chair.

'What I have to say, Miss Lewis, may come as a surprise, a shock even.'

His manner had altered, become brisk and business-like. It made her nervous.

'Although I'm only a very distant cousin, as your mother has so kindly pointed out, I have an interest in your circumstances by virtue of my profession as a lawyer in Natal Province. In January my senior partner instructed me to manage the legal affairs of Mr Ernest Bancroft, a Durban gentleman who died a few years ago. Whilst working on his estate papers I came across some documents which directly concern your family's claim to one of his properties.'

He hesitated, shifting uncomfortably in the tight clothes, and glanced again at her parents, silent on the sofa. She saw her mother give a little nod, he should continue.

'I made contact with your parents as soon as I could and, since I was coming over to London on other business, we agreed I should make a journey to Wales to meet them – and you – in person. The matter was too important to communicate by letter alone. There are some legal complications which concern you in particular.'

The room was suddenly too warm; she longed to open a window. Her father's face was drawn and pale; the fluttering fingers had escaped again but this time he took no notice.

'Mr Flynn has unearthed a bit of a mystery, Margaret. It

appears the farm called Thorneybrook is not my inheritance as we all supposed. It belongs to you.'

The words made no sense. How could she be the owner of a property she'd never heard of until a year ago. Percival Flynn was waiting for her to respond, fixing her with his cold lawyer's eyes. She sensed her parents, too, were looking at her expectantly.

There was a gentle knock on the door and Betsan shuffled in with the heavy tea tray. She placed it carefully on the occasional table and her mother rose from the sofa to commence the tea ritual. With relief Margaret left her chair and went to help as she usually did, whilst the two men sat in awkward silence – nothing further could be said while a servant was in the room.

She got on with the business of handing round the teacups and the dainty plates of sandwiches, her thoughts racing. If she owned the farm she could sell it. They could stay at Bryntowy. Make all those improvements Father talked about before the war: repair the crumbling walls of the estate; install a proper bathroom in the Hughes's farmhouse so they didn't need to use the outside privy, that would please Wil's mother. Put a decent roof on the schoolroom, get rid of the leaks, buy more books and pens for the children.

'That will be all, Betsan. I will ring when we've finished.'

Mother's curt dismissal brought her back to the present. Betsan closed the drawing room door and Percival Flynn reached for the brown leather briefcase beside his chair. He opened it and drew out a large manila envelope. He paused and glanced across at her father on the other side of the room.

'Colonel Lewis, as we agreed earlier, I will explain the conditions of the inheritance to Miss Lewis so that she understands her position.'

He opened the envelope and withdrew some stiff folded papers which crackled as he straightened out the creases.

'This is a copy of the original will and testament, made on

the 18th July 1904 by your father's maternal uncle, the late Mr Ernest Lewis Bancroft, formerly of Mount Pleasant, Durban, Natal.' She saw him exchange a quick glance with her parents. 'Mr Bancroft had no children of his own – he was never married. His will states that the Durban house, its contents and all his money are bequeathed to a distant cousin on his father's side residing in Melbourne, Australia. The farm known as Thorneybrook is bequeathed to the heir of Colonel Arthur Lewis of Bryntowy Hall, Carmarthenshire, South Wales.' He paused, waiting for her to respond.

'I don't understand, how can I be the heir?'

Percival Flynn's face reddened; he fiddled with the papers on his lap. Nobody said a word. Then she realised: of course none of them had expected this inheritance would be hers. Flynn was addressing her again, his features composed into a thin smile.

'I understand your question, Miss Lewis. Had circumstances been different, your brother would have inherited, but now Thorneybrook passes to you as the only surviving child of your parents. It's not altogether unusual for property to be willed to a different generation, though I admit it has its… complications.'

'But it's not complicated. I'll sell the farm and then we can stay here and spend the money on improving Bryntowy. Do you remember, Father, all those plans you used to talk about?'

But her father was looking at the lawyer. 'Go on, please, Mr Flynn.'

Her throat felt dry, why was he ignoring her? She heard Percival Flynn clear his throat.

'I'm afraid the situation is not as straightforward as you would like it to be, Miss Lewis. In the first instance Thorneybrook only passes to you when you are of age. As your legal guardian your father has responsibility for any decisions regarding the farm until you reach your majority.

Secondly, there are certain financial matters which make a sale impossible.'

'Mr Flynn, I think perhaps it is more appropriate for my daughter to hear the truth from me. Selling Thorneybrook won't cancel our debts, Margaret; the upkeep of an estate the size of Bryntowy is simply too great; we haven't the capital. I'm sorry, but there really is no alternative. We have to do this…'

She saw her mother reach out and take his hand and then she understood. Their plans weren't going to change; they wanted to leave. Percival Flynn started to speak again but Mother was quickly on her feet, smoothing her skirt and straightening the cuffs of her grey jacket.

'You can stop now, Mr Flynn, my husband is tired. Margaret doesn't need to hear any more at this juncture, she has quite enough to be thinking about.'

Flynn stood up hastily, his lanky frame towering over her small, precise figure. She held out her hand in a formal gesture of dismissal.

'You will have an early start tomorrow to catch the London train. I'm sure the rest of the arrangements can be conducted by correspondence with Colonel Lewis once you are back in Natal.'

'As you wish, Mrs Lewis.' He carefully folded the documents back into their envelope, placed them inside the briefcase and snapped the lock shut. Mother could silence the most persistent of men.

'We eat at six. I am going to the dining room to see that everything is ready. Margaret, please ring for Betsan to show Mr Flynn to his room.'

Once she had left, Margaret rose from her chair and crossed the room to the tea table. As she picked up the little bell she sensed a movement behind her. Turning, she saw Flynn bend over her father and press a piece of paper into his hand. He took a quick look at the note, nodded, and put it in his pocket. Both men must have sensed she was watching for they turned towards her at the same moment. Like a pair of guilty conspirators.

'I expect Betsan's waiting for you in the hall, Mr Flynn. I'll take the tray to the kitchen.' She made a show of gathering the tea things while he picked up his briefcase and left the room. Her father rose stiffly from the sofa; on his way to the door he suddenly paused and laid his hand on her arm.

'I apologise for dashing your hopes, dear girl, but this move is an opportunity for our family, a chance to put the past behind us. South Africa will be just the thing, you'll see.'

Another bout of coughing halted him at the door; he drew the handkerchief from his pocket and something fluttered, unnoticed by him, to the floor. Margaret waited for him to leave then picked it up. Percival Flynn must have been in a hurry; the handwriting was a scrawl, barely decipherable. *Codicil destroyed as agreed. She must not know.*

Her heart was thudding. She'd read enough Wilkie Collins and Conan Doyle mysteries to know that a codicil could change lives, for good or ill. One thing was certain, for some reason this man and her father were determined to keep it a secret. She stuck the note hastily inside her sleeve and picked up the tea tray. Well, she could be determined, too. While Percival Flynn was around, she, like the best of detectives, would be on her guard.

Wil

The buzzards were circling by the time he reached the top of the field. He could hear their distinctive high-pitched mews alerting other predators to the feast. He didn't spot the lamb at first. Its mother was standing near the corner where the hedge straggled a turning. She backed away at his approach, watching him warily, reluctant to leave her offspring. He could see the dried blood matting her backside where she trailed a pale ribbon of afterbirth. He knelt beside the small shredded corpse, breathed the stink of entrails puddling the frosty grass. Poor dab. The eyes were gone already, crows' work. Once the other birds had their fill there'd just be bones.

The third dead lamb this week. It had been a bad idea to turn the pregnant ewes out so early after such a harsh winter, they should have kept them in the field close to the house. Pity not to make the most of the dry weather, Dad insisted – the sheep could do with some fresh grass. But they couldn't afford to lose any more spring lambs, not with the price of meat so low. Last Wednesday's market, people were talking about farms going out of business up and down the valley. Ifor Thomas was giving up his tenancy; that was the biggest shock. Moving to live with his daughter in Llandeilo. Three sons he'd lost to the war, Wil remembered. Jack, the youngest, was only two years up from him at school. Strange to think there'd be no more Thomases farming Y Wern.

Wil held out his stick and gently tapped the ewe's flank to turn her away from her lamb. There was nothing more to do here. He'd drive her down to the bottom field to join the others. She had enough milk in her for the orphaned lambs born yesterday; their dead mother would be off to the hunt kennels in the morning.

Below him, two fields away, a thin plume of smoke rose into the chill March air. He blew on his chapped fingers, raw and roughened by the winter; it would be good to get home, thaw out a bit by the kitchen range. He'd been up since five as usual. There might just be time to snatch a cup of tea before afternoon milking.

'*Dere, nawr*, get a move on!' The ewe wouldn't budge,

wanting to stay close to the bedraggled carcass of her lamb. Wil gave her a sharp prod with the stick and reluctantly she started to shuffle off down the field. He followed her, thinking about the conversation in the shop that morning. If the Lewises were dividing the estate, like Doris Jones said, selling it off farm by farm, how many tenants could afford to buy? Dad had no money; it was all he and Mam could do to pay the monthly rent for Hendre. The three of them were working as hard as they could just to make ends meet. Why hadn't Margaret said anything about this? She'd been over only last week to collect the egg basket. Chatting about this and that, a stream of questions as usual – had he noticed the wren's nest in the wall above the stable door? That fresh hole below the fence by Coed Mawr, could it be foxes again? And did he know the red kites were back? Not one mention of the sale.

Nansi's bitter comments had really got under his skin. She knew full well he and Margaret had been friends for years, ever since they were children. But if that were true then why the silence from her? He shunted the ewe through the open gate into the bottom field and watched her trot away to join the rest of the flock. Moments later she was cropping the thin grass as though nothing had happened. Why did people have to make everything so complicated? He finished retying the gate and gave a last glance back up the hillside. On the horizon two birds of prey with distinctive forked tails had joined the buzzard ring. Margaret was right – the kites were back.

When he came in later Dad was at the kitchen table; he didn't look up from his reading when Wil went to the sink to wash the dirt off his hands. A large foolscap envelope lay on the table, very official-looking, *Mr Emrys Hughes, Tenant, Hendre Farm, Bryntowy Estate*. Wil dried his hands on the rough towel and waited. In a moment his father leaned back in his chair and took off his reading glasses.

'Read this for me will you.' He thrust the letter towards him with an irritable shrug of his shoulders. '*Sa i'n deall y geiriau*, I can't understand all this English.'

Wil noted the dark shadows below his father's eyes, the deep worry creases in his forehead. You never really knew what was going on in Dad's head, other than farming business. Today though, he looked harassed, bone tired.

Wil was used to translating for Dad when Mam wasn't around. She had stayed on longer at school and could speak English quite well when she had to. The letter was written in terse, formal language, like those articles from *The Times* Miss Roberts made them read at school. He'd been top of his class back then; Mam wanted him to try for a place at the Grammar in Carmarthen, only there was no money for school fees. He was wanted at home, on the farm.

The name and address were in heavy type at the top of the letter:

Bradbrooks Solicitors, Grays Inn Road, London WC1.
Dear Mr Hughes
Notice is hereby given that the Bryntowy Estate is to be sold at public auction on 30th April 1920.
As tenant of Hendre Farm within the said Estate you are eligible to make an offer to purchase the said farmhouse and a parcel of land. Should you wish to take up this opportunity you should contact the Estate solicitors at the above address. The closing date for application is 31st March.
Yours sincerely
Kenneth Marshall (clerk to Messrs Bradbrook & Son)

Dad was listening intently as Wil translated the letter, staring across the table at the window opposite which looked on to the yard. His calloused workman's hands gripped the edge of the table. When Wil had finished a kind of silence fell between them, broken only by the frenzied buzzing of an early fly against the window pane.

'What are you going to do?'

His father stirred, pushed his chair back from the table and stood up.

'Going to check on Dan – that front leg was lame again this morning. Don't want it getting worse before the ploughing starts.'

Through the window Wil watched him limp across the yard to the barn. He was avoiding the question of course. Better to wait for Mam to come home; she'd give him a direct answer like as not. He thought about the Dolau Estate up the valley, the big public auction of the farms last summer. Even the *Carmarthen Journal* had a story about it – local tenant farmers forced off the land by English buyers who were only after shooting rights and the weekend fishing on the Towy. Wales was cheaper than Scotland.

The old clock in the *parlwr* struck the milking hour. No time for that cup of tea now, the cows would be waiting at the gate. He put the letter back into its envelope and went to pull on his boots. Outside, the sky above the hillside was empty; the birds had taken their fill and gone.

CHAPTER 3

Margaret

A month gone already since Percival Flynn's visit; the date was in her diary. Bryntowy was full of bustle, endless activity. Father travelled up to London most weeks on estate business, agents and tradesmen called, Mr Howard the accountant from Swansea came and went. These mornings she woke to the noise of hammering; outside in the empty stables the carpenters were flat out constructing the travel containers for the furniture. Some of the crates were the size of small sheds.

She rose stiffly from the rug in the library where she'd been sent to pack up the books. Father had arranged them in neat piles on the floor. Apart from his guns and fishing rods, books were his great delight. That was something they had in common, at least. His lists were on the large walnut table in the middle of the room, each item meticulously entered in his careful sloping handwriting: the books in front of the fireplace were for shipping; the smaller pile below the window for the valuers; those in the corner to be donated to the county library in Carmarthen. She admired his thoroughness for such a dreary task. He had attached cardboard labels to the two display cabinets – like the leather-bound stamp books, the guns and fishing rods, this collection of moths and butterflies was an indissoluble part of him. Outside the tall library windows spring was calling her. Wild spurts of sunlight after days of rain, casting bright shifting patterns across the gloomy parquet.

The *Times Atlas* was lying on the table next to the lists, open at the map of the world. There was a similar map on the classroom wall in Rhydfelin school – half the world smeared in British Empire red. Miss Roberts talked a lot about India – a cousin was in the Civil Service there – and they had studied Egypt and the pyramids, but Africa was a mystery. Margaret turned over the heavy pages to the map of Southern Africa. She found Cape Town on the edge of the coast at the bottom of the map. Durban was also a port city; their furniture and the large household items were being shipped there ahead of their arrival. She traced the shoreline with her finger, searching for the name.

The library door opened. A scrawny, red-haired girl in maid's uniform. Nansi Davies, the girl from the village.

'Mrs Lewis sent me to find you; you're wanted in the morning room.'

Margaret closed the heavy atlas and wiped the dust from her hands. The girl was lingering at the door, watching her. Another of Betsan's cousins, hired to help with the packing. She dimly remembered her from the schoolyard, the ringleader in a gaggle of children from the class below. She stepped aside as Margaret approached and leaned against the doorjamb, staring at her with her arms folded insolently across her chest. Margaret had to squeeze past her. As their eyes met, she detected a mocking expression on the girl's face.

The morning room hadn't been sorted for packing yet; it looked the same as always, a comfort when all the other rooms seemed to be vanishing before her eyes. She loved this place, tucked into the east wing of the house looking out over the valley and the distant hills. In contrast to the formal drawing room with its austere portraits and fussy expensive ornaments, the morning room was small and cosy, the walls cluttered with family photographs and a few of Mother's fine watercolours of local views, bits of embroidery poking out of the wicker basket beside the fireplace. So many times, she'd sat here reading, often with a large dog curled warmly beside her on the rug. Unless David were home, bursting with energy as usual, urging them to play another hiding game. Sometimes Mother joined her: the two of them would crouch behind the sofa stifling the giggles, knowing he would find them. These days, Margaret avoided his photograph on the mantelpiece, so solemn and grown up in his Welsh Guards uniform. Someone should pack it away with all the other memories.

Mr Jenkins must have brought the post early. Mother was already at her writing bureau in the corner of the room, a pile of correspondence teetering on the stool beside her chair. Wisps of pale hair had escaped from the tight bun and the spring light streaming through the window spun them into gossamer about her head. Hearing Margaret's presence in the room, she stirred but did not turn around.

'Mr Flynn has written to us from South Africa. He enclosed a second letter addressed only to you. I wasn't aware you were corresponding with him.'

She indicated an envelope on the top of the pile, then bent again to her writing. Since the lawyer's visit her parents had made no mention of her inheritance, as if they had agreed never to speak of it. Margaret took the envelope from the pile. How ridiculous of Mother to think she and that odious man were exchanging letters. What on earth would they have to say to each other?

She sat down on the window seat, propping herself comfortably against the soft cushions embroidered with tiny leaping dogs – labradors and spaniels, her favourite breeds. The envelope was addressed to her in black looping handwriting, **Miss Margaret Lewis**. The letter inside had a Durban address – **King's Buildings, Smith Street** – and it was dated the 28th March. He must have written it soon after his return.

My dear Miss Lewis,

It was a great pleasure to meet you at Bryntowy and to renew my acquaintance with your parents. I am delighted to hear from the London office that Colonel and Mrs Lewis have secured a purchaser for the house. No doubt that will bring an end to what must have been an anxious time for you all.

I have just returned from a visit up country to some old friends, the Jamiesons, whose property lies a few miles east of Thorneybrook. Whilst I was there I made a brief visit to the farm, to ascertain what preparations should be made for your arrival. I am not much of a writer but I hope the following will help you imagine the place before you see it for yourself.

Thorneybrook is a fine old homestead, though not so grand as Bryntowy. I gather Mr Ernest Bancroft never actually lived there, though he visited from time to time. I'm sure you and your parents will enjoy 'putting your stamp' on it, as they say. The farm is two days drive west from Pietermaritzburg, through some splendid high country.

The house is situated on the left bank of the Amanzimnyama river and has magnificent views of the southern Drakensberg mountains. Although the Natal uplands are still quite green in late March, the autumn colours are beginning to show themselves now. This is quite the best time of year in my opinion, but I am sure you will love the winters too when we experience many days of bright, dry weather. The highest peaks of the Drakensberg are often snow covered. A far cry from your mild wet climate!

Mr Jamieson has a daughter, Mary. I have asked her to write to you by way of introduction to the country. She's a little older than you, but I know you will appreciate her friendship and wise advice when you arrive; the ways of Southern Africans can feel a little daunting at first.

Please be assured of my willingness to offer whatever

assistance I can to you and your family as you settle into your new life in Natal.

Yours ever, Percival Flynn

Margaret closed the letter, irritated beyond words. What made him think she would be interested in all this detail? He knew nothing about her. She would make her own friends, not some stranger he wanted to foist on her. He was not to be trusted, the hasty note to her father made that clear; she would make it her business to uncover their secret once she got to South Africa.

Through the window she observed Gwennie stretched out on the terrace below, dozing in the watery sunshine. Mair passed by with a basket of washing heading for the laundry room next to the stables. Margaret watched her old dog stir, sniffing the air as she raised herself to follow on stiff legs; Mair's apron pockets were always full of titbits. In the distance a rabbit skittered across the bottom lawn and disappeared into the shrubbery. A flurry of rooks rose cawing out of a clump of conifers at the edge of Coed Mawr. The familiar scratch of her mother's pen.

She sighed and opened the envelope to replace the letter. Inside, was another piece of paper. A sketch – hastily drawn, an afterthought perhaps. A low-roofed, single-storied house framed by tall, thin pine trees. A narrow verandah running the length of the house, a flight of steps leading from it to the front door. Below the sketch, the name *Thorneybrook*.

There was nothing grand about that mean-looking house, Percival Flynn had been truthful in this regard at least. The Bryntowy Estate buildings with their solid stone walls and clustering ivy were far more appealing. She could make nothing of it. She thrust the letter and the alien sketch into the envelope. Her heart was sore. Flynn already knew Bryntowy had been sold and neither of her parents had bothered to inform her.

'I didn't know you'd sold the house.'

The words lodged in her throat, thick as river mud. She watched her mother slowly place the fountain pen on the blotter beside her writing pad, straighten her shoulders then turn in her direction. She had been preparing for this moment.

'Yes, we have, Margaret. Colonel Fairhurst has bought it, he's ex-Indian army, your father knows him from Sandhurst days. They're a good family and keen to settle in this area. Bryntowy will suit them very well.'

She turned back to her papers, picked up her pen again. Margaret's face was burning. Was that all there was to say?

'Have the Fairhursts bought the whole estate, the farms, the cottages? What about the people at the Lodge and the other tenants? Will the Hugheses be staying on? Have you told Mair and Betsan yet?'

'That's quite enough, Margaret.'

Mother's tone was icy. She'd gone too far, there'd be no answers now.

'Your father is dealing with everything, that's all you need to know. The carter from Carmarthen will be here tomorrow for those library books. When you've finished packing them I need you to take these letters to the post office. Betsan and Mair are busy in the linen room all afternoon.'

There was no point in pursuing the matter. Margaret rose from the window seat and deliberately placed Percival Flynn's letter on top of the pile of correspondence. Mother could read it if she liked; she would not be accused of keeping secrets.

Some hours later, crossing the hallway, she encountered Mair Thomas and Nansi Davies on their knees polishing the oak floor. They were giggling and whispering to each other in Welsh but stopped when they saw her coming. Mair, a thin, wispy-looking girl with a permanent worried expression, gave

Margaret a guilty-looking smile and returned to her polishing. Nansi rested her back against the bottom stair and regarded her with that same mocking expression.

'Mrs Lewis said to tell you the letters is ready.' She raised an arm and pointed to the hall table by the front door. 'You'll have to hurry to catch the post.'

As she gathered the letters Margaret heard Nansi mutter something in Welsh, drawing a suppressed snort from Mair. She closed the front door on their laughter and took a deep breath of spring air. That girl's tone bordered on rudeness. Mother should get rid of her; they could easily find someone else to take her place.

She dropped the letters into the bicycle basket and pulled on her hat. This time she'd take the short cut down to the village through the wood; the track wouldn't be so muddy today. She pedalled swiftly around the corner of the house, free-wheeled down the path skirting the shrubbery and bumped over the cattle grid separating the garden from the fields and woodland. The beeches were greening into leaf at last and birds called brightly from the deeper shadows inside the wood. Below on her right the glimmer of water marked the western edge of the lake. There was no time now to turn on to the path to the summerhouse. She hadn't been back there since the day they received the telegram.

The track came out at the bottom of the wood and joined the main road into Rhydfelin. The school was at the edge of the village and she cycled slowly past the building, hoping to catch a glimpse of Miss Roberts through one of the windows. She usually stayed on after the children had gone home to tidy up and prepare the next day's lessons. But there was no sign of her old teacher, only Dai the caretaker sweeping leaves in the corner of the schoolyard. The youngest Morris children were playing with a ball outside the Butchers Arms and they waved to her as she rode past.

The post office was at the other end of the village adjoining Penlan Stores. From behind the counter she could feel Mrs Jones watching her stick the stamps on to the letters.

'Busy with all that packing, Miss Lewis, I expect you are?'

She nodded, dreading the next question.

'You got a buyer for the Hall we heard. Someone from England is it?'

'Yes, that's right.' So the village knew too. One more stamp, then she could escape.

'Well, you'll soon be off to Africa, isn't it? Very hot over there they say. My uncle Tom was there in 1901. He was with the 1st Battalion, Royal Welch Fusiliers; lots of Carmarthenshire boys killed in that war you know. Those Boers, wouldn't trust any of them; shoot you dead soon as look at you, that's what my uncle used to say. You be careful now.'

Margaret handed over the last letter. People were talking as though she had already left. She pedalled slowly back through the village, deciding to take the longer way home. She would take her time, avoid the lists, Mother's coolness and Nansi Davies's insolent looks for as long as she could. This route would also take her past Hendre; she hadn't seen Wil in a while; it would be good to spend some time with him before she went away.

She turned off the main road at the milk churn stand and followed the narrow lane enclosed by high blackthorn hedges towards the cluster of farm buildings. She rode into the yard, scattering the hens in a flurry of dirt and feathers, and propped the bicycle in the usual place against the low stone wall separating the farmhouse from the outbuildings. From around the corner of the house a scruffy sheepdog, great gouts of brown and white hair hanging off its flanks, sprang at her, growling. She held out her hand towards him.

'It's alright Ceg, it's only me. Lie down good boy.'

The dog sniffed at her fingers then lay still, his tail thumping the ground. She was no stranger. Margaret stroked his bony head. From inside the milking shed on the far side of the yard she heard the busy clank of buckets. She should have realised this was the wrong time to call round; they would be busy for a while yet. She would sit on the wall and wait until Wil had finished the milking.

'*Prynhawn da*, Miss Lewis.'

Mrs Hughes was at the doorway of the farmhouse. In the past she would have run to her for a hug, burying her head into the warm floury bosom. These days she had a feeling Wil's mother was avoiding her; whenever they met Mrs Hughes spoke with a kind of guarded politeness. Her frostiness might be even worse today, now the sale was proceeding. She longed to explain, none of this was her fault.

'I'm sorry to disturb you, Mrs Hughes. I thought Wil might be free.'

'You know it's milking time.'

She wasn't wanted, that was clear, but she badly needed to see Wil; it might be the last time.

'If you don't mind Mrs Hughes, I'll wait here until he's finished.'

Wil's mother hesitated then she seemed to change her mind.

'You'd better come inside the house; it's too cold to wait out here. Going to be rain soon.'

She'd much prefer to stay outside with Ceg than sit alone in that dark parlour on a hard chair with nothing to look at except the black-bound family Bible and those ugly china dogs on the mantelpiece. But in these altered circumstances it would be rude to refuse.

To her relief Mrs Hughes was heading towards the kitchen not the parlour. It was good to be in this familiar room again, warm from the fire and smelling of newly baked bread. The little wooden stool she used to sit on as a child was in its usual place in the corner; instinctively she made towards it but Mrs Hughes was pointing towards the kitchen table.

'Sit down by here, Miss Lewis.' She indicated the high-backed chair, the one where Mr Hughes usually sat. 'It will be more suiting for you.'

She was being put in her place, thought Margaret, as she took the hard, uncomfortable seat while Mrs Hughes collected the cups and plates from the tall corner cupboard. The room was darkening; through the window she could see rainclouds gathering above the roofs of the outbuildings. There was Ceg at the cowshed door, waiting for the signal to drive the cows back to the fields after milking. Then the men would be here.

Mrs Hughes lifted the heavy iron teapot from its warming stand on the hearth. The usual routine, strong tea and bread after milking, then the last rounds of the farm before the light went.

'Will you have some tea?'

Such politeness, like she was talking to a stranger!

'No thank you, Mrs Hughes. I promised Mother I wouldn't be long.' Very well, she would be just as formal. 'I was in the village and I thought I would call by on my way home to see how you are.'

Mrs Hughes bent to replace the teapot on the hearth. She was taller than Mother and physically much stronger; a stout attractive figure with brown curly hair just beginning to grey, a round face and the dark, intelligent eyes she'd passed on to her son. She straightened up, wiping her hands on her apron.

'We are doing as well as you can expect. That is, since we had the letter about the sale.'

She pulled out a chair opposite and sat down. Margaret stole an anxious glance towards the window. Surely the men would be in soon. Mrs Hughes sat very still, her hands folded in her lap and Margaret squirmed under the stern gaze.

'I expect you know that Emrys has told the solicitors we are not buying the farm. William has written the letter for him.'

Margaret felt her cheeks flushing. 'No, I didn't know. But you can't leave Hendre, you've always lived here!'

'Some of the farmers are buying, the ones who can, that is.'

'But surely you can stay on here as tenants?'

Mrs Hughes shook her head. 'They don't want tenants, they are only asking for buyers. And the work is hard, you know, harder than it used to be. Emrys is getting tired, with the sheep, the milking, always such a lot to be doing. Lost the heart for farming, he has.'

'But you have Wil to help. He can take over most of the work, can't he?'

It seemed such an obvious solution. Mrs Hughes was staring at her, frowning, open mouthed.

'You have no idea, do you, how it is for us? We haven't the money to buy this farm. There's no future for William in farming. He is a clever boy, could have gone to the Grammar. There's work up in Cross Hands at the colliery, he was there yesterday to see about a job in the office. Good with numbers he is and they want workers who can speak tidy English. '

'But what will you and Mr Hughes do?'

'We are going to my sister's place over Brynamman way. She is on her own since her husband died. There's a bit of land, enough for a few sheep. William can walk to work over the mountain.'

They heard the men's footsteps coming across the yard towards the back door. Suddenly she didn't want to see Wil, or his father. She wouldn't know what to say to them; this was all her family's fault even if Mrs Hughes wasn't saying so directly.

'I won't stay after all if you don't mind, Mrs Hughes. It's getting late and they will be expecting me at home.'

She got up hastily. Wil's mother followed her out of the

kitchen into the narrow passageway leading to the front door.

'Please don't be speaking to William about this, Miss Lewis. It is a difficult time for all of us and I don't want you upsetting him with your questions.'

On a different occasion she would have resented this. Wil was used to her questions; he wouldn't be upset, whatever his mother thought. Everything had changed, there was no place for her here.

'Of course, I do understand. But could you just tell him I called? In case he's wondering why I haven't been in touch for a while.'

There was no reply. The door closed firmly behind her. Feeling like an intruder, she crept around the corner of the house, fetched her bicycle and began the weary pedal up the steep rutted cart track which led from the back of the farm in the direction of the Hall. The spring light had completely faded now and a soft drizzle was already turning the earth into slippery red mud. She would have to push the bicycle most of the way home. Halfway up the track she paused to catch her breath and looked down at the farm, now dissolving into greyish outline through the thickening rain. Turning its back on her. Bryntowy, too, was shrugging her off. Drawing down the blinds and waiting for its new owner. You could love a place with all your heart, but it still wasn't yours to keep.

She heaved the bike up the sodden track, the wheels sliding on the loosened stones, rain matting her hair. The track came out on the lane that ran alongside the boundary wall. She pushed the bicycle through a gap in the stones and followed a narrow deer path through the trees. It was very quiet, only the shushing of rainwater on leaves.

She stopped. There was something up ahead, where the path curved to the right. A tall figure muffled in a long greatcoat standing just beyond the fallen beech. His back was turned towards her, but there was something familiar about the alert stance, the tiptoe look of him, poised for action. He had come back, of course he had, just when they needed him! She flung the bike to the ground and ran towards him, stumbling over roots and bramble, but he was moving away, sliding between the trees. She shouted his name, and then he wasn't there any longer. Just a trick of the fading light. *This shall end when one is dead.*

She walked slowly back to her bicycle, shaken and foolish. She picked it up and continued along the path until it emerged on to a gravelled clearing behind the Hall at the servants' entrance. One of the huge shipping crates was blocking the doorway; it was draped in a tarpaulin against the rain and the men were busy loading the marked boxes of china and glassware. The house was ridding itself of them all.

Her thoughts turned to that other house, the one Percy Flynn had sketched for her. Reluctantly at first, she allowed it to enter her imagination. Mysterious Thorneybrook, with its low roofs and verandah, waiting for her in the shade of the pine trees, silent and shuttered against the African heat. A house of secrets. Could the 'she' referred to in Flynn's note, be herself? Perhaps it was time to find out.

Durban, South Africa
Early Winter
(Southern Hemisphere) 1920

Chapter 4

'I can see the Bluff!'

The small boy, immaculately dressed – grey shorts, red-tipped blazer, neat school tie – clutched at his mother's sleeve, pointing into the greyness. Margaret watched him wriggle his head into the gap between the deck rail and the ship's side to get a better view. His mother took a languorous drag at her cigarette and watched the smoke slowly wreathe about her head then dissolve. Although she was standing next to them Margaret could see no shape of land beyond this thick sea fog. She squinted into the distance. Nothing. That boy must have second sight.

The air up on deck was warm and fragrant. A shrubby scent, buttery like gorse. Whatever it was, it made a welcome change from the cloying mix of brine and engine oil they'd been breathing on the long voyage out from England. The wooden rail felt clammy, salt-sticky beneath her palms. After so many weary weeks at sea, the huge liner moved sluggishly towards her final port on the Indian Ocean, the familiar throb and judder of engines now just a distant subterranean thrum beneath their feet. Margaret became aware of other voices gathering around her, passengers coming up on deck from cabins and staterooms, eager for their first sight of Durban. Through the fog she heard a gull's harsh cry and caught the white swoop of wings alighting on the ship's middle funnel.

The boy was right. A hulk of land loomed out of the greyness on their portside. Through the thinning air she spotted the steady blink of the lighthouse on the top of the Bluff, just as Mary Jamieson had described in her letter. *'This will be your first landmark.'* A slick of dark green vegetation ran across the lower slopes of the headland, its summit still necklaced in mist. Margaret felt the ship slow as it began the wide turn towards the narrow neck of the lagoon.

Her grey winter coat clung to her body, the damp wool heavy with sea vapour. At Cape Town, their first stop in South Africa, the weather had been surprisingly cold and breezy, like an autumn day in Carmarthenshire, and she'd been glad of the coat's warmth. *'Durban will be much milder than you expect,'* Mary had written. *'Nobody wears coats here, even in winter.'* Margaret shrugged the coat off her shoulders and folded it carefully over the rail. Some white hairs were caught in the wool and her eyes filled at the thought of dear Gwennie, now so far away.

The Indian Ocean swells receded as the ship entered the calmer waters of the bay through a narrow channel between the Bluff and a curving spit of land. Rising above the shoreline Margaret could see a densely wooded ridge. To her right a long sweep of sandy beach slowly disappeared behind the jumbled roofs of storehouses lining the entrance to the harbour.

After days of flat horizons and empty skies, her senses were assailed by the clamour and bustle of the busy port. Wooden crates of bananas stacked high as houses; thick coils of hawsers heaped along the quayside; a row of grimy coal trucks waiting to be unloaded on a siding. Everywhere the noise of hammering, the screech of metal on metal. Two men in red tunics fishing off a jetty waved as they passed. Small sailing boats bobbed alongside the ship, curious dark faces staring up at them. On the far side of the harbour she could see the jagged outlines of cranes and the bulky smokestacks of the cargo ships; the words *Hulett & Sons Sugar* emblazoned in black across the face of a huge brick warehouse. Margaret looked up, shielding her eyes against the sun. The sky was the palest, warmest blue.

The ship was moving alongside the pier now, flanked by the Union Castle building. In one of the offices on the first floor a fair-haired woman in a green patterned dress was busy at her typewriter. She glanced up and their eyes met; her expression was blank, indifferent. She turned back to her work, the arrival of the weekly liner from Southampton only a brief distraction. The dock's heavy timbers creaked and juddered as the huge ship slowly berthed against them. Down on the quayside a team of dark-skinned men in blue overalls secured the heavy ropes around the moorings.

'Quite a sight isn't it?'

She hadn't noticed her father come up beside her. He was leaning over the rail to watch the activity below and his face was alight with interest. It seemed an age since she'd seen him smile like that: the habitual frown lines softened and his thin face was relaxed, attentive, younger somehow. Even his fingers seemed at ease, she observed, resting lightly on the rail. He turned his head to look at her.

'I knew you'd be up on deck for your first view of Durban. I can still remember my first time, back in '99, when the regiment came ashore. We were billeted here for a few weeks before we went north.'

For a moment she was puzzled, she had no idea he'd been here before. Then she remembered, the photograph of him in the morning room at Bryntowy – a young officer in regimental khaki, sun helmet in one hand, the other resting on his sword. He touched her arm and pointed towards the distant wooded ridge.

'I stayed somewhere up there – lovely house overlooking

the bay. We felt rather sad when furlough was over and we had to travel up country to fight the Boers.'

He inhaled deeply, lost for a moment in some distant memory. He was happier here, she thought, in those years before he met Mother, before David and me, before the war and the debts. Perhaps he was right, South Africa would be 'just the thing'. She saw him straighten up and turn towards her.

'Your mother sent me to find you. Problem with the hand luggage. The girl can't carry it all, apparently. Such a complaining type, don't know why we brought her with us, Betsan would have been much more agreeable. Be a dear, won't you, and sort it out. It's going to be a while before they let us disembark.'

He gave her shoulder a brief squeeze and walked off along the deck to take a closer look at the doings on the quayside. She wished she could stay out here with him, do what she wanted for once. Throughout the tedious voyage she'd coped with Mother's bouts of seasickness, played endless games of whist and gin rummy with the other ladies, endured the dreary meals, longing to escape into her books, stop missing home. She gathered up her coat from the rail and pushed irritably through the throng of passengers at the bottom of the stairway leading to the cabins on the upper deck.

It was her mother who insisted Nansi Davies should travel with them. The girl had been such a help, she said, so practical, goodness knows how they would have managed the move without her. With Betsan getting married and Mair not really the right sort of servant material for life overseas, Nansi was the obvious choice. And poor Mrs Davies would have one less mouth to feed in that crowded family. No one had asked Margaret's opinion. Fortunately, she hadn't seen much of the girl on the voyage out, she kept to her quarters in third class, somewhere on the lower decks. Sometimes she complained of feeling seasick and there were dark circles beneath her eyes. Perhaps she too was missing home. Well, serve her right, at least she'd been allowed to choose her future.

An hour later Margaret took her first uncertain steps on land. After so many weeks afloat she felt the ground unsteady, shifting, as though she were a child learning how to walk. Behind her, the *Llanstephan Castle* was already loading for its return voyage to Southampton. They'd laughed at the coincidence – to be travelling on a ship named for a village on the Towy estuary. Now, as she took a farewell glance at the liner, her heart ached to be parting from this final link with home.

She heard a man's voice call her name amongst the small crowd on the quayside gathered to watch the arrivals. People shifted position to let someone through. In the sun's glare she couldn't be sure until she felt him grasp her hand.

'Welcome to South Africa Miss Lewis, Margaret!'

It was Percival Flynn, of course, doffing his cream panama hat and beaming at them. She had been right about one thing: the man looked far more at ease in his linen tropical suit and crisp white shirt than he had at Bryntowy, trussed inside that suffocating tweed. Her parents were smiling at him, even Mother looked relieved to see a familiar face. Nansi Davies stood some way off beside the portmanteaus and hatboxes, awkwardly clutching her green felt bag. She looked so out of place that for a fleeting moment Margaret felt almost sorry for her.

Flynn was taking charge, marshalling them through the crowd, out along the quayside. She could hardly breathe for the press of people and the unexpected warmth. Her dress clung to the back of her legs and her hands felt clammy inside her woollen gloves. She should have heeded Mary Jamieson's advice and worn something cooler. Three brightly painted vehicles the size of a large handcart, padded with embroidered cushions and shawls, were waiting at the kerbside. Beside each one stood an African in traditional dress – white buskins studded with coloured beads, a scarlet sleeveless tunic adorned with feathers and yet more beads. Each man wore a fantastical headdress, horned and plumed like some exotic creature from myth. She tried not to stare. Father caught her eye and grinned.

'It's a Durban rickshaw, Margaret; famous in these parts. You look just as surprised as I did the first time I saw one. I don't need your help thank you, Mr Flynn, I've travelled in one of these before.'

He handed Mother into the second rickshaw, settled her amongst the gaudy cushions then climbed in beside her. Flynn was all busy attentiveness. Margaret felt his hand grasp her elbow as she clambered awkwardly into the leading rickshaw. Over her shoulder she glimpsed Nansi being bundled with the luggage into the third contraption. Next thing Flynn was at her side. He leaned forward, shouted some curt instructions to the rickshaw puller and settled himself comfortably into the seat. She watched the man step between the heavy shafts, the muscles of his broad shoulders tensing to take their weight. Feathered tendrils swung from his headdress, swirls of gold, iridescent blues, the brightest emerald. She felt Flynn's hand again, resting on her sleeve, and flinched at this unwanted familiarity. He took no notice.

'Hold on to me, Margaret, it takes a bit of getting used to.'

The rickshaw tipped backwards on its wheels and she clutched the wooden side, avoiding his arm. Then they were off, swaying and jolting on the rough dirt road towards the town. The wide embankment was fringed with exotic flowering trees and bright fragrant shrubs. A chorus of seagulls shrieked above their heads as Flynn grabbed her arm again, pointing to a pale imperial-looking building set back from the road amidst tall clustering palms.

'That's the Durban Club. I'll take you to tea there if you

like. That tall red-brick building behind it with the dome is our central Post Office. Wonderful architecture isn't it? The British Empire at its best, I always think.'

He searched her face, the pale eyes unsmiling; he wanted her to be impressed. She glimpsed wide avenues – a blur of rickshaws and carriages, throngs of people on foot, on horseback – and his commentary continued. 'That's Aliwal Street, then Smith Street, named for the first colonial secretary. Oh do look, there's a hoopoe, it must have flown down from the Botanic Gardens.'

She wished she were sitting with Nansi, silent among the suitcases.

Later that day, when they had settled into their seafront hotel, Margaret sat in her room and read over her diary account of the day. She never liked her own writing – she stumbled over words as she did objects. But it would do as a record, she could always turn her account into a letter to Miss Roberts who would want to know all the details. The day before they left, Mr Jenkins had brought up a small parcel from the village: a volume of Emily Bronte's poems and a postcard of daffodils, '*Cofiwch eich gwreiddiau, remember your roots, my dear Margaret. Affectionately, Elen Roberts.*' Those last weeks had gone by in such a rush, there'd been no time for last things: a walk down to the lake; a lingering view of the valley from the top of Dryslwyn castle; a last walk with Gwennie. When Mair took the old dog home with her Margaret contrived to be away from the house, it was too much to bear.

The little clock on the bedroom mantelpiece showed five in the afternoon but outside the window of the Marine Hotel it was already dark, the dull flicker of gas lamps along the Esplanade a reminder they were no longer at sea. She remembered something else Mary Jamieson had written – '*Night falls very quickly in Africa; we don't have your long British twilight.*' At home now the early evening light would be starting its slow western fade across the valley, blushing the Towy's meanders, and the geese would be sweeping in long graceful arcs, calling down the night. With a sigh she laid her pen on the table beside the diary.

In the room next door Father was coughing again, perhaps the cooler evening had brought it on. Dr Morris had told them there would be a significant improvement in his health once he'd had a good dose of African sunshine. After all, this was only their first day overseas. Their final week in Bournemouth, staying with her mother's sister Rose, had been terrible, a bereavement all over again. Father paced the promenade each morning, watching the tide, anxious to be gone, to be done with it all. The furniture and glassware, the paintings, books and china, had sailed weeks before; they would be at Thorneybrook by now, stored somewhere until their arrival.

She wondered what Wil was doing. After that last visit to Hendre she'd heard nothing from him. She tried to picture him sitting in an office at the mine, head bent to sums and invoices, but she could only conjure him against fields and sky, busy with his farm work. He wasn't an indoors person. She should have searched him out, in defiance of Mrs Hughes, said a proper goodbye. Drawn a line. Perhaps she would write to him next week as soon as they were at the farm; he'd like to know what she thought of it.

She picked up the pen; laid it down again. She was too tired to write, the diary could wait for another time. They were staying in Durban for a few days; Father had bank business to attend to, lawyers, old acquaintances to meet. There was a list of provisions to buy for the farm and the necessary clothes for the climate. The Army & Navy couldn't supply everything from London, he said; Durban had one or two department stores and Percival Flynn would advise, they were fortunate to have the services of such an excellent, trustworthy chap, he thought of everything. Indeed he did, Margaret thought, remembering the furtive exchange in the drawing room at Bryntowy. What other secrets was Flynn hiding?

Father's cough was worsening; she could hear faint voices in the adjoining bedroom, furniture being moved, a window opened. Mother always insisted on fresh air to ease congestion. Somebody knocked rapidly at her door and she rose quickly to open it. Nansi was still wearing her brown coat from the ship; her thin face was flushed, she must have sprinted from the room next door.

'Mrs Lewis needs you, miss. The Colonel's not too good; the doctor's sent for.' Then she was gone.

When Margaret entered her parents' room her father was at the open window, leaning out and sucking in the night air with shallow, urgent gasps. In one hand he held a crumpled handkerchief. From outside she heard the loud, rhythmic plash of waves against the breakwater below the Esplanade. Bent over like that in his shirt sleeves, collarless and bereft of his usual formal clothes, her father looked frail and old, so different from his bright morning self. Perhaps Dr Morris had been wrong.

Mother was standing beside him. She turned and beckoned to her, but as Margaret stepped forward she realised Mother was calling to Nansi, not herself. The girl was busy at the bedside table, pouring water from a glass decanter into a small tumbler. She brought it to the window, whispered something in Father's ear. He took the glass in both hands and sipped at the water, pausing every few moments to take another labouring breath; when he had finished Nansi placed her arm gently around his waist and led him away from the window to a chair beside the bed. The painful gasping began to ebb. At Nansi's insistence he drank more water, wiping his mouth with a piece of cloth she gave him. When he returned it to her

Margaret saw the material was flecked with blood. He leaned his head against the back of the chair and closed his eyes.

'Better now.' His voice was barely a whisper.

'Margaret, would you go down to the foyer and wait for the doctor, please. He should be here any moment.' Mother gave a little tug at her cuffs; they were still in place and she was in command again. 'Close the shutters, would you, Nansi. Best leave the window open though, Colonel Lewis still needs the air.'

Nansi crossed to the window and closed the heavy wooden shutters; the noise of the sea receded.

Glad to have something to do, Margaret left the room and made her way down the thickly carpeted stairs to the foyer. The hotel decor looked expensive and depressingly familiar – gloomy panelling, ugly flock wallpaper, thick velvet curtains. Disappointment weighed on her; this wasn't how she had imagined Africa. They might be in Bournemouth or some stuffy hotel on the south coast, were it not for the large ceiling fans lazily stirring the sultry air.

A turbaned Indian servant in white tunic and red sash crossed the hallway in the direction of the dining room. He saw her on the stairs and inclined his head respectfully. Unsure how to respond, she blushed and looked the other way, at a portrait of the King, hanging on the opposite wall, looking faintly ridiculous in his medals and feathered tropical hat. She spotted a wicker chair near the main entrance dwarfed by an enormous tropical fern in a large earthenware pot. She would wait for the doctor there, where she could look out through the door's glass panels into the salty darkness. The day's energy and brightness had diminished to a single question now, would her father recover? What was the point of them leaving what was precious and travelling so far, if they ended up with nothing? She noticed her hands were shaking.

A small motor car drew up outside and she saw a tall

bearded man emerge, carrying a Gladstone bag. She got to her feet as he came in and he doffed his hat to her, revealing a bald domed head. Dr Ian Ewart – she detected a slight Scottish burr beneath the South African accent. He followed her briskly upstairs to her parents' room and she waited with her mother at the window while he made his examination. Nansi, standing beside Father's chair, answered the doctor's questions in a low steady voice.

Margaret followed her mother out of the room with Dr Ewart. In the corridor his verdict was brisk, to the point. A few weeks' rest at the coast and Colonel Lewis should be 'well on the road to recovery' but travel up country was 'out of the question' for the time being. Her father's lungs were in bad shape, no doubt worsened by the stress of the move and the long voyage. They had lost a son, hadn't they? Ah, that might have contributed to Colonel Lewis's ill health. Cheer up dear ladies, these old soldiers were a tough breed; he should pull through.

A few weeks? They hadn't planned for this. Margaret thought of the plush sofas downstairs, the imposing dining room with its silver cutlery and crystal glassware. The Marine Hotel must be expensive. She stole a look at her mother. From the troubled expression on her face she realised they both had the same thought: if they'd known how seriously ill Father was, they might have stayed in Wales. Now, it was too late.

Chapter 5

A message arrived after lunch the following day. A Mr Flynn was in the foyer, enquiring after Colonel Lewis's health. On the small landing at the top of the staircase Margaret halted for a moment to observe him. He was standing near the potted fern, dressed in the same light-coloured suit and panama hat, talking to his companion, a short, neat woman in a light blue skirt and matching jacket, the broad brim of a cream straw hat obscuring her face. They seemed to be having an altercation. The woman was talking rapidly, jabbing her finger at him, as though he were a child in receipt of a telling off. Flynn spoke very little during this tirade, but the sardonic expression on his face gave him the advantage, Margaret thought. It was like watching a performance. Suddenly he seized the woman's arm and pulled her close, dislodging her hat. He bent over and muttered something into her ear. She burst out laughing, jerked herself out of his grasp and, still chuckling began to adjust the brim of her hat. Flynn straightened up, stiff-limbed, and his face was flushed with something like anger, difficult to read from this distance. He cast a quick look around the foyer then turned to the woman once more. Margaret hesitated on the stairs – should she go down to join them or stay where she was, pretend she hadn't seen them. Flynn's voice floated up the staircase.

'Everything will be fine so long as you keep quiet about this, do you understand? I won't have you ruining things!'

The mood between them had changed; there was an ugliness in the air. The woman took a step backward, seemed about to retort. Margaret turned to go back to her room; it would be wiser to leave them to it. Percy Flynn must have noticed her movement on the stairs for she heard him call out, 'Margaret! Don't go!' She turned around. He was at the foot of the staircase, clutching his hat.

'Do come down, we've been waiting for you.'

He threw a quick glance back at the woman. Margaret couldn't discern her features beneath the hat, but she did see her place a quick finger on her lips. Another secret. She hesitated, clutching the banister rail. She should invent an excuse to leave them – Nansi needed her help with Father – but Flynn was now bounding up the stairs. He made an awkward lunge for her, as if he intended an embrace. She backed away and he seized her right hand instead.

'My dear girl, I came as soon as I could. You and Mrs Lewis have no need to worry; I've made sure the Colonel is in good hands. Ian Ewart's a capital chap, one of the best medical men in the colony. He's told me everything. Please come down so we can talk properly.'

With an effort she prised her hand from his sweaty grasp and followed him down the stairs. How dare he 'dear girl' her, she hardly knew him. She disliked this eagerness to assume control of her. In the foyer Flynn tried unsuccessfully to take her arm again, to lead her towards one of the chairs.

'I gather you have to delay your arrival at Thorneybrook until Colonel Lewis is recovered. Believe me, I do appreciate how frustrating this must be when you are longing to settle into your new home. However, in the meantime we'll endeavour to find plenty to entertain you in Durban.' His expression was rather smug, she thought.

'What Percy means, Miss Lewis, is that we shall endeavour to keep you from being bored stiff!'

The woman had come up behind them. Her hands were tucked into her skirt pockets and she was smiling broadly. She looked about Percy's age, in her early twenties perhaps.

An attractive face, heart-shaped, with a strong nose and chin and surprisingly pale skin for someone used to a hot climate. Though she seemed to be addressing Margaret there was something odd and unfocused about her expression; the look was unnerving.

'I keep telling him Durban's not London or Paris; it's a dull backwater, even if it is a pretty one. Dear Percy's a true colonial; he thinks there's nothing better than lying under the African sun, preferably with a gin cocktail to hand!'

It seemed a mild form of teasing but Margaret rather enjoyed Percy's discomfiture. He threw the woman a swift, tight-lipped glare. She had evidently struck a deeper nerve.

'Forgive me, Miss Lewis, I forgot to introduce my tiresome friend.' Margaret detected a note of anxiety beneath his cold politeness. 'This is Mary Jamieson. You will remember I first mentioned her in my letter to you; I gather you young ladies have been in regular correspondence.'

The woman gave a short laugh. 'That's not quite correct, Percy. I have written three fulsome letters to Miss Lewis, in which I provided an invaluable guide to the delights and vagaries of our climate, gave her some useful advice on suitable clothing, and an introduction to the manners and customs of our privileged community. She, on the other hand, has sent me one brief note in reply. Though it was very polite.'

She spoke with only the trace of a South African accent and her voice was surprisingly deep for such a small person. Flynn's expression stiffened.

'Take no notice of her joshing, Margaret. Mary does this to everyone. She thinks it's amusing. You will forgive her, won't you?'

There was an awkward pause. This confident, brittle manner of conversation was quite beyond her experience. She had nothing witty to say. Mary Jamieson came to her rescue.

'In this instance, I will allow Percy is correct about me.

It's a bad habit. I apologise.' She extended a small white-gloved hand. 'Welcome to South Africa, Miss Lewis, or can I call you Margaret? I'm sure you must be finding all this very difficult, with your father suddenly taken ill when you've only just arrived. And you're probably missing your home too, if you're anything like me. Perhaps you'll tell me about Wales some time, when you've got used to being here. Your little note didn't give much away, you know.'

Margaret felt a sudden, embarrassing welling of tears. Mary moved closer to her, a look of concern on her face, and Margaret realised why she had found her so disconcerting. Her left eye was colourless, the pupil obscured in an opaque, milky film. She tried not to stare.

'Please don't worry; I'm quite used to it.' Mary seemed unperturbed. 'River blindness it's called out here; a little worm burrowing under the skin, causes lots of itchy lumps and worse. Many people lose their sight completely, so I've been lucky. It doesn't stop me doing things, like driving or riding. Though Percy wishes that worm had got my tongue instead, don't you?' She tilted her head in his direction.

Margaret sensed another barb being thrown. Flynn looked irritated again.

'If you're not needed by your parents this afternoon, Margaret, we shall introduce you to some of the Durban sights. We shall wait over there while you get ready.'

He took Mary firmly by the arm and propelled her towards one of the large sofas. As Margaret climbed the stairs she heard Mary's ringing voice. 'You won't need a coat, remember!'

When she came down again, wearing the ugly pale straw hat Mother insisted she take for the walk, her companions seemed in better spirits. Margaret, too, felt a lightness. She had left Father sitting up in bed surrounded by books and newspapers.

He looked rather better this afternoon; his eyes were brighter, there were spots of colour in his cheeks and he seemed to be enjoying the view of the ocean through the open window. They had not minded her going, though Mother had hesitated for a moment, pausing from her letter writing to cast an anxious look towards the bed before giving her reluctant consent. A light sea breeze plucked at the heavy curtains behind the little writing table and Margaret noticed the old photograph positioned where it could be seen from the bed – David, in schoolboy cricketing flannels, tousled hair and a wide grin. Nansi sat in a small easy chair on the opposite side of the room, sewing. Such a peaceful scene, like a painting she remembered from a visit to the Tate Gallery one time. The bedroom of a country house. Surrey, not Africa.

Mary took her arm as the three of them stepped out of the hotel into the sunshine. The air was balmy, like a summer's day at home, on the other side of the world. Along the wide Esplanade people were strolling, couples arm in arm, children playing, dogs on leads, one or two older individuals on benches gazing out to sea. Elegant horse-drawn vehicles parked in the shade of palm trees. Bournemouth again.

Except that it wasn't. She felt something nudge at her shoe and looked down. A child, squatting on the edge of the pavement, in a torn dirty vest; alongside him an older woman, his grandmother perhaps, huddled in a brightly patterned blanket, her head swathed in green material, an extravagant turban. On the ground beside them, carefully arranged on a frayed tablecloth, were small objects and trinkets designed to catch the eye: a clutch of little woven baskets studded with coloured beads; tiny animals carved from some dark wood; squares of cloth embroidered with leaves; bright feathered headdresses – smaller versions of the ones worn by the rickshaw pullers. She disengaged herself from Mary's arm and stooped to pick up one of the little ebony carvings – a resting rhino, its rounded flanks velvet smooth and cool to the touch. The little boy's large eyes fixed themselves on her. Perhaps he was afraid she would pocket the animal and leave without paying for it. She knelt down beside him.

'This is lovely! Did you make it?'

That was better. She was at eye level with him on the dusty road. He stared gravely at her, silent. The old lady muttered something and he nodded, brushing a grubby hand across his face.

'Yes, I make it, *Nkosazana*.'

'And these too?' She pointed to the other animals. The boy's face broke into a broad grin. She smiled back at him.

'You are very clever to make such beautiful things. Where I come from people would be amazed to see them.' His smile faded– this was too much English. She tried again, holding out the little rhino. 'I would like to buy this one. How much is it?'

'Only give him half what he asks for. If you pay full price they won't leave you alone, they always want more money.'

She squinted up through the sunlight at Percy's white flannelled legs, imagining how it would feel to see him always like this, from the ground, bestriding the earth.

The child whispered, 'Five pennies, *Nkosazana*.' Margaret fumbled in her purse and found a shilling. She held it out to the boy. He glanced over at the old lady. From the folds of her blanket a thin dark hand emerged holding a cracked teacup. Margaret dropped the coin into it and got to her feet. Flynn was stony faced.

'On your own head be it. You'll soon find out you don't know the first thing about this country.'

He turned on his heel and strode off down the Esplanade. Margaret took out a handkerchief from her bag and folded it carefully around the little rhino. Mary was watching her, head cocked on one side, a quizzical smile on her lips.

'I say, good for you. Percy's always scared that if we show

we're a soft touch the Empire will immediately collapse!' She threaded her arm through Margaret's again. 'Come on, let's catch him up. We'll walk to the end of the Esplanade and have tea in Albert Park. They do wonderful scones there.'

Dr Ewart was coming down the stairs as she entered the hotel some hours later. The tea had indeed been delicious, served at round, white-clothed tables in the lilac shade of the graceful jacaranda trees. Birds called brightly among the crowding bougainvillea and hibiscus, the sea a melodic, drowsy undertone. Mary and Percy – he insisted she drop the formal Percival, far too English – were attentive and good humoured, naming the plants and shrubs for her, patiently answering her many questions. The rhino incident might never have happened. After tea Margaret insisted on leaving them at the entrance to the park and walking the hundred yards or so back to the hotel on her own. Her head was aching from the strain of making conversation. As she turned to wave she saw they were already walking away, their arms around each other, Percy's head bent towards Mary's, whispering. She felt suddenly uneasy, out of kilter. They were keeping something from her, she was sure.

The doctor's expression was grave. 'I'm afraid Colonel Lewis has taken another turn for the worse. I thought he was on the mend this morning but I was wrong; his lungs are struggling to cope. I've advised your mother he should be moved away from the seafront up to the Berea where the air is fresher and rather better quality.'

He must have seen the bewildered look on her face.

'I do apologise, Miss Lewis, I forget you're a stranger to Durban. The Berea is the ridge overlooking the city, you see it when you sail into the harbour. Lots of space up there, lovely homes, gardens, sea views, that sort of thing. I will make some enquiries. Peter Clarke, the rector of St Anselm's, might be able to help.' He cleared his throat rather awkwardly. 'The church has some... accommodation which might be suitable. I'll call again tomorrow morning to check on the patient.'

He doffed his hat to her and the turbaned doorman held the door, bowing as he passed. Margaret felt dreadful, overwhelmed with guilt. She should never have agreed to the afternoon walk with Percy and Mary, knowing how ill he was. Mother wasn't pleased. Why hadn't she put her foot down and stopped her from going out? Outside, it was already dark again; a small wind had got up and she could hear the urgent slap of waves against the sea wall. An ocean continent lay between here and home and Father was now seriously ill. They had no idea what would happen next and they were among strangers, however well intentioned. She hugged her arms tightly to her chest and moved towards the staircase. Nobody – Mother especially – must see how truly terrified she was. There were no certainties any more.

CHAPTER 6

It was Mary who saved them from the indignity of a poky annexe adjoining the Anglican Church, which was all the rector could offer them. A letter addressed to Mrs Lewis arrived the following morning. Miss Jamieson would be delighted if the Lewis family would be her guests for the duration of their stay in Durban. Her family's town house on the Berea was at their disposal until Colonel Lewis was well enough to travel north.

'She says we must treat the house as our own; she will be staying with a friend. How very kind of her! Miss Jamieson says she will collect us from the hotel on Friday afternoon. You must have made quite an impression, Margaret, for her to be so generous to us. I'm sure Percival had a hand in this too. Such a thoughtful man.'

Margaret thought of that odd little scene between the two of them in the hotel foyer; none of their behaviour quite added up. No point in bothering Mother with her reservations. She had quite enough to be worrying about.

The Jamieson's house – No. 3 Fraser Lane – was at the end of a pretty tree-lined street just off Berea Road, the main thoroughfare running from the city up to the Ridge. As Mary's little car slowed to turn in at the gates Margaret, seated behind her mother on the back seat, glimpsed an elegant red-brick, double-storied villa with a steep curved roof of grey corrugated iron and tall windows framed in white-painted wood. At the front of the house were two shady verandahs supported on slim pillars thickly entwined with purple bougainvillea and white jasmine. The Jamiesons must have money; the houses they had passed on their climb up Berea Road were mostly small, single storied dwellings.

Mary drove them slowly up the short gravel driveway, past a neat circular lawn lined with flowering shrubs. She stopped the car in front of the house and Margaret stepped out. Dr Ewart was right; the air did feel different up here, fresher than at sea level. A tang of woodsmoke reminded her of one of those sharp autumn days back home; Father's health was sure to improve up here. He was already installed at the house, having travelled up that morning in Dr Ewart's motor car accompanied by Nansi. And there he was, sitting in a large wicker chair on the verandah by the front door, a tartan rug tucked around his knees. He cast it aside and rose to greet them. Beneath the panama hat his features were still drawn and pale but it was good to see him smiling again.

'Well, my girls, this is a turn up for the books! Wonderful to be staying on the Berea again. The view over the bay is simply marvellous; you must see it from the top floor.'

An elderly black servant was struggling up the verandah steps with their heavy suitcases. Instinctively, Margaret moved to take hers from him. The man looked confused and seemed reluctant to give up his burden; for a moment there was an awkward tussle between them.

'I think you had better yield, Margaret. Simon won't thank you for interfering; it isn't done out here.'

Mary's face wore that same look of wry amusement Margaret remembered from the episode with the African child. She felt awkward, wrong-footed again; after all, she'd grown up with servants herself, she knew the protocol. But this was different. He was an old man; it wasn't right to leave him struggle on like this. She gripped the handle tighter.

'Margaret, please!'

Mother was frowning at her; she looked embarrassed.

Reluctantly, Margaret let go and the old man staggered on with the luggage into the house.

A sudden flurry of movement in the nearest tree deflected their attention. Something grey, lithe, was skimming the leaves, bouncing across the slim branches. Strange clicking sounds, bursts of noisy chatter. Twigs showered on to the grass below.

'Blast them, they're after the figs again. Precious!'

At Mary's shout a young black woman, neatly dressed in a blue overall and matching headscarf, came running from the side of the house brandishing a wooden broom. She ran to the foot of the tree, hoisted herself on to the lowest branch and poked the broom handle up through the thick leaves. From inside the canopy came a chorus of piercing screeches, then a group of small grey monkeys – half a dozen at least – emerged at the top of the tree, leaping long-tailed from branch to branch like deft trapeze artists. They disappeared into the denser foliage at the bottom of the drive. The young woman retrieved her broom and jumped down.

'Thank you, Precious,' Mary called from the verandah steps. The maid gave a brief nod then walked swiftly away in the direction from which she had come and disappeared from sight. Mary shook her head irritably.

'Those monkeys are vermin; they'll steal anything. Make sure you close your windows at night. Pa likes to take a shot at them when he's here but they're quick little devils, you've got to be lucky to catch one.' She was rubbing at her blind eye. The puckered skin around the socket was inflamed; it looked sore. Margaret moved away from them towards the tree and gazed up into its branches, hoping the monkeys would return. Until today she had never seen one in the flesh; vermin seemed a harsh term for such exuberant, confident creatures.

'Come on Margaret, tea's ready,' Mary was calling. She turned and saw that Simon had silently reappeared on the verandah bearing a large wooden tray. He placed it on the wrought iron table beside her father's chair. A plate of neatly arranged sandwiches, another of little buttery scones, a pot of strawberry jam, tiny iced cakes. Even the china was dainty, painted with a smattering of pink roses, like an English garden.

'Do let me pour.'

Mother was standing by the table, looking rather wistfully at the silver teapot. It must be the relief of habit, Margaret suddenly understood. Mother wasn't one to show her feelings. Perhaps this dislocation from the familiarity of home was difficult for her, too.

Mary gave a bright laugh. 'Goodness me, please do, Mrs Lewis. The tea always slops into the saucer when I'm pouring; you need two eyes for this kind of thing, you know.'

For a moment, nobody spoke. Mary plonked herself onto one of the comfortable wicker chairs; she seemed entirely unconcerned.

'Please do sit down all of you. A cup of tea will be lovely. I'm simply parched after the drive up here!'

Margaret took one of the other chairs and moved it into the shade to be nearer her father. Indeed, the tea was welcome, this dry air did make one thirsty. As she sipped, unfamiliar sounds teased her ears: the gurgling call of laughing doves, crickets buzzing in the long grass, the rhythmic scratch of a broom sweeping leaves in a neighbouring garden. Distant chatter of African voices on the road below the house. Her father leaned back in his chair with his hands folded on his lap; he looked very peaceful. Mother busily handed round the plates.

'We really are tremendously grateful to you, Miss Jamieson. It's so kind of you to let us use your house for Arthur's recuperation. I do hope it's not a fearful nuisance.'

Mary took the proffered plate and helped herself to a sandwich.

'It's no trouble at all, Mrs Lewis. As you can see there's plenty of room here. We only come down to Durban a few times in the year, mostly in July and August to escape the winter up country. The city's such a trial in the summer – clammy and horribly hot. I spend most of my evenings sitting in a cold bath just to cool down!'

'The upkeep of a house like this must be very expensive if you use it so seldom. Do the servants stay here throughout the year?'

'Do forgive me, I should have explained. This house doesn't belong to us; we rent it on a long lease. The owner lives in Australia, hardly ever comes to South Africa. In fact, I've never met him.' Mary reached across the table for one of the little cakes. 'Pa needed somewhere to stay when he comes to Durban on business and his lawyer found this house for us. Percy keeps an eye on the place when we're not in town, manages the accounts, that kind of thing.'

'Ah, the indispensable Mr Flynn.' Mother brushed away some crumbs from her lap. 'That young man has quite a knack for earning one's trust. A secret would be quite safe with him, don't you agree, dear?' She glanced affectionately at Father.

He did not reply. His gaze seemed fixed on some point on the distant horizon and his right hand moved restlessly up and down the arm of his chair.

Mary's voice broke the silence. 'Well, I'm not sure I'd tell Percy everything, Mrs Lewis, but he's a reliable, thoroughly decent friend.' She swivelled in her chair to look at Margaret. 'And he's good company, I'm sure you've seen that already. He's always full of ideas and schemes to bring me down to Durban, stop me being bored. I know you won't agree with me, Colonel Lewis, but country life can be a little dull!'

Father dragged his gaze away from the sea and cleared his throat. 'You are quite right, Miss Jamieson, I cannot agree with you on that point. When one's been in the thick of two wars, here and in Europe, and seen such terrible sights, dull country life is exactly what one needs.'

He dabbed at his mouth with his handkerchief, frowning, and Margaret felt her stomach tighten. The subject must be changed. She tried to recall something from the earlier conversation.

'Does your mother still enjoy coming to Durban, Mary?'

'My mother died when I was ten – a riding accident. After that I went to boarding school in Scotland, her old school in Edinburgh. I would have been sent there in any case; she used to say she didn't want me growing up with a dreadful South African accent.'

Margaret watched Mary's finger stirring the tiny cake crumbs on her plate. For a while nobody spoke. With something like relief they all stirred at the sound of a car turning in at the drive and Mary scrambled to her feet.

'Oh look, Dr Ewart has arrived. I'll just move my car to the side of the house so that he can park.' She seemed relieved to be diverted.

What an odd creature Mary was, Margaret thought. Underneath that confident exterior was a more complex personality. Mary had made an effort to befriend her even before she arrived in South Africa; she should at least try to reciprocate. Despite the difference in their ages and upbringing, perhaps they could find common ground. Without Wil to confide in, she was in need of a friend.

CHAPTER 7

She had missed all the signs. Father's relapse had been so swift, barely a month after they had settled into the Jamieson's house. Before then everyone said how well he looked, how much the climate on the Berea suited him. He willingly followed the daily routine designed by Dr Ewart to aid his recovery. Most mornings he would walk in the garden then rest for a while in a chair on the verandah. Sometimes Margaret walked with him amongst the shrubs which bordered the front lawn. He was learning their names.

'Do you see that one with the bright yellow flowers? It's a sunbird bush. The plant next to the fence is strelitzia and, if I'm not mistaken, that's an African dog rose climbing into the coral tree, it has the most wonderful deep red petals.'

And he would pause, leaning on his cane, smiling at this new pleasure. In Wales he never took much interest in Bryntowy's garden, there was always so much estate business to be getting on with. Here, in contrast, after his afternoon nap, he often sat at the desk in the study with a copy of *The Flora of Natal* and transcribed into his diary, in his distinctive fine handwriting, the botanical names of the trees and shrubs he'd identified that morning.

At the end of their first week Percy arrived with a borrowed wheeled chair. From then on someone – usually Nansi, occasionally Margaret – would take Father on a daily outing along Fraser Lane to admire the elegant colonial houses with their white porticos and graceful verandahs, their tidy lawns and sweeping views across the bay. The weather was a constant delight: balmy, sun-filled days followed by cool, crisp nights. At home spring would be advancing into summer, the hawthorn in full flower, the tall beeches greening along the drive. It would probably be raining.

There had been moments, watching her father push aside his plate of barely touched food at the dining table, or carefully lower his thin frame into a chair by the window overlooking the garden, when Margaret witnessed the unmistakeable, disturbing changes: the shortness of breath, the deeper shadows beneath his eyes, his skin's translucence. And the trembling in his fingers had returned, though this didn't trouble him in the way it used to at home.

The signs were all there, but she didn't want to see them. Neither Mother nor Dr Ewart appeared concerned and, even if they were, she was too preoccupied to notice. Mary and Percy had gone out of their way to fill her days with activity, all of it 'delightful' – Mother's word – and all of it a welcome distraction from Father's irresistible decline. Outings along the wooded lanes of the Berea in Mary's little car or visits to the Botanic Gardens to see the rare orchid collection, supper at the Durban Club. She was beginning to think of them both as her friends.

Until the Sunday tennis party. They were at The Heights again, another grand house on the Berea belonging to Mary's regular tennis partner, Bridie McAllister. Another long gin-stoked lunch after the morning's awful doubles match. Margaret was no good at the game, Percy knew that by now – he'd seen her stumbling around the tennis court on too many occasions – but he was persistent. She had to partner him for the first set, then he'd let her go. It was so humiliating. She kept missing shots, dropping the ball, ducking at the net each time he served another self-consciously blistering ace. In the end she let him play for both of them and simply gave up pretending. Mary was partnering Howard, a cousin of Bridie's from Cape Town, a rangy, sunburnt man with a vacant expression and no obvious interest in the game. Mary was a skilful player: the accuracy of her shots, her speed on court, gave no indication of her disability. For all the attention she and Percy paid to their partners they might as well be playing a singles match.

It was Percy's turn to serve. Howard, at the receiving end, was straightening up after retying a loose shoelace. Margaret, hugging the net and longing for the set to be over, saw Mary catch Percy's eye and raise her racquet. He smiled, raised his own and hit the ball so hard it slammed into Howard's chest, knocking him backwards. Percy called out, 'So sorry, old chap, thought you were ready.' His opponent, clearly winded and in some pain, tried to laugh it off, 'My fault, should have been concentrating.' But the game had clearly soured for him. At the end of the set he lurched off the court to pour himself a beer from the tray of drinks the maid had brought out to the terrace overlooking the tennis court. Mary and Percy resumed their game. Neither paid any attention when Margaret followed Howard off the court.

The long afternoon wore on into the evening. Indoors, she declined Percy's invitation to partner him at bridge – was this another game expressly chosen to humiliate her? – and left the four of them to their play. On the other side of the drawing room were books and a comfortable sofa facing away from the bridge table. She picked out *Gardens of the Cape Colony* and settled down to read. Father would like this, she would make a note of the title for him.

'Your friend doesn't seem to be enjoying herself, Percy.' Bridie's voice, just above a whisper. 'You'd better go and cheer her up; you don't want to lose your golden egg, do you?' Howard sniggered and then she heard Mary snap, 'It's your call Bridie, get on with the game, please.'

Percy said nothing though she sensed him twisting round in his chair to see whether she had heard. She made a show of turning over the pages, absorbed in what she was reading. His 'golden egg', for heaven's sake! There must be something he wanted from her, since he was cultivating their relationship so obviously. From now on she would be even more careful around him; no part of Margaret Lewis would ever belong to Percival Flynn.

What Mary was up to, she couldn't be sure. There were occasions when she seemed genuinely interested in her, asking about life in Carmarthenshire, about the boarding school she'd attended near Hereford, the books she enjoyed. One afternoon, dropping her back at the house after a drive up the coast, Mary produced a small leather-bound book from her handbag.

'When you told me about the novels your teacher used to lend you, I thought you might be interested to read this.'

Margaret took the proffered book. The title was embossed in gold letters on the cover, *The Story of an African Farm*.

'I don't expect you to like it. Olive Schreiner's not everyone's cup of tea. Percy would be horrified if he knew I'd given it to you; he likes women to be adoring and mostly silent and they are the opposite in this novel. But you won't be in the city for long and the book has interesting things to say about life in the wild. Durban isn't Africa, you know. You're heading for a shock if you don't pay proper attention.'

Surprised by the gravity of Mary's tone, Margaret looked up from her perusal of the cover. Today the damaged eye was covered by a black patch. Earlier, Percy had joked he would bring her a parrot next time. But in that moment the effect was more disconcerting than comic. Clearly, this was no casual gift; Mary expected her to take the book seriously. She would begin reading it tomorrow. But she didn't, because that was the day when she knew for sure Father was dying.

She woke early to the sound of a car's engine idling outside the house. She opened the bedroom shutters to see the top of Dr

Ewart's bald head disappear rapidly through the front door. The driver's door swung open, abandoned.

Hurried footsteps climbed the uncarpeted stairs. She pulled on her dressing gown and went out on to the landing. Her parents' bedroom door at the end of the corridor was ajar and she could hear Mother's voice. Nansi came out carrying a bundle of sheets; this time there was no concealing the bloodstains. The maid, Precious, was already on the stairs, a pile of clean, neatly ironed sheets in her arms. The women swiftly exchanged the sheets and Precious disappeared back downstairs, the bloodied tangle she had been handed held discreetly close to her body. Nansi avoided looking at Margaret as she returned to the bedroom and closed the door behind her.

Margaret sat down on the edge of the top stair, hugging her knees. The polished wooden treads and banisters smelled familiarly of warm beeswax. The early morning spilled through the open window above her and the space filled with scattered light and the scent of honeysuckle. Downstairs in the hallway she heard the clock chime six times. She buried her head in her lap. If she kept her eyes shut she could imagine she was sitting on the stairs at Bryntowy, hearing her father calling Gwennie for their brisk daily walk to the stables to check on the horses. Please God, don't let him die.

She sensed movement, someone sitting down next to her. She straightened up. Mother's hair was unpinned, tied into a long loose plait at the back of her neck. She was still wearing her nightclothes: her shoulders were covered by an Indian paisley shawl and her feet were bare. Margaret would always remember that shock of seeing her mother's naked feet, surprisingly large for such a small neat woman, the toes misshapen and calloused from a lifetime of being cramped into shoes too small. At least they had their big feet in common; she always felt lumpish and ungainly in comparison. Her mother's arm lightly touched her own.

'Your father is very ill, Margaret. The doctor has given him a sedative and he's breathing more easily now.' Her face was pale and there were dark shadows beneath her eyes. 'Dr Ewart says the tuberculosis is more advanced than he initially thought and we have to prepare for the worst. He says it's only a matter of time.'

What did that phrase really mean? They'd been living in a kind of suspended time for weeks. She had barely given a thought to Thorneybrook, all their belongings waiting there to be unpacked, that new life Father had looked forward to. She felt her mother's arm steal softly around her shoulders and rest there. On the wall opposite hung a large painting in an ebony frame, a landscape depicting some wild part of southern Africa. She'd passed it so often but never properly looked at it until this moment. In the foreground a rock-strewn river tumbled between high banks of grassland stretching to the horizon; in the background a dark twin-peaked mountain range beneath a turbulence of gloomy cloud, patched here and there with sky. Unpeopled. Unknowable.

Leaning into her mother's warm body, Margaret summoned a different landscape: her beloved Towy pooling beneath the castle rock; Father casting his fishing line out over the water below Dryslwyn bridge; Wil driving Dan along the lane with a cartload of hay; in the foreground, herself and David sitting on the riverbank, with Gwennie tucked between them. She would put Mother in the picture too, though less clearly observed. In the background perhaps, upstream from the bridge, with a sketchbook on her lap, drawing the scene. A comfort it was, this illusion of another life, if only for a few, brief minutes.

CHAPTER 8

Death should be short-lived. Father's dying dragged on and on. Perhaps he was reluctant to give up this new country, where the warmth eased his lungs and he still clung to the promise of a different future. For a few days he rallied, was well enough to be brought downstairs to the front room to sit near the window and watch the sparrows pick delicately at the seeds on the bird table, or smile at those raucous birds they called 'hadedas', poking for crickets in the front lawn with their long thin beaks. He seemed content to be there, spoke little, ate less, whilst the three of them learned how to care for him.

That afternoon it was her turn to be on duty. Mother had decided to take Nansi with her to tea at St Anselm's Rectory. Mrs Clarke, the rector's wife, had an English maid about Nansi's age; it would be good for her to meet someone of her own class, pick up some tips about how to be a lady's maid in Africa. Margaret wondered briefly what Nansi thought about this arrangement. The two of them had barely spoken to each other since they moved to the Jamieson's house; here Nansi seemed altered from that watchful, insolent girl at Bryntowy, kinder, more dependable. 'A rock', Mother called her one time. 'I don't know what I'd do without Nansi.'

Margaret settled herself in one of the easy chairs in the far corner of the room from where she could keep a watchful eye on her father who was reading near the window. She opened the first page of the long delayed *Story of an African Farm*.

'*The full African moon poured down its light from the blue sky into the wide, lonely plain. The dry, sandy earth, with its coating of stunted karoo bushes a few inches high, the low hills that skirted the plain, the milk-bushes with their long finger-like leaves, all were touched by a weird and an almost oppressive beauty as they lay in the white light.'*

She read the description a second time, allowing the unfamiliar landscape to breathe and colour her imagination. Father's book clattered to the floor. Margaret started from her chair, heart pounding, and rushed over to him. With relief she saw he was only asleep, his chest quietly rising and falling. His reading glasses had slipped to the end of his nose. She removed them gently not to disturb him and stooped to pick up the fallen book. It was one he had asked her to bring him from the bookcase in the study – *Birds of South Africa* by Arthur Cowell Stark. The cover of the book was open and an inscription on the flyleaf caught her attention. *For Josephine with fondest love, Ernest. 10th July 1898.* At the bottom of the page was an address: *Mount Pleasant, 3 Fraser Lane, Durban.*

She pondered the names for a while then left the book on the little table beside her father's chair. He was still deeply asleep, his breathing even and regular. Mary always referred to the house as Number 3, but the name *Mount Pleasant* she had heard before. She stared out of the window, beyond the vivid canna lilies and the purple fuchsia fringing the lawn. The leaves at the top of the fig tree were shaking; those monkeys must be back again. Why hadn't Flynn told them this was Mr Bancroft's house? It was not a coincidence, surely.

Perhaps one of the servants would know. Father was still sound asleep; this wouldn't take long. She had never been beyond the front rooms on the ground floor. At the end of the hallway was a door through which Precious and Simon came and went with trays of food for the dining room. She pushed it open and walked into a large airy kitchen, empty of people and spotlessly clean. A clutch of flypapers fastened to a hook in the ceiling flapped in the draught from an open doorway on the other side of the room.

She walked out into a small dirt yard enclosed by high wooden fencing. Two metal dustbins, a mop and bucket, and a basket of wet clothes. A washing line strung between two wooden poles. Across the yard a rickety shack with the top half of its stable door hanging from a rusty hinge. The sound of voices inside.

'Hello? Is anyone there?'

The sounds ceased. In the silence she sensed someone was listening.

'Precious? Is that you?'

She crossed the yard and peered through the top half of the door. The room was pungent with the smell of burnt wood and cooking. A candle stub burned in a jam jar on top of a small table covered with a brown striped cloth. Beside it an old wooden chair and a maid's blue overall hanging from a nail driven into the rafter. The floor was just beaten earth. Something stirred under a heap of blankets in the corner and she heard a muffled cough. Someone was living there.

Precious's face appeared out of the gloom, inches away from her own. Startled, Margaret withdrew her head. The girl regarded her in silence. Behind her the coughing began again. Precious turned from the doorway and she heard her whisper something in her own language. There was a mewing sound – some small animal – then Margaret heard the bolt being drawn back. Precious stepped out into the yard, closing the door behind her. The girl's hands were clasped in front her in that demure servant's pose Margaret had seen so often at the dining table.

'*Nkosazana*, may I help you with something?'

'I'm sorry to disturb you. It wasn't anything very important, just a quick question. This house, do you know its name?'

'Yes, madam. Number 3 Fraser Lane, Durban.' Her voice was low, but each word was clear and precise.

'Does it have another name?'

The girl hesitated, a look of mistrust in her dark eyes. 'I do not understand you, *Nkosazana*.'

'Who does the house belong to?'

She shrugged her shoulders, as though the question made no sense. 'Jamieson family.'

'Miss Jamieson and her family have been renting the house for a long time. Do you know the person who owns the house, or perhaps used to own it? Was his name Bancroft?'

Precious's face was a careful blank. She knew the answers, Margaret was sure.

'Very well, I will ask Simon. Perhaps he will be able to help me.'

Precious was looking at the ground now. She folded her arms across her chest and her thin fingers plucked at the sleeve of her grey blouse.

'Simon not here. I am sorry, *Nkosazana*.' The words were delivered in a flat, distant tone.

Another voice was calling from inside the shack. 'Ma! Ma!' A child's thin, querulous note.

'Is that yours?'

Precious did not reply. The child began to wail, a high-pitched, insistent crying, impossible to ignore. The girl glanced over her shoulder at the door, turned again to face Margaret. There was a pleading expression in her dark eyes.

'Please, *Nkosazana*, do not tell the other madam. It is not allowed to have family stay in the city. My mother's home is too far; she is sick, too sick to look after the child. He must live here with me.'

'But surely Miss Jamieson will understand.'

The girl shook her head vehemently.

'If you tell her, the police will come. I will lose my job. Please, *Nkosazana!*'

She'd never seen fear like this. What kind of country was it that separated mothers from their children?

'I won't tell anyone, Precious, I promise. Can I help you in any way? Bring some food for your child. Clothes, medicine?'

'No, madam, thank you, we have everything. He has a small fever, that is all. Will be better soon.'

She fell silent, eyes on the ground again. The child's cries grew louder; Precious mustn't ignore him, someone might hear. The girl seemed to be waiting for her to leave first.

'You don't need to worry, I do understand. You should go to your child.'

In an impulse she reached out her hand, a gesture of sympathy. Precious hesitated, then extended her arm, clasping the elbow with her other hand in the African greeting Margaret had often seen in gatherings outside the church or on the street. Their hands touched, briefly.

'Now you must go.'

Precious nodded and turned away. The door of the shack closed behind her and the child's wails quietened.

It was nearly dusk; over the Berea the air was cooling. Margaret shivered in her thin dress. How did Precious manage to care for her son, hidden like a stowaway in that dilapidated shed? In Bryntowy, Mair, who lived in, had her own room off the back stairs and cooked her meals in the kitchen. Out here, her parents expected Nansi to be accommodated under the same roof, often sharing their food. That outside shack was hardly fit for human habitation. Why should the discovery of a child living with its mother be a matter for the police? It certainly wouldn't be, if the child belonged to Margaret or Mary or even Nansi. In this country it seemed, what mattered most was not your identity, but the colour of your skin.

CHAPTER 9

The afternoon of her conversation with Precious turned out to be Father's last one downstairs. They took turns to sit with him, a shrunken figure half-buried already beneath the heavy bedclothes. She was standing at the open window one morning, the distant ocean a deep, serene blue, the scent of honeysuckle filling the room.

'Are you thinking of Bryntowy?'

She turned, startled by his voice; he spoke so little these days. He was sitting up in bed with his eyes closed, enjoying the warm sunlight spilling through the window.

'It's the smell, isn't it? A summer's day on the terrace, that's what I think of. You and your brother playing tag on the lawn; your mother with her shears, ravaging the honeysuckle. It survived though didn't it, came back every year without fail.'

His voice faltered, tired from the effort of speech. Such shallow, labouring breaths. Margaret came over to the bed and drew the chair closer to him. He reached for her hand; his skin felt cold and dry, the knucklebones brittle beneath her fingers. She hadn't been thinking of home, as it happened; she'd simply been enjoying the lovely view. He was still struggling to speak.

'Moving here has been hard for you, don't think I haven't noticed. I see the sadness in your face sometimes.'

She felt her face flush at this unexpected intimacy; Father never talked about feelings, unless it was to do with horses or his days in the regiment.

'I'm fine, really, just getting used to the change. I suppose I'm still missing the old familiar places.'

His grip on her hand tightened a little. 'I want you to promise me something, Margaret. Don't give up on this country after I've gone. You will grow to love it in time, as I have; you're a strong person, you have your mother's resilience.'

Her eyes were swimming. She turned her head so he wouldn't see. Concentrated on the wallpaper pattern, doves and pale roses intertwined.

'I'm not strong, I won't know what to do if you're not here.' The words she wanted to say; instead she was silent.

'You won't be alone. I've instructed Percival Flynn to manage any legal business, keep an eye on the finances so your mother doesn't worry. He'll be a good friend to you both, I've no doubt of that.'

He released her hand and lay back against the pillows, exhausted by the effort; he needed to sleep. She got up and drew the curtains to shut out the sunlight. Nansi would be taking over shortly. She was on her way out of the room when he called her name.

'Margaret, one more promise. Before you make any decisions, go to Thorneybrook, see the place for yourself. Everything will feel quite different then, believe me. I think it will be the making of you, my dearest girl.'

He was looking directly at her and it felt like a farewell. She couldn't be truthful and disappoint him. Yes, of course she would go. He gave her a last, faint, smile and closed his eyes again.

Mother and Dr Ewart were with him when he died. When they called Margaret into the room, his face against the starched sheets was the colour of putty and he didn't look like Father any more.

She knew her mother was grieving, though they did not speak of it. She sometimes heard her, late at night, weeping for him behind her bedroom door. One time she got up and knocked on the door, hoping to be let in, but there was no reply. Mrs Lewis had lost her son and now her husband; women of her class weren't supposed to show their feelings, even to a daughter.

They buried Father in Durban at her mother's insistence.

'Arthur was happiest in South Africa even though we hadn't been here long; he had such fond memories of his time out here during the Boer War. He was looking forward to starting a new chapter after all he'd been through.'

She was sitting with Mr Pretorius the undertaker in the dining room at Number 3, dressed in her darkest clothes and draped in the awful shawl with the black fringe lent to her by Mrs Clarke. Her hair was scraped back from her face and secured in a tight bun. She reminded Margaret of one of those stiff-limbed Victorian dolls with china faces and tight, unsmiling mouths.

'It feels right to bury him here.'

Her long fingers fiddled with the black lace at her neck. Margaret knew the tone of voice; once Mother's mind was made up she would not be persuaded to change it. And there was another, unspoken, reason: they simply couldn't afford the considerable expense involved in shipping the body home for burial.

Three days later they walked behind the coffin out of St Anselm's to the little graveyard overlooking the bay. The horizon was an empty blue haze; in the light sea breeze the palm trees fringing the graveyard rustled their dry leaves. Mary helped Mother choose a suitable wreath – white chrysanthemums, yellow roses, a spray of golden honeysuckle. At home Margaret would have picked him a bunch of wild daffodils, the ones that always bloomed in late spring at the edge of the lake below Coed Mawr. He would have liked that; the flowers were an annual pleasure they both looked forward to at the end of a sodden winter.

A small group of mourners attended the service besides herself, Mother and Nansi: Mary and Percy of course and Dr Ewart; Mr Harding the lawyer; an associate from her father's military time in South Africa, Captain Armstrong – a tall, distinguished looking man with a thick black moustache; a clutch of ladies from the church in fashionable sombre clothes and solemn faces. Mother had written to relatives in England and Wales but they knew nobody would make the long journey in time for the funeral. As she stood by the graveside listening to the rector speak the last rites Margaret thought she glimpsed Precious and Simon in the distance near the gate. Later, she recalled the fragrance stealing from the yellow blossoms of a stubby tree near the boundary fence.

The day after the funeral she returned to the graveyard on her own. The earth mound looked ugly and raw and the flowers were already wilting in the stiff wreath. Mother had chosen a burial plot next to the grave of Father's only relative in South Africa. Margaret stooped to read the inscription on the grey marble headstone.

Sacred to the memory of Ernest Lewis Bancroft Esq
Born Portsmouth, England 1863.
Entered into rest Durban, August 1904

Dark moss and lichen speckled the marble and a raggedy shrub straggled along the base of the stone, snared by creeping tendrils of ivy. She dropped to her knees and began to pull the ivy away from the stone, in an impulse to tidy the neglected memorial; he was a relative after all. Beneath the ivy was another inscription, the lettering thin and rather crudely done, as if someone had scratched it into the marble with a sharp knife.

Also Josephine, died 1901

She had seen that name somewhere. Was she a wife, a sister? Unlikely since the inscription on the marble was so poorly executed, scribbled like an afterthought at the bottom of the gravestone. She thought of Gwennie. People often had their favourite animals buried in the same grave. Josephine seemed an unlikely name for somebody's pet; it jogged no memory for her.

During the days following the funeral she tried to make herself useful. There were letters to be written: to the vicar of Rhydfelin, requesting prayers for the family at the Sunday services; a long obituary notice for the *Carmarthen Journal* and a briefer one for the *Natal Mercury* – the editor wanted details of his service in the South African War. *The London Times* required a succinct biography – education, military service, his DSO 'for conspicuous gallantry and devotion to duty'. (A surprise, Father never having mentioned it to her.) What about David; should they include him in the obituary? Mother said people would think it odd if they didn't, so they agreed some suitable words: *'Colonel Lewis had been deeply affected by the loss of his only son, 2nd Lieutenant David Lewis of the Welsh Regiment, mortally wounded in France, March 1916.'*

That was when Mother mentioned the picture.

'The little photograph of David playing cricket in his first year at Shrewsbury, do you remember it? I decided to put it with your father before they closed the coffin.'

She put down her pen and reached for the blotting paper to dry the ink. She looked tired, older; there were more grey streaks in her hair.

'He was very fond of that photograph, always kept it by his bedside at Bryntowy. David's death was a bitter blow, I'm not sure he really recovered from it.'

Bitter for all of them, thought Margaret. She'd done her grieving alone, all that damp spring and summer, hiding away in the woods or in the old summerhouse where nobody could see. And Gwennie rescued her as she always did. But in this place there was no loving animal to hug, nowhere to hide from this terrible new grief. For Mother's sake it was better to keep busy, fill the hollow space with other thoughts.

The mysterious Josephine, for instance; that was a mystery to be solved. She couldn't be a much-lamented pet, surely, that idea led only to a dead end. A woman of secrets, then, her name forever linked with Ernest Bancroft, concealed at the bottom of his gravestone. Unacknowledged, like Anne Catherick in *The Woman in White*. Suddenly it came to her: she had seen the name before, in the book her father was reading during those last weeks of his illness.

Alone in the study, she hunted through the shelves of the bookcase until she found it. *Birds of South Africa*. This time the inscription had meaning – '*For Josephine with fondest love, Ernest*'. Odd that she had completely forgotten its existence, but then so much had happened in the intervening weeks. Who was she, this mysterious Josephine? Had she lived in Mount Pleasant? The house seemed emptied of its past. There was one small portrait on the wall above the hall table – a fair-haired, refined-looking young man, seated at his desk looking into the middle distance. Melancholy, wistful eyes. He could be Ernest Bancroft, but there was no name on the painting to prove it.

She examined the books crowding the study shelves. A few were inscribed with his initials, *ELB*. One in particular drew her notice, a large leather-bound book entitled *The Wildlife of Southern Africa*. The chapters on different species were beautifully illustrated: detailed drawings of cheetahs, lions, various birds of prey. When she attempted to return it to its place in the row, the book resisted her pressure. Something was wedged at the back of the shelf. A crumpled brown exercise book. Each page was crammed with detailed sketches of birds, some drawn in fine pencil, others painted in delicate watercolour. Whoever made these drawings was an accomplished artist.

'What are you doing?'

Percy's voice. Seated at the study table, utterly absorbed in the pages, she hadn't heard him enter. The room felt distinctly chill.

'Nothing really. Just looking at these drawings.'

He was suddenly at her shoulder. She felt his hand resting lightly in the small of her back and flinched but the hand stayed put.

'Gosh, those are good. Where did you find the notebook?'

'On one of the shelves, it must have fallen out of here.' She indicated *The Wildlife of Southern Africa*.

He bent over her to take a closer look and she could feel his warm breath stirring her hair. The sensation was uncomfortable.

'Who is Josephine?'

She might have pricked him with a needle. He gave a sharp intake of breath and abruptly withdrew his hand.

'I have no idea. Why do you ask?'

'Her name is in one of the books my father was reading.' She got up from her chair and went over to the bookcase.

'Here it is.' She placed *Birds of South Africa* on the table in front of him, opened it at the dedication on the flyleaf.

'This is Father's relation, isn't it? Mr Ernest Bancroft, the man who left us Thorneybrook; they're his initials. Why didn't you tell us we were staying in his house?'

It was a surprising moment of triumph. Underneath the suntan she could swear his face had paled. He was swallowing hard, adjusting his lips into the semblance of a smile.

'Well, you've been quite the sleuth, Miss Lewis! Mr Conan Doyle should write you into one of his detective novels. You're quite right, I should have been more honest with you. This was

Ernest Bancroft's house, quite a coincidence really that Mary's father should be renting it from the current owner. I thought the Jamiesons would have cleared out these old books by now; they're not much use to anyone.'

He reached forward to take the book but Margaret was swifter. She snatched it up, tucked the notebook inside the back cover and returned it to the shelf. Percival Flynn would not have the upper hand.

'I think it should stay where it belongs, don't you, Percy?'

There was no reply. When she turned round he was near the door on the other side of the room.

'As it happens your mother and I have just been discussing a related matter. She sent me to find you; we're out here.'

The study door opened into a sunny conservatory on the west-facing side of the house. They often sat there to make the most of the late afternoon light. Her mother was seated on one of the small sofas covered in a faded chintz.

Percy removed a clutter of papers from the chair opposite.

'Here, Margaret, have my seat.'

He went to perch on one of the small upright chairs nearest the door. Margaret sat down; this awkward formality made her think of the headmistress's study, Miss Ainsley with a copy of her end of term report, waiting to deliver her verdict.

Mother removed her reading glasses. She looked a bit flustered.

'Mr Flynn has been helping me set our affairs in order after the funeral. We need to talk about your inheritance, Margaret, and decide what is to be done about it.'

It sounded like the beginning of a well-rehearsed speech.

'When Mr Flynn came to Bryntowy to inform us that Thorneybrook had been left in trust to you by Mr Bancroft, the intention was that your father and I would manage the property until you came of age.'

She glanced at Percy, as if to check her lines were correct. He smiled his approval.

'As you know, Margaret, we have very few assets left at home, mainly items of furniture we decided not to send out here, a few paintings, some shares.' Mother's tone sounded more confident, now she was on surer ground. 'Your father was scrupulous in repaying his debts; he wanted us to make a good life for ourselves in the colony. Now he is no longer with us I feel we should honour his wish and settle in South Africa.'

So this was their plan and they were delivering it to her as a fait accompli. Mother's fingers plucked at her lace collar; either there was something else she wanted to say or she was waiting for Margaret to reply. Well this time she wouldn't oblige; she would keep them waiting as long as she liked. Father had called her strong, resilient – in this moment she remembered the words so clearly. She had a different plan and she would choose her moment. She listened to the seagulls squawking on the roof, the sighing of the palm trees. Holding her nerve.

In the end Flynn was forced to speak.

'I appreciate this is a difficult subject to broach so soon after your father's death, Margaret, but Mrs Lewis is right, decisions have to be made. Thorneybrook is now legally yours in terms of the will, and no doubt you believe this gives you the right to dispose of it as you please. But there are other considerations.'

He paused. Outside the window a sudden gust of wind blew over one of the wooden chairs at the end of the balcony. The sky was gunmetal grey, it was about to rain. Mother reached over, took her hand in her elegant cool fingers.

'Percival says the land at Thorneybrook is excellent. He has already made enquiries about finding a suitably experienced farm manager. And people have been so very kind to us since your father's illness and afterwards. I've made some loyal friends out here.'

She was gently stroking Margaret's palm, her eyes seeking

out a response. She would not give way; heavens above, Mother was even calling him by his first name.

'My dear, Mary Jamieson says we can have this house for the rest of the winter. Her father has no need of it by all accounts; he's about to make a long visit overseas, three months at least she said. It will give us time to look for another Durban property to rent.'

Mother's choice. A lifetime of tea parties, interminable games of tennis and bridge. Having to endure those enervating Durban summers everyone complained about. She would not bear it. She pulled her hand away. They would not determine her future; her father may have instructed Flynn to handle their affairs, but the farm was her property now.

'Since Thorneybrook has such excellent land I shall sell it.' She rather enjoyed the sudden consternation on her mother's face. 'If I can't find a South African buyer I'm sure there'll be lots of interest at home. These days people are keen to move to the colonies, I remember you and Father telling me that.'

She looked over at Flynn. He should understand she was making the decisions.

'I expect you know how one sells property out here. I'd like you to have the farm valued as soon as possible so that we can place advertisements, here and at home.'

Her mind was already racing ahead: once the farm was sold she might travel for a while, go to Europe. She could learn to type, find some interesting employment. The war had opened opportunities for women, Miss Roberts often said; perhaps she would study, go to university. Mother would be happy to move in with Aunt Rose, she liked Bournemouth. Selling Thorneybrook would take them home again, that was the main thing.

Flynn called again the following morning. Sitting on the verandah with their morning coffee, the two of them tried another tack.

'Before you dispense with your property, Margaret, your mother and I thought you should see the place for yourself.'

She was instantly suspicious. Those had been Father's last words to her; had they hatched this idea with him before he died? Percy was leaning towards her across the table with an earnest expression on his face, the look of a disinterested friend.

'Of course that doesn't mean we are disregarding your wishes. I will arrange for the farm to be valued with a view to selling. However, I sincerely believe you will regret not having seen Thorneybrook before you return to Wales. It might help you to understand exactly what you are giving up. Mary would be delighted to organise a visit, the farm's in her neck of the woods, you could stay at her place which would be more comfortable. Mrs Lewis, I take it you are happy to part with Margaret for a few days?'

Mother could barely hide her approval; she was more than happy, it seemed.

'I think that's an excellent idea. It will do you good to have a change of scenery, Margaret, after all you've been through. You mustn't worry about me; I have plenty to do over the next few days, finishing these letters, seeing people. And Nansi will be here if I need anything.'

She rose and went back into the house to her correspondence. Flynn got up to leave; she must speak to him.

'You're not going to change my mind, you know, making me do this. I'm not stupid, Percy, I know you and Father were in some kind of conspiracy. There's something important you're not telling me. I wonder if Mother knows what it is.'

He stopped in his tracks, his face suffused with anger. She'd called his bluff.

'You've been reading too many detective novels, Margaret. Try some South African history instead, you might learn something. Facts, not fiction. Believe me, I have only your best interests at heart.'

He was off down the drive before she could think of a suitably stinging response.

As if on cue, Mary called on them that afternoon. Flynn must have briefed her. Margaret, busy addressing envelopes in the dining room, heard her quick footsteps crossing the verandah. She had brought a map.

'I thought you'd like to know where Thorneybrook is before you visit.'

She smoothed out the wrinkles in the stiff cloth and spread it out across the table.

'Africa isn't like Britain, you know, where every stream and lane has a name and all the houses have histories and you can't walk anywhere without trespassing on someone's property. There's such freedom here, miles and miles of empty country to explore. I hope you like riding; we can show you some lovely places you can't reach by road. Thank you for sparing her for this visit, Mrs Lewis.'

Mother was beaming. They believed their plan was working, Margaret thought irritably; she would capitulate in the end, like all obedient daughters. Mary moved her chair closer to the map.

'Now, Margaret, follow my finger along this road. That blue squiggle near the top of the map is the Umzimnyama, the river that runs through the farm.'

The map was a confusion of black lines, a few place names, lots of empty space.

'You see those tiny black dots?' Mary's finger tapped the middle of the map. 'That's the drift – you'd call it a ford. There's a track leading off to the right just beyond it and Thorneybrook's about a mile on from there. Let's see if I can find it for you.'

She brought the map closer to her face; it must be difficult to pick out details with only one eye.

'Ah, there it is. Take a look.'

She leaned back, keeping her finger on the place, and Margaret took a closer look. A tiny square in the middle of nothing. Mary must have read her thoughts.

'Don't look so worried, you won't be too far from civilisation! Pieterskloof is only ten miles away, just a morning's easy ride. Pa will be thrilled to have you with us for a few days. Percy says you can't possibly stay at Thorneybrook; everything's still in crates, waiting to be unpacked.'

Or shipped home again, Margaret thought to herself. Her mind was already made up. Nevertheless, a promise was a promise, David always said, when they played their games of dare. No matter whether you crossed your fingers behind your back when you made it. She would make this journey because she had promised her father, then she would sell the wretched place and be done with the lot of them.

NATAL PROVINCE

END OF WINTER, 1920

Chapter 10

With a sudden jolt the teacup slid across the table towards the window, only coming to a halt when it hit the bottom of the ledge. Margaret made a grab for the little jug of milk before it followed suit. From the tilting window of the first class carriage she could see the engine several carriages out in front, cresting the steep curve along the edge of the escarpment. Gouts of steam plumed in the frosty air. Beyond the train a vast landscape opened out: hills unfolding as far as the eye could see, the earth still felted with the ochres and yellows of winter grass, dissolving in the distance into the brown smoke haze of a hundred small fires. She had never seen anything like it. Winter at home was always green.

Perched on a little plateau near the bottom of the nearest hill a circle of mud huts, topped by conical hats of thatch grass. A gaggle of barefoot children waving beside a railway crossing; two women walking single file along a winding dirt path, vivid red skirts swaying in the dust, long bundles of sticks precisely balanced across their heads. This was the Africa she had imagined, like a scene from one of Father's beloved Rider Haggard novels. She wished he were sitting opposite her, sharing this journey. There was so much she wanted to ask him now it was too late. Thorneybrook would 'surprise her', he had said. Was this another secret she would have to uncover on her own?

The carriage righted itself and she retrieved her teacup. She downed the last lukewarm dregs and reached for another egg and cress sandwich from the picnic basket. Strange she hadn't lost her appetite yet. Food seemed to be everyone's medicine for grief. 'Have some more fruitcake, Margaret, you need to keep up your strength.' 'Mrs Holmes has sent round a delicious chicken stew, Mrs Lewis. She says there's plenty more at home.' The day after Father died a hamper arrived at the house: more fruitcake, cheeses, pastries, a whole ham. Accompanying the bouquet of white carnations and freesias was a black-edged card, '*To Mrs Lewis and Miss Lewis with deepest sympathy from St Anselm's Mothers Union.*' Margaret and her mother had eaten everything. With gusto sometimes, when nobody was looking. Only Nansi seemed to have no appetite, moving palely about the house like some visiting ghost.

The train was out of the bend now, beginning to slow. She glanced at her wristwatch. It was just after noon, they must be near Inchanga station, the halfway halt on the route from Durban to Pietermaritzburg. Percy's notes said the train waited here for half an hour to take on water after the three-hour journey up from the coast. She would walk to the end of the platform and back, then return to her seat to continue writing her diary; she'd neglected the routine these past weeks. There were more sandwiches in the picnic basket and a slice of lemon cake to keep her going until they reached the terminus.

She stepped down from the train and edged past a noisy clutter of African women on the platform, selling trinkets and woven baskets. It felt rude to refuse the proffered bead necklaces and wooden bracelets but she had no need of them; perhaps she would buy some on the way back to Durban, presents to take home to Wales. Wil wouldn't thank her for a necklace, of course, but she already had his gift set aside: the little rhino she'd bought from the boy at the beachfront.

She reached the end of the platform beyond the station

buildings. The rail track stretched into the distance, back towards the ridge of lumpy hills and valleys they'd passed earlier. Spears of scarlet aloes poked up from the thin red soil on the opposite side of the track, fiery fingerposts in the smoky blue. She breathed in a pungent mixture of earth and woodsmoke. The air was much colder up here than on the Berea; her skin was tingling beneath the cotton fabric of her travelling dress as she returned to her seat.

The guard slammed the door behind her and whistled them off. Steam blanketed the window. An elderly man with a walrus moustache doffed his hat to her and enquired whether the seat opposite was free, looking pointedly at the picnic basket she had placed there. Reluctantly she wedged it under the table, cramping her feet. As the train picked up speed the man opened his copy of the *Natal Mercury*. Thank goodness, she wouldn't have to make polite conversation all the way to Pietermaritzburg. She checked the notes she had made at the back of her diary, following Percy's instructions. The train would arrive at four-fifteen. Mary had arranged for her to stay at a boarding house close to the station.

Jacaranda Villa. The stationmaster will give directions, only a short walk. The driver will call for you at 8am tomorrow morning. Name Moses. Does not speak English.

The carriage darkened and Margaret looked up from her notes. The train was in a cutting, the view blanked by immense rocks, criss-crossed with black scars from the dynamite. Her fellow traveller sighed and turned over another page of his newspaper. She turned to the front of the diary and began to write.

'Might I borrow that for a moment, young lady?'

He was looking at her pencil.

'My pen has dried up, just as I was about to fill in the last clue.'

It took a moment to recall where she was. She handed over

99

the pencil and he went back to his crossword. They were now travelling across a wide plain. Grassland as far as the eye could see, broken by small outcrops of rock and stunted thorn trees; on the horizon the darker outline of a mountain range.

'Thank you so much.'

She took the pencil from him and watched him fold the newspaper into a neat square. He pulled out a pocket watch from his waistcoat.

'Almost four o'clock; nearly there. Good old SAR&H, always on time.' He snapped the lid shut and returned the watch to his waistcoat. 'Not like the railways back in the old country, eh? Hopeless lot those Liberals, should have given that dreadful Welshman the boot after the war.'

She bristled at the insult; even Father would have defended Lloyd George from such ignorance. The man was still talking. 'Are you just visiting Pietermaritzburg or going further on?' Reluctantly, she supplied a few details of her journey.

'Ah, Pieterskloof. Grand country. Scotland on a bigger scale. Wonderful shooting, fishing. Mind you, the nights can be jolly cold up there, I hope you've brought something warmer than that to wear, young lady.' He indicated her thin Durban clothes.

She chose not to reply; he wasn't the type to listen to a woman. Outside, across the greying plain, she could see the flickering lights of Pietermaritzburg. She stowed her cup and plate inside the picnic basket and retied the stiff leather straps; the piece of lemon cake had lost its appeal.

The boarding house was spotless, smelling of beeswax and camphor oil; the rooms were crammed with dark overbearing furniture and framed embroidered Bible texts. The landlady, Miss de Vries, a terse, thin-faced Afrikaner in a shapeless purple dress and thick black stockings, took her up to her room.

'A long journey, *juffrou*, you will sleep good tonight.'

She spoke English with a heavy guttural accent. On the bedside table was a pale cream envelope bearing her name. The note inside was from Mary.

My dear Margaret, I hope the journey so far has not been too tiring or dull. Percy told me about that little altercation you had the other day. The poor boy's quite upset to think he may have lost your good opinion. Beneath that lawyer's cold exterior he's a soft-hearted old stick. Believe me, he has your best interests at heart.

It will be good to see you tomorrow afternoon. Mary

Why was Mary so anxious to defend him? What was really going on between those two? So many secrets. Margaret lay in the creaky uncomfortable bed, unable to sleep and wishing she could talk to Wil. At this moment what she needed most was his common sense, his practical outlook on things. He would quiz her, of course, say she was imagining non-existent conspiracies, but he always listened first before making a judgement. She would trust Wil with her life.

The cart appeared at the front of Jacaranda Villa at 7am sharp the next day. According to Percy's notes they had a long morning's drive ahead of them. Moses, hooded and muffled in a thick blanket against the cold, acknowledged her greeting with a brief nod. His transport was not the sturdy, comfortable trap she had imagined. Filled to the brim with sacks of grain, rice, bristling farm implements, it looked like the Hendre farm cart on its return from the farmers' market in Carmarthen. Her travel case and the picnic hamper were wedged in tightly behind the driver's seat, the only space available. Wil would feel quite at home here.

It was a beautiful morning, the sky a brilliant clear blue, the sun beginning to melt the frost that had formed on the lawn during the night. The two sturdy bay cobs shifted in their harness, breath steaming in the icy air. She climbed into the seat beside Moses and turned up the collar of her jacket against the cold; she was glad to see a pile of rugs on the floor beside her feet. Her head ached from the sleepless night. Miss de Vries waved them off from the steps as they lumbered away. It didn't take long to become accustomed to the rocking motion of the cart; with the sun warming her face Margaret closed her eyes and dozed.

She woke with a start to find the horses had stopped. They had reached a wide shallow river, the Mandhla. Some large rocks, carried downstream by the current, were blocking their passage through the drift. Moses climbed down from the cart, untied the strings holding together his battered leather boots, placed them carefully side by side on the bank, and waded into the river. Margaret watched the icy water swirl around his thin ankles as he strained to lift the first rock clear. She scrambled down from the cart and started to unbutton her boots.

'Please let me help…'

He looked across at her, then down at her boots, and his face broadened into a toothless grin. He shook his head and pointed to the cart. She climbed back into her seat, a little annoyed by the rebuff. At home she'd often helped Wil clear the winter debris from the ford at Nant Gwyn; this job didn't look any different.

It was very still and peaceful. Above the noise of the river she could hear doves calling – two long throaty notes followed by three short ones – and the dry rasping of unseen grasshoppers. The horses chomped at the stubbled grass on the road verge. On the other side of the drift the river valley narrowed between steep hillsides, crested by seams of dark rock. In Wales these would be mountains. Something screamed, high and shrill above her head. Shading her eyes against the sun's dazzle, she thought she saw a movement in the blueness, some bird of prey perhaps, wheeling in wide, slow circles. Her father would have identified it immediately; she pictured him with her, marvelling at it all.

The drift was clear. Moses retied his boots and guided the horses slowly across; the current parted around their fetlocks as they splashed, sure-footed, towards the opposite bank. Ahead of them the road stretched away towards a distant rise, then disappeared into the dust haze. She brought up one of the rugs and wrapped it around her shoulders. The scratchy cloth smelled of smoke and animals, like Gwennie's old dog blanket. She buried her face in the dusty fabric and tried not to think of home.

Hours later she watched Moses tighten the harness before the final steep descent; the horses were sweating heavily from the haul up the last hill. Margaret watched him brace his feet against the struts and lean back, keeping the reins taut; thick ice crusted the potholes and the horses were struggling to keep their footing on the slippery surface. At one point the cart suddenly tipped and she imagined herself somersaulting over the edge, tumbling into the rock-strewn abyss below in a chaos of splintered wood and flailing hooves. Then at last they were on even, flatter ground, and the horses broke into a sprightly trot after the awful downhill slither.

They came to another smaller stream, the water a mere trickle amongst the stones. Moses slackened the reins to let the horses pick their way across. Immediately to their right a track, barely the width of a cart, branched off the main road into a long narrow valley. Here the horses quickened their pace, scenting home, and suddenly her stomach was churning with anxiety; until now Thorneybrook had just been a name, the idea of a place.

The track hugged the valley contours alongside the river. In the distance a thin curl of smoke rose into the air above a stand of tall pine. The thick grass tussocks bordering the track gave way to bare earth and they entered a long drive lined with pale gum trees, dry slivers of bark crackling beneath the horses' hooves. The air was fragrant with the spicy scent of crushed eucalyptus. She knew that smell – in an instant she was back in Bryntowy, standing on the path beyond the kitchen garden watching Wil plant two eucalyptus saplings. Father's voice in her ear – 'They're Australians, Margaret, they won't like Welsh damp.' He had sounded almost sorry for inflicting their climate on these innocent trees. He bent down, pulled off one of the leaves and crushed it between his fingers. Held out his palm. 'Isn't that a wonderful scent?' She had recoiled. 'Ugh! It's like toothpaste. You smell it, Wil.' He shook his head, grinning, and finished his task, treading in the soil around the roots. To everyone's surprise the trees had thrived, foreigners asserting themselves amongst the natives.

At a fork in the drive the cart turned left into a short grassy avenue half-buried in a thicket of laurels. They came to a halt at a rusted iron gate, tied to a wooden post by a length of fraying rope. Moses jumped down, loosened the rope and the gate swung open. He walked the horses through into a dusty clearing in front of the house.

Margaret gasped. Thorneybrook was not at all the romantic dwelling she had conjured from Percy Flynn's little sketch. The long low roof was patchworked with pieces of rusty corrugated iron and coarse thatch grass; thick gobbets of the stuff lodged in the saggy guttering above the verandah. There were bare grey patches on the walls where the cement had cracked. The whole building looked utterly forlorn and unkempt, as though it were past caring what face it showed to the world. Her heart sank. Who on earth would buy a place like this?

Moses looped the reins over the cart shaft and the horses stretched their necks and shook out their dusty manes, grateful to have reached the end of the long journey. She jumped down and stood unsteadily beside the cart, her head buzzing with the deep stillness of the winter afternoon, the fluting of unseen doves, the sharp smoky tang of burned wood.

She walked towards the house. At the edge of the verandah steps was a small statue, made of pale marble. The goddess Flora, her graceful arms entangled in the carved roses encircling her head. Margaret paused, surprised. The statue could almost be the one that used to stand on the front terrace at home. Moses passed her, carrying her case and the picnic basket, a rug tucked under his arm. He negotiated the cracked, uneven steps, pushed open the front door and disappeared inside the house. She should go after him, see where he was putting her things. He should have left them outside the house, Mary would be arriving any minute to collect her.

She took a closer look at the statue and her heart missed a beat. This Flora's left foot was also missing, like the one David smashed with a cricket ball one summer practising his bowling technique; they had never got around to having it repaired. She reached out her hand and touched the cold mossy head. Flora's stone eyes regarded her reproachfully; perhaps she too was missing her old home.

Moses emerged from the house and without a word climbed back into the cart. He gathered up the reins and the horses moved forward, disappearing out of sight around the corner of the house. She was alone.

Chapter 11

The front door was wide open. She walked up the steps and paused at the threshold, waiting until her eyes adjusted to the interior gloom. The hallway smelled dank, musty, as though nobody had lived here for some time. Wooden floorboards wobbled unevenly, creaked underfoot; flakes of plaster chalked her sleeve as it brushed against the wall. There was no sign of her luggage. On opposite sides of the hallway were two doors. The one on the right was open; Moses might have put her things in there. The large room was in darkness, save for a sliver of light filtering through some thick curtains at the far end. She started to feel her way forwards, towards the window. Without warning she stumbled against something hard, sharp-sided, and let out a scream, feeling a stabbing pain in her knee. A piece of furniture – a small table perhaps – teetered under her clutching fingers, sending an object crashing to the floor. Panic seized her. She daren't turn around, she had to get to that window somehow, escape this suddenly smothering dark.

Fragments of glass or china crunched under her boots as she set off again, arms outstretched, blinded; her clutching hands felt the velvety spine of a sofa, a chair's solid shape, a sticky patch of damp along the wall. At last she reached the window. The curtains were made of some heavy embroidered material; she fingered the raised stitches in the fabric and tugged. Glorious afternoon sunlight spilled through the cracked and dirty panes of glass.

She turned and looked about her. The room was crammed with furniture. Thick wooden beams criss-crossed the plastered ceiling; the walls were smeared with damp, with ugly patches where the limewash had peeled. A brownish rash mottled the plaster on the underside of the window sill. In front of the massive stone fireplace dominating the room were two mahogany armchairs covered in a faded blue velvet and a matching sofa; they suggested the odd illusion of comfort. Elsewhere, other larger pieces of furniture jostled for space against the walls: a bureau, a marble-topped washstand, a pair of ladder-backed kitchen chairs.

On the floor at the foot of a small octagonal table, tiny shards of glass glittered in the sunlight and nearby lay the shattered remains of a photograph frame, the photograph itself still intact. She limped back across the room, stooped and picked it up. Held it to the light. Her father in his riding clothes sitting on the bench at the end of the terrace, looking relaxed and young, with a cigarette in one hand and Gwennie posing at his feet. Perched on the arm of the bench grinning at the camera was her six-year-old self, gap-toothed and wearing a pair of David's old cricket flannels rolled up at the bottoms and tied round her waist with string. The day he shattered Flora's left foot.

She could hardly breathe; her heart was bursting. She looked around the room. It was all Bryntowy. The Persian rug from the library spread itself in front of the fireplace; on the opposite wall the portrait of her great grandfather, Captain Henry Lewis, which used to hang in an alcove in the drawing room, fixed her with his baleful stare. She recognised the old dining room curtains, Mother's favourite blue armchairs from the morning room. Betsan always left the tea tray on that wobbly table. Dear God, even that awful stuffed fox with the mangled rabbit in its bloody jaws had found its place here. There it was, leering at her from the corner cabinet. 'Fancy you being frightened of that old thing, Margaret; you know it's not real.' Father was laughing at her on the stairs, as she balled her fists into her eyes and whimpered. 'Let's find a different place for it, shall we?' From behind her hands she watched him lift the ghoulish creature from the hall table where every day for as long as she could remember she'd endured its glassy menace. He carried it away in his strong arms to some remote part of the house and she never saw it again. Until now.

But he would never come again, ever. Those warm strong arms would not return to banish the horrors.

She doubled over from the sudden rush of pain, the knowing that this was real. All that pent-up grief smouldering inside her, burning holes beneath the skin where no one could see. With a kind of relief she felt herself give way, let the hot tears flow, soak her cheeks, her hands, her clothes. No David to tease her. No Gwennie for comfort. No Bryntowy. All lost. Heartbreak was physical, like fracturing a limb.

'Margaret? Is that you in there?'

Mary's voice, loud in the hallway; she must have heard her wailing. How long had she been in the house? Margaret scrubbed at her slimy face – why did she never carry a handkerchief? – hastily pushed the damp tendrils of hair behind her ears. Nobody, Mary least of all, should see her like this.

'Good gracious, what's been going on?'

Mary was now inside the room, a neat figure in khaki jodhpurs, tight tweed jacket, the black eyepatch. She was gazing at Margaret, at the photograph in her hand, the broken glass all over the floor. She couldn't think of an answer; it was like being caught trespassing in someone else's property. Mary came over, knelt down and started collecting bits of glass. She was shaking her head.

'I'm so terribly sorry, Margaret. I've no idea who's responsible for this outrage. Your furniture was securely locked in the packing crates; Percy told me he'd ordered them to be stored in the sheds behind the house. Moses lives in the compound; I know he won't have touched a thing. He wouldn't dare.'

The idea of a motive hadn't entered Margaret's head.

Impossible to imagine someone breaking open those huge wooden cases, unpacking her family's belongings, carrying the furniture into this room and arranging it like this on purpose. Perhaps she should be outraged like Mary, but she didn't feel that way. The furniture, the pictures, the rugs – they looked perfectly at home in their new surroundings. Even the mangy fox and its bloody prey.

Mary's cupped hands were full of glass and wood splinters. She got to her feet and heaped them on the little table.

'I'll get to the bottom of this, I promise. Word's probably got around that your property is here. I'm not altogether surprised this has happened; you can't trust the natives, the area's full of thieves. We should have made the house more secure. I'll get Moses to put everything back into the crates.'

'Oh, I don't think there's any need for that. Someone's gone to a lot of trouble to make the room look nice.'

She saw Mary stiffen; as usual her words had struck the wrong note. She tried again.

'I mean, isn't it better, now that this furniture's been unpacked, for everything to stay where it is? Where it's dry...' She was going to say 'comfortable' but that sounded sentimental.

Mary was heading briskly for the door as if she hadn't heard.

'I'm going to check the rest of the house, see if anything else has been disturbed.'

Margaret heard her footsteps recede along the hallway towards the back of the house. She placed the photograph gently on the table and left the room. The door opposite was ajar. Sunlight poured through a large jagged hole in the window shutters on to dusty floorboards, peeling wallpaper and a small square wooden crate lying in the middle of the empty room. The lid had been opened; scraps of newspaper and wood shavings spilled over the sides. On the floor, propped against the crate, was her old doll Semolina, her brown cloth legs in their knitted red boots tidily crossed at the ankles. She was wearing the purple felt coat and hat Wil's mother had made for her sixth birthday. Strange how a memory could be so instant, so specific.

She picked up the doll and held it close. Semolina's solemn china face with its vacant blue eyes and painted lips stared back at her. Tucked into the doll's hatband was the little downy wood pigeon feather David had given her the day before he went away to school for the first time. Odd that Mother had chosen to keep this relic of their childhood when she'd donated all their other toys to the Carmarthen workhouse.

'Hurry up Margaret; you need to see this!'

Mary sounded cross. Reluctantly Margaret put Semolina down, settled her against the packing case as before and left the room.

The hallway was surprisingly long, with other rooms leading off it. From the outside Thorneybrook had seemed quite small for a farmhouse; inside, it revealed itself to be a rabbit warren. At the end of the hall beyond an archway Margaret entered a large light-filled space, with a further passage beyond that. From every wall familiar pictures regarded her: the gloomy oil painting of Manorbier Castle framed against a turbulent sea; several of Mother's gentle watercolours of the lake at Bryntowy in spring and autumn; her charcoal sketch of David as a young child which hung above her desk in the morning room.

'I'm in here!' Mary was calling from a room behind her on the left of the hall. Margaret joined her. This room had also been furnished. The washstand from Father's dressing room was next to the window, the Chinese blue porcelain bowl decorated with a motif of butterflies had been carefully positioned on the marble top. Beside the washstand stood the walnut chest of drawers where he kept his socks and handkerchiefs. The bed from David's room was by the wall facing the window, draped with the green counterpane from her own bed, the one with the pattern of daisies and trailing ivy. She recognised her dressing table in the opposite corner. On the floor a large rug waited to be unrolled.

Mary was standing by the bed holding a paper in her hand.

'This was on the dressing table.'

It was one of the calling cards Mother used to leave behind when the person was out. The message was written in red ink, dark as blood.

Welcome home Miss Margaret Lewis.

Mary snorted in disgust. 'This must be someone's pathetic idea of a joke. Neither Moses nor his wife can write English, so God knows who's responsible for this.'

Margaret sat down on the bed and heard the old springs creak under her weight, the way they always did when David jumped on it. She noticed her little bookcase near the window. At Bryntowy it used to be next to her bed; she rather liked this new position. Some of the books she had chosen to bring from home had been unpacked and arranged on the shelves in neat rows, taller ones on the bottom, shorter above. She could never be bothered with such details, no matter how much Mother and the servants told her off for being untidy. Her books, the green bedcover, the china bowl; it was all rather lovely. She couldn't imagine this was Percy's idea, though it was the most obvious conclusion. He and Mother would never dream up such charming silliness.

'I don't think we should be too alarmed. Perhaps Percy's organised this as a surprise, to make me feel at home.'

'Don't be so absurd. How could you even think such a thing? He would never do this!'

The outburst was so unexpected, so violent, that Margaret

111

flinched in self-defence. Mary's face was white, the patch a black slash of anger. She took a step backwards and ran a hand through her hair, sensing, perhaps, that she had gone too far.

'Forgive me, Margaret, I didn't mean to be rude, it's just been a bit of a shock, that's all. I assumed the house would be empty, it certainly was the last time I was here.' She moved towards the door. 'We should be going, it's getting late.' She gave a rather terse laugh. 'Perhaps you're right, we should leave things as they are for the time being. Once you've moved in you can rearrange everything. I've left the trap at the side of the house. Why don't you get in while I have a quick word with Moses. Don't worry, I won't scold him too much. I've brought a warm coat for you; it's on the passenger seat, you'll need it once the sun goes down.' And she was gone.

Margaret turned the card in her hand. There was more writing on the back. Two words: *Zenzile Grace.* It could be a greeting, in the local language perhaps. Another of Percy's jokes? Though Mary had been so adamant this had nothing to do with him. Now Margaret wasn't sure either; the note gave her the creeps.

She tucked the card into her skirt pocket and out of habit smoothed the creases in the counterpane to avoid a scolding from Betsan. Mary had left the door open and it was only when she went to close it behind her that she noticed her suitcase, the rug and the picnic basket in the corner. Moses must have assumed she would be staying. She picked them up and took them out into the sunshine.

The sides of the house were even more dilapidated than the front. Pieces of corrugated iron littered the ground, shards of broken wood, stones, rubble were heaped against the walls; a shutter swung on its broken hinge from one of the windows. At the base of a wall where the brickwork had worn away, huge holes were clogged with weeds. The rusting remains of a ploughshare lay on its side near a pile of roughly cut logs.

In the shade of the pine trees opposite the house a pony and trap were waiting. The grey mare dozed in her harness, twitching at the flies clustering her neck. Margaret hoisted her belongings into the small space behind her seat and climbed in. The mare, roused by the movement, shifted her scabby rump, then closed her eyes again. Margaret unfolded the fawn tweed coat on the passenger seat and draped it over her shoulders. She was exhausted. Her knee was very painful; she winced as she touched the tender place where the bruise was forming. The house's long shadows reached across the path, as if drawing her back into their silence. The decrepit state of the farm oppressed her. Father would have known what to do; he loved a challenge. She could imagine him and David hatching their plans, then rolling up their sleeves and organising a work force to transform the place. With them gone, she knew she wasn't equal to the task. Those furnished rooms, her old books, Semolina, the fox, that note – it was ludicrous, a sick joke. Mary was right. They would find out who had thought up this stupid prank and then she would sell Thorneybrook as soon as she could and go home, even if Mother and Percy Flynn tried to dissuade her. It was not their decision to make; it was hers alone.

Mary climbed into the trap. She had taken off her eyepatch and the puckered skin across the dead eye looked red and sore.

'Sorry to have been such an age. I've spoken to Moses. He says he was away in Pieterskloof for a couple of days; when he got back the rooms were as we found them. He thought your father had ordered someone to do it before you moved up here; he hadn't heard the news of course. You'll be pleased to know the other packing cases are intact. I checked the ones which were opened; they aren't damaged, someone had just unpicked the locks. I'll send a message to Percy as soon as we get home.'

She reached behind her seat and brought up a wide-brimmed brown felt hat, clamped it over her head so that her face was in shadow, and took up the reins, shaking the mare out of her doze.

'Come on Petra, time to get going. Do you have everything you need?'

Margaret nodded; the trap was certainly more comfortable than Moses's farm cart. She slipped her arms through the sleeves of the coat and fastened its large horn buttons.

'I've told Moses to leave the furniture and stuff in the house for the time being and put extra padlocks on all the doors. He'll patrol the place at night, get one of the farm boys to help him. I assume you're happy with that. Move on, old girl.'

Mary was back in control. She turned Petra on to the laurel drive. The sun was low on the horizon as they reached the river crossing and turned right on to the main road to Pieterskloof.

'It will take us a couple of hours to reach town, our place is only twenty minutes from there.'

The trap lurched to the left as the wheels bounced over a pothole and Margaret clutched the side. Mary laughed.

'Don't worry, you'll get used to this kind of thing after a while. I expect you'll be glad to get out of those clothes, though; the dust gets everywhere. Look at this!' She held the reins in her right hand and patted the front of her jacket; thin whorls of dust lifted into the air.

'That reminds me; I need to give you this letter.' She felt inside the breast pocket and brought out a small envelope. 'Moses gave it to me, said it arrived some while ago. The post comes up to town from Durban once a week; if there's anything for Thorneybrook he collects it when he comes to market. There's never anything much, Percy deals with all the important correspondence at the office.'

The envelope was addressed to her. *Miss Margaret Lewis, Thorneybrook Farm, near Pieterskloof, Natal Province, South Africa.* Strange to see her name attached to a property she had no intention of keeping. The envelope bore a British stamp. A letter from her aunt perhaps; not many people knew this address. She was about to open it when Mary put a hand on her arm.

'I wouldn't try to read that now; the road's pretty bumpy from here on.'

She clicked the mare into a slow trot. Clouds of dust billowed up from the wheels. Margaret glanced over her shoulder at the receding road. She'd seen enough; she wouldn't be back.

CARMARTHENSHIRE, WALES
TWO MONTHS EARLIER

CHAPTER 12

'*Wil, wyt ti 'na*? *Dere nawr*. Dad needs the liniment.'

He'd forgotten to keep an eye on the time. That note of impatience in Mam's voice; his father would be wanting his bed. He placed the draft of the letter to Margaret inside the cover of the book he was reading, *The Young Colonists – A Story of the Zulu and Boer Wars* by G A Henty. Mam wouldn't look in there.

Dad was sitting in a chair next to the empty stove when he came downstairs. Mam was at the sink cleaning the pan of warm water she'd used to soak his sore feet, the nightly routine. Seeing those lumpy misshapen toes, the mottled skin stretched tight across the bulging knee, he felt a surge of grief. When they were at Hendre Dad never sat still for one minute, always busy about the farm he was with one thing or another. These days the liniment was the only thing giving him relief from the pain. Wil took the bottle of Sloan's from the cupboard in the dresser and poured a few drops on to the clean rag Mam had left beside his father's chair. The strong burny smell reminded him of Dr Morgan's waiting room. His father's mouth was a tight grey line; he could see the muscles in his jaw clenching against the pain. Wil wrapped the cloth gently around the sore knee and held it there for a bit, to allow the balm time to work its magic, ease the throbbing, inflamed joint.

'*Ydyw e'n iawn*, Dad? Is that better?'

His father's face was relaxing, the frown lines smoothing out. He nodded. '*Mae'n well.*'

Wil applied more pressure to the rag and saw his father wince and brace himself against the pain's return. 'Like lubricating an engine joint,' Dr Morgan told them at the surgery, 'you have to persevere before you see results.' No different really from that stuff they used to rub on Dan after a hard day's ploughing. Though his legs weren't holding up so well at the end. They'd decided to put the old boy down before they left Hendre, no one wanted to send him to the knacker's yard. Even Dad, never one to be sentimental about animals, was crying that day.

'That's enough for tonight.' He withdrew the rag, gently rolled down his father's trouser leg and eased the swollen feet back into their slippers.

'*Diolch, Wil bach.*' His father closed his eyes, dozed. Mam was at the table, taking out her knitting from the bag next to the chair. She was no use with the liniment, she said, couldn't abide the nasty smell of it. Aunty Sara-Ann had gone to her room already; she was good like that, giving the three of them some time together at the end of the day. Wil replaced the bottle of Sloan's in the dresser cupboard and turned towards the stairs to finish the letter.

'I saw Mr Watkins at the chemist's yesterday when I was in for bandages. He says you're in line for promotion. Why didn't you tell me?'

Mam wasn't looking at him, but he knew she expected a reply.

Something sharp pressed into his shin – Mabli, Aunty Sara-Ann's tabby. The evil creature clung to him, needling her claws through his thin summer trousers. He scooped her up and felt the animal nestle warmly into his chest, having her own way again. He didn't get on with cats; funny how they always made a beeline for him.

Mam was still waiting for his answer, needles clicking, another sock for Dad. She'd lost weight recently worrying about him and the fresh colour in her cheeks had faded. Mabli settled into a deep contented purr in his arms, curling and uncurling her claws in delight, hooking threads in his jumper.

'Sorry, Mam, it slipped my mind. Mr Watkins hasn't said anything definite, it was just a quick remark he made in the office, after I'd given him the figures for the annual report.'

'Well, it seems to me you've made an impression already. I knew you would. There's a good career ahead of you in that business if you put your mind to it. Best thing we did was move off the farm, though I wasn't happy about it at the time.'

She broke off with a look of exasperation and held up the knitting.

'*Mawredd*, look at this, missed another stitch!'

He watched her supple fingers unpick the row and start again, counting the new stitches under her breath. The cat was getting heavy. He dumped her on the ground and made for the door before she turned on him for vengeance.

Back in his room again he read over the letter.

Dear Margaret,

I hope this finds you well. I was sorry to learn that Colonel Lewis has been poorly again. My parents and I send him our best wishes for a good recovery.

We are living now at Cwmbach, my aunty's place near Brynamman. My father is not so busy as he was at Hendre, the rheumatics in his legs are bad. My mother misses Rhydfelin but she has good friends here. We do not hear much news from Bryntowy. The new owners keep very private, not like it was with your family. Emrys Williams has been felling the big trees in Coed Mawr and the beeches in the avenue have gone. Likewise the old summerhouse down by the lake, remember we used to play there when we were young.

My work in the office at Cross Hands colliery is quite easy, I am good with numbers and such like. Mr Watkins the manager wants to train me to be his assistant, but to tell you the truth my heart is not in it. I miss the land, being with the animals.

Nansi Davies said in her last letter that you will be moving to the farm when Colonel Lewis recovers. I wondered whether he might be looking for a stockman, or perhaps a manager? I hear the prospects for agriculture in South Africa are excellent and I would welcome the opportunity to try my hand at farming there. I have saved enough money to pay for my own passage to Durban.

I hope you will not think me too forward in writing to you like this, but ...

How should he finish? '*In view of our old friendship I thought I would write to you.*' '*Would you be so kind as to raise this with your father when he is well enough?*' '*I look forward to hearing from you by return of post.*' What was the right form of words?

It was Nansi's suggestion he should write to Margaret. Her letters were full of details about Durban, the posh house they were staying in, the black servants, the marvellous weather. All chatty stuff, a mix of Welsh and English like she was in the same room so he could imagine it all. Not a word about missing home or her family. And it was true what she said about him, he wasn't suited to office life, even though Mam thought different. If he made a good fist of running the Lewis's farm in Natal, who knows, one day he might be able to buy his own place. Land was cheaper there than at home, Nansi said, there were good prospects for young people.

He read the letter again. The tone wasn't right, too formal; Margaret would be on to that in seconds. He pictured that sharp look she'd give him if she thought he was hiding something; she'd stand foursquare, on a level with him, with her arms folded and staring him out until he gave her the truth. She knew him too well.

There was so much more he wanted to tell her: someone had filled in the badger setts at Cae Morgan; he'd spotted a little herd of fallow deer in the woods above Pwll Du; Miss Roberts had been asking after her. And there were otters in the river again, near where she'd fallen from the alder tree, remember? She'd be interested in that. Most weekends he cycled over to Hendre to check the land was still in good shape, see if there was any news of Bryntowy. She loved that old place; she'd be wondering how it was coping without her.

But perhaps it was a different Margaret he was thinking about. She hadn't been in touch since they left, hadn't even called round to say goodbye. Mam said the Lewises had forgotten their old friends in the valley now they were living the high life in Africa; Nansi grumbled about Margaret's new friends taking her off to play tennis, leaving her and Mrs Lewis to cope with the Colonel. '*Hunanol*' she called her. 'Selfish.'

He picked up his pen and changed *Dear Margaret* to *Dear Miss Lewis,* crossed out the last sentence and wrote:

> *I should be grateful if you would discuss this proposal with Colonel Lewis when he has recovered his health, and let me know at your earliest convenience whether he would be willing to consider it.*
> *Yours sincerely etc.*

He was different too. Margaret wouldn't recognise him in his neat office suit and white shirt with the starched collar. A smart office clerk. Someone who knew how to write a formal letter.

He rewrote the letter once more, folded it into the envelope and placed it in the inside pocket of his jacket. He lit the little oil lamp beside the bed and settled down to read another chapter of *The Young Colonists*. Dai Pritchard, the mine foreman, lent it to him; he'd fought at Colenso with the 1st Royal Welch Fusiliers. 'Have a read of this, *bachan*, being as you're interested in South Africa. Clever buggers the Boers, farmers they are mostly, ran rings round us half the time, no doubt about it.'

The picture on the cover depicted a soldier in khaki mounted on a handsome black horse, a rifle in one hand and a bandolier sashed across his chest. His wide-brimmed hat was tilted over one eye, giving him a rakish, devil-may-care look.

That Boer War stuff was old history now even if it was still fresh for Dai. Wil was more interested in the chapters on farming: how Dick Humphries and his family built their cattle business in Natal, protected the livestock from predators, learned how to turn that wild country into good agricultural land. If they could do it so could he, if Colonel Lewis agreed to give him the chance. In the meantime he would stick it out at the mine office and wait. People like the Lewises were never in a hurry; they would take as long as they chose to reply to the likes of him.

NATAL PROVINCE

CHAPTER 13

'You must miss your friends in Wales, Margaret. Such a pity your letter was sent all the way to Thorneybrook instead of going straight to Mount Pleasant from the sorting office. It's not like Percy to allow that kind of thing to slip through his net.'

Mary finished buttering her piece of toast, broke it into two neat pieces and fed them, one by one, to the drooling terrier at her feet.

'No more, Fly. That's your limit. Off you go. *Voetsak*!'

The dog obediently withdrew to its basket in the corner of the breakfast room. Mary wiped her hands on her napkin and leant across the table.

'Good news?'

She was looking pointedly at Wil's letter which Margaret was reading at the table. She hastily folded it and put it back in her pocket, feeling her cheeks burn as though the letter were some kind of guilty secret.

'Just the usual stuff friends write about – holidays, gossip, that kind of thing. Nothing important.'

She hated having to lie but this was no business of Mary's. She seemed content with the answer.

'Oh well, at least you've plenty of interesting things to tell your friend when you reply, especially now you've seen Thorneybrook. Though perhaps you'd better keep quiet about the state of the place until we've found out who broke into the crates. I've sent one of the boys into town to post my message to Percy.'

She picked up the little silver bell beside her plate and rang it. Moments later the door opened and an older African woman in maid's uniform – blue checked overall, matching headscarf – entered, bearing a large wooden tray. She set about silently clearing the breakfast things.

'Come on.' Mary pushed back her chair and stood up. 'I want to show you the farm while you're here; you'll see it best from the back of a horse. Come over to the stables when you're ready.'

Such efforts they were all going to, to make her feel at home. Aviemore, the Jamiesons's home, was a smaller, modern version of Thorneybrook, furnished in the style of an English country house, oak furniture smelling of beeswax, pictures of hunting scenes, Scottish landscapes. From what she had experienced so far white people seemed to treat Africa as if it were the home counties, only with more space, more servants to do their bidding. What would Wil think of all this? She checked the thought, remembering what she had just decided. He would have to find a way of getting to Africa without her help.

His letter irritated her beyond words – that absurd formal tone, the too careful language. Calling her 'Miss Lewis' as if they barely knew each other! And not a word in it about the things she really wanted to know – news of Gwennie, Miss Roberts, the garden, were the red kites nesting again this year. She didn't want to know they'd cut down her beloved trees in the avenue or that the summerhouse wasn't there anymore. Wil, of all people, should have known she'd be upset by this news.

There was something else, too, grating on her nerves. Nansi was keeping in touch with him, writing regular letters. It was obviously her idea he should write this begging letter;

she'd probably calculated Father could be persuaded to give Wil a job if Margaret asked him. She was a sly one, always so attentive around her mother, but she barely spoke to Margaret, never met her eyes unless she had to. Well, Nansi's schemes would come to nothing; there was no job for Wil, she was selling Thorneybrook; he would have to stay on at the mine office, work his own way up the ladder. At least Mrs Hughes would be pleased with her precious son's choice of career.

She went upstairs to change. Someone had put out a set of riding clothes on the bed. Horses and riding were not her favourite occupation. She'd endured the lessons years ago, learning how to trot and canter around the paddock and cling on for dear life over the little jumps Father set up in the field below the house. Thank goodness the elderly pony he'd borrowed from Mr Griffiths Waunllwyd turned out to be a kicker and had to be sent back. David was always the better rider, spending all his time on horseback during the school holidays, talking bloodlines with his horsy friends. He'd been dead set on joining Father's old regiment; if only he'd chosen the cavalry he might have galloped his way out of trouble.

She studied herself in the long mirror. She had none of Mary's petite gracefulness. She was big boned and clumsy, always tripping over things. Her nose was too long, her thick eyebrows met in the middle, her hair had a mind of its own. Surprisingly, once she ignored her face, the mirror showed that the clothes fitted her well; the breeches and tweed jacket, even the white canvas sunhat, could have been made for her. She wondered whether they belonged to Mary's mother. There was a photograph of her in the drawing room, sitting astride an elegant horse, wielding a polo stick. A tall, confident-looking woman, staring into the sun. Perhaps wearing her clothes would miraculously transform Margaret from a clumsy duckling into a swan.

She left the house and followed a sloping path along the edge of the front lawn to a wicket gate. Beyond it stood a cluster of whitewashed buildings. She found Mary in the yard outside one of the looseboxes, holding the grey mare's halter while her father examined the animal's legs. Nearby a tall bay gelding tethered to a ring in the stable wall stamped its hooves impatiently. Donald Jamieson looked up from his inspection of the mare. He was a short, stocky man, with a rather florid complexion and fair wavy hair turning to grey.

'It's a no go I'm afraid. She's not fit for riding today – must have picked up a stone on the way over from Thorneybrook yesterday; she's lame in the left foreleg.'

He patted the mare's neck. 'Give her a day or two and she'll be sound again. You girls will have to find something else to do this morning. Johnson can take your horse back to the field, Mary.'

As if on cue a man in labourer's overalls silently appeared from one of the sheds next to the looseboxes. He untied the bay and led him across the yard towards a gate at the side of the hay barn. Mary turned to Margaret and shrugged her shoulders.

'Sorry about that, we'll have to use shank's pony instead. Do you see that little *koppie* behind the house?' She pointed to a rocky outcrop rising from the grassland about half a mile away. 'There's a good view of the farm from the top; it's not too much of a climb. We could head straight there if you like, get back in time for lunch. Is that alright with you, Pa?'

She tucked an arm inside her father's and they leaned into each other comfortably, smiling at Margaret. Mr Jamieson was not much taller than his daughter.

'Those old riding clothes fit her perfectly, don't they? Just as well you didn't get rid of them with the rest of Mummy's things.'

'Yes, clever old you for remembering where they were after all this time. I hope they don't smell too much of mothballs,

Margaret.' His pleasant voice had the faintest trace of a Scottish accent.

Margaret shook her head; in fact the jacket smelt faintly of old roses, the ghost of a perfume. Standing so close like that, arm in arm, Mary and her father reminded her of a photograph from one of Mother's magazines, *Country Life Illustrated*. 'The Jamiesons at home.' She smiled to herself and pretended to adjust the cuff of her jacket.

'Please keep the clothes, Margaret, we don't need them. I don't think little Mary here is going to grow any taller. I'm heading back to the office, work to do.' He gave his daughter's nose a playful tweak and said goodbye, striding briskly out of the yard in the direction of the house. Margaret heard him give a short whistle. Fly shot out from underneath the loosebox door and ran after him, stubby tail quivering with excitement.

'Pa's planning his visit overseas – he's not going until next year, but he's excited about it already. The last time he went to Scotland was with me, after Mummy died; he left me in Edinburgh to start school and went off to visit some cousins near Aberdeen. Had a wonderful time fishing and riding about the place. He's planning to go back there on this trip. I'll just have to get used to managing without him.'

Margaret followed Mary across the yard towards another gate leading into open country. The borrowed riding boots were a bit tight for her large feet; there would be blisters by the end of the day. She thought about what Mary had said.

'Weren't you homesick at school, being so far away? I know I was, and my school was only three hours travelling, just across the Welsh border.'

Mary didn't answer immediately. She reached up to untie the rope which fastened the gate. Today she was wearing a blue eye patch which matched her riding shirt; the lighter hue softened the sharp angles of her face.

'Here's my answer to your question, Margaret. "Of all the

cursed places under the sun, a girl's boarding school is the worst." My sentiments exactly, though the words are Olive Schreiner's. Perhaps you haven't read the book yet. "A woman who has been in one of those places will carry the mark of the beast upon her until she dies." Isn't that a terrific sentence?'

She swung the gate wide and grinned. 'I don't imagine that was the answer you expected!'

It certainly wasn't; Mary looked the sort of person who loved her school days. For Margaret school was something you had to endure between holidays, not a place that damned your soul. She had almost finished reading *The Story of an African Farm*. It was an odd, tormented mishmash of a book; she admired the ideas but there wasn't much of a plot to hook the reader. It certainly wasn't *Jane Eyre*.

She followed Mary through the gateway into a billowing grassy landscape which stretched to the horizon – 'the *veld*', as people here called it. Her boots crunched on tussocks of frost-nipped grass, drawing puffs of dust from the dirt track they were following towards the *koppie*. Tiny flowers – pale yellow, white, with hairy leaves – sprouted among the bare stones and from the edges of deep ruts made by farm vehicles.

They reached the bottom of the *koppie*. It looked a stiff climb to the top and Margaret's feet were already pinching inside the tight boots. Aside from her half-hearted attempts at tennis she hadn't taken any vigorous exercise since she came to South Africa and she had to keep stopping to catch her breath. There didn't seem to be any obvious pathway; they had to clamber over rocks and squeeze between thickets of prickly bush. The mid-morning heat was a bother too; in the end she shrugged off her jacket and tied it around her waist, glad to have her back and shoulders free of the heavy cloth. Mary, smaller and more nimble, had already reached the summit. She was perched on a large boulder, dangling her legs over the edge. No doubt she was already laughing at Margaret's uphill toiling. She reached the boulder at last, panting heavily and conscious of her burning, sweaty face. Mary shuffled across to make room.

'I'm surprised you're so out of breath, Margaret, I thought you'd be used to this kind of thing. They have hills where you come from, don't they?' She fished out a packet of cigarettes from the pocket of her breeches, opened it and took out a cigarette. From her other pocket she produced a small gold lighter, flipped it open and lit up. She waved the packet in Margaret's direction.

'Do you smoke?'

Margaret shook her head; she'd tried it once but the taste of tobacco made her feel sick. Men like her father – and David in those last days when he was home on leave – smoked cigars after dinner. A manly thing to do, she supposed. Mary took a long drag of her cigarette and blew a thin column of smoke into the air.

'I used to love walking in Scotland; the mountains reminded me of home. Though they aren't as grand as our Drakensberg. I've never been to Wales; it's a pretty poor relation to Scotland, isn't it, just coal mines and singing, I've heard.'

She watched Mary settle herself comfortably against the side of the rock and tilt her face into the sun.

'Bliss! My favourite place in the world.' The blue eye patch cast a shadow across her skin like a pale smear of ink.

Margaret thought of Coed Mawr's moist greenwood, of autumn leaves dabbing the surface of the lake, the call of rooks settling in the dusk. She wouldn't swap any of that for this place, wild and beautiful though it was. She thought of Wil whistling to his sheepdog, tenderly reuniting a stray lamb with its mother. She pictured him at a cramped office desk, head bent low over his paperwork. *'My heart is not in it.'*

'Blast, there's Pa. He's probably got his binoculars out and spotted the smoke!'

Mary was sitting up, frowning at the sprawl of rust-red roofs below the *koppie*. Mr Jamieson, a diminished figure from this height, was standing on the front lawn, a tiny blurred shape racing in circles around him. She stubbed out her cigarette.

'He doesn't like me smoking; says it's not very ladylike, such nonsense. South African women will be getting the vote one day, like they're starting to in Britain. I'll do as I please then, whatever Pa thinks.'

She put her hands to her mouth and made a loud hallooing cry. He waved something white, a handkerchief perhaps, then turned back towards the house. They sat in silence for a while. A light breeze was beginning to creep up the hillside; Margaret felt the coolness brushing her cheeks, stealing their heat. She thought of Precious and her child, the maid who cooked their meals at Aviemore, the ragged girls who swept the pavements. Would those South African women be allowed to vote?

'Do you see that fence down there in the veld, to the right of the *koppie*?'

Mary pointed out the dark line of a firebreak stretching across the open grassland, a skein of barbed wire skirting its length.

'That's our boundary; everything you see this side of the fence is Aviemore property; it's about 800 acres, that's quite small for this province. The farm's more of a hobby for Pa than a business, he only keeps it for rough grazing and riding.'

Margaret gazed at the landscape below her. How could you really know a farm this size, all its nooks and crannies, its secret places? She knew every inch of Bryntowy; she only had to close her eyes and she was there walking the paths, slipping through the woods. She leaned over and plucked one of the pale star-shaped flowers growing out of a crevice in the rock; the petals were dry and rather brittle, like fine tissue paper. Mary was looking at her thoughtfully.

'Thorneybrook is probably three times the size of Aviemore,

did you know that? It's better land than ours, of course, and most of it is river valley so it's protected from the worst of the weather. You're very lucky to have inherited it. Pa says the property could be a goldmine for anyone who knew how to farm it properly. Have you decided yet when you will be moving in?'

Margaret focused on the tiny petals, plucking them from the stem, one by one. Mary's gaze was a shiver at the back of her neck.

'I mean, so many of your things have already been unpacked. You said yourself that the rooms looked nice. Someone obviously wants you to live at Thorneybrook, don't you think?'

These questions were so deliberate. Mary was pinning her down like one of those moths in Father's display case. Was she a little afraid of this woman, that she couldn't be truthful and tell her she had no intention of living at Thorneybrook?

A high, thin scream, somewhere in the brightness above them. A dark shape – immense, terrifying – plunged at them out of the sun. Instinctively, Margaret threw out her arms to protect her face, heard something beat at the air and the whirr of great wings passing over her head. Then silence. She uncovered her face, her heart pounding. Mary hadn't moved position; she seemed quite unperturbed, shielding her good eye with her hand as she gazed into the sky above them.

'Lucky you; it's not often you get so close to one of the biggest eagles in Africa. Oh look, it's given you a present.'

It was lying on her lap: a long feather, greyish-brown striped with black; it stirred in the stiffening breeze. Margaret picked it up and ran her fingers through the soft filaments along the shaft.

Mary leaned over. 'The tail feather of a martial eagle. You must keep it; in Africa when an eagle gives you one of its feathers, it's considered a sign of luck, a good omen. It means you belong here.'

Was she being serious or teasing again? Margaret looked at the feather. She didn't believe in omens, good or bad. But this was Africa not Wales; these things meant something different here. She shivered. The wind was blowing up the *koppie*, whirling dust and bits of dry grass into the air. Mary had turned away and was waving again; down below them Donald Jamieson was back on the lawn with the white handkerchief.

'We'd better go; Pa wants us home. There's a nasty Berg wind coming down the valley. Be careful you don't get dust in your eyes.' She took the feather and tucked it into Margaret's hatband. 'You don't want this precious gift to blow away. We'll take the quicker route down; it's a bit of a slither but we need to get out of this wind. Hope you're not scared of heights!'

She launched herself off the boulder and disappeared. Startled, Margaret inched forward and peered over the edge. Mary was already some distance below, on a narrow pathway winding between rocks and thorn bush. From here the drop looked almost vertical. Margaret untied her jacket and put it on, grateful for the immediate warmth, then lowered herself carefully over the edge of the boulder. She located the path and started down it, her boot soles slipping on the dry uneven ground. Mary was now more than halfway down the hill, a small figure scrambling sure-footed as an antelope towards the bottom where the path seemed to level out. All the time the wind was strengthening; small stones, stinging bits of soil whipped at her face and hands. The brilliant clarity of the winter morning, the sun's warmth, vanished in a choking cloud of dust. She felt her legs slide away from under her and she clutched wildly at clumps of spiky grass, rocks, thorny branches, anything to stop herself falling. It wasn't fair. Mary should have waited for her, guided her down, not abandoned her like this. The air tasted gritty and her eyes were smarting; she could barely see what was in front of her. Mary was too far away to hear her calling into the bludgeoning wind. She was losing control, her body insisting on this terrible, precipitous falling. She let go.

She was looking up through thin spears of yellow grass into a cloudless sky framed by the spindly branches of a tree. There was a sharp pain somewhere in her right side and her throat felt clogged with dust. The back of her head ached. She remembered the shock of pain as it slammed into the rock, when her feet slipped and she fell. Someone was speaking, though the voice was far off.

'Margaret, can you hear me? Can you move your legs?'

She could wiggle her toes, her fingers; they were good signs, she knew that. She felt an arm reach around her waist and lift her up. A new, sharper pain skewered her right arm.

Mary's face swam into view. Her skin was very white against the blue patch.

'I thought you were just behind me, coming down. It was the wind. I couldn't hear you. Where does it hurt?'

She could move, her legs were fine, just the awful pain in the right arm. She struggled to kneel and felt with her left hand to the back of her head where the other pain was; the hat must have fallen off and her hair was damp. She brought her hand away, sticky with blood.

'You've got a nasty cut on the back of your head. I need to get you to the house. Could you try walking?'

Mary's arm came around her waist again. She tried to get to her feet but the light darkened and her sore head filled with spinning, watery noise. Her stomach heaved. She daren't lift her right arm, she might be sick.

'It's no good, you'll have to stay here while I fetch help. I'll be as quick as I can.'

With Mary's help she manoeuvred herself into a sitting position, propped against the tree trunk. The ground underneath her was hard and unforgiving and her whole body ached. She watched Mary take off her jacket and fold it into a pillow, tucking it in snugly behind her back. She closed her eyes. When she opened them again Mary was gone.

The wind had passed on and the sunshine was warming her face and limbs, dulling the worst of the pain. The lazy drone of cicadas, the faint rustlings of some creature in the long grass around the tree. Please God, don't let it be a snake, at least not one of those poisonous ones, the puff adders Mary and her friends loved talking about – how quickly the venom would attack the vital organs if you were unlucky. Wil had shown her a dead grass snake once, scythed almost in half by the tractor mower, its olive-green body caked in mud from the ditch where someone had thrown it. The same day she'd slipped off the alder branch. They were walking slowly back to the farm when he showed her the snake, wanting to take her mind off the pain. Wil would never have left her on her own like this.

She felt again for the sore spot at the back of her head. The hair was now stiff with congealed blood. There was her hat, lying on the ground near the tree, the white canvas streaked with dirt and something darker, her blood probably. The martial eagle's feather was still attached to the band. Not such a good omen after all, Mary Jamieson. Wil believed in that sort of nonsense, too, so she'd kept the red kite's tail feather all this time 'for luck', whatever that meant. What would he say about this feather, would he agree it meant she belonged here after all?

Perhaps she would ask him herself. He should be with her; this country would be so much better for him than life in a dingy mine office. She'd been wrong to judge him on that letter; it was too long since they'd seen each other. As soon as she got back to Durban she would write to him, tell him to book his passage. Her mind was racing. Wil would manage Thorneybrook and she and Mother would move up here. Nansi would easily find another job in Durban; they could manage perfectly well without her. The past was over and done with, it was time for something new. There was nothing wrong with changing your mind.

She heard hoofbeats pounding the dry hard ground. Mary and her father on the bay gelding, its glossy coat dark with sweat. They dismounted and Mr Jamieson made a swift examination. Yes, the right arm was probably broken. A nasty cut on the head but no other damage as far as he could see though you could never be sure about broken ribs; does it hurt when you breathe? Her arm cradled in one of Mary's scarves, they lifted her gently on to the saddle in front of Mr Jamieson. Mary walked alongside them. On the slow journey back to Aviemore Margaret closed her eyes and let her imagination blossom. The pain in her arm and the headache, the shock of the fall, all diminished in the bright future she was creating for herself and Wil.

DURBAN

CHAPTER 14

He was holding her hand when she woke up, his face inches from her own. She tried to pull her hand away, struggling to sit up but his grip only tightened.

'Dear Margaret, such a dreadful shock. Thank goodness it was just your arm; I can't bear to think what else could have happened.' The accompanying look of concern was almost convincing. The room was full of an overpowering, sickly fragrance. She turned her head and saw the garish lilies.

'Just a small gift to cheer you up. I decided pink was your colour. When you're feeling stronger I'll take you to the Botanic Gardens to buy some more.'

Her broken arm itched inside its plaster casing and the headache was still there, though duller than before, thank goodness. On her return to Durban Dr Ewart had insisted on a proper cast to protect the broken bones. No one in their right minds should be up on a *koppie* in a Berg wind, he said; what were they thinking of? She had enough severe bruising, cuts and bumps to remind her how lucky she was to survive the fall.

Percy released her hand and stood up. He was on his way to the office, just looked in to see how she was. He leaned over the bed and to her horror, made an attempt to kiss her cheek. She averted her face swiftly and he moved away. There was no trace of embarrassment on his face.

'Tomorrow's Wednesday, my afternoon off. I'll call round and we'll make some plans to get you out and about. Durban winters are so mild compared with where you've been, it's a pity not to make the most of the sea air. Soon put some colour into those pale cheeks.' He gave her a little wave as he closed the door.

The letter to Wil must be written immediately. Her mind was made up, she needed him. What if he'd changed his mind, having waited so long for a reply to his letter? He might have concluded from her silence that she wasn't interested in his proposal. If tomorrow was Wednesday then the weekly Union-Castle ship would be leaving Durban for Cape Town this afternoon, en route to Southampton. She couldn't let another week pass.

Her right arm was useless for writing and with her left hand she'd only produce an indecipherable scrawl. Mother had placed a small brass bell on the little table next to her chair; if she needed anything Nansi would be downstairs, she had mending to get on with. Margaret got out of bed and walked stiffly to the table – her whole body ached with the effort. She rang the bell. In moments Nansi was there, brisk and dutiful, her face shuttered as usual.

'Is there anything you need, Miss Lewis?'

'Yes, I want you to write a letter for me. It has to go on the mail boat today, I wouldn't ask you otherwise.' It was better to be business-like. Nansi wouldn't thank her for trying to be friendly. 'I'm sure you know where the writing materials are kept. Could you fetch them please; I'll dictate the letter here.'

Nansi withdrew, returning quickly with pen and paper. She settled herself in a chair beside the table, a blank sheet of writing paper in front of her. Margaret was ready. She had been composing this letter in her head since the morning she and Mary got on the train at Pietermaritzburg.

'William Hughes has written to me, he wants to know whether we would employ him at Thorneybrook as a farm manager. It seems a good idea to me.'

Nansi was quiet, looking at the writing pad in front of her; a long curl of auburn hair had escaped its pin and fell across her cheek. Her fingers were gripping the pen; Margaret noticed the nails were bitten to the quick.

'Nansi, I'm not a fool. I'm aware you've been writing to Wil; he told me so in his letter. This was your idea, wasn't it, that he should write to me first. You knew I would persuade my father to agree. You took advantage of the fact that Wil and I are old friends.'

Nansi lifted her gaze from the paper and their eyes met, hers the colour of bracken, flecked with green. She looked anxious, less sure of herself than usual, and Margaret felt her advantage.

'His letter went to Thorneybrook instead of here, that's why it took so long to reach me. He must have heard about my father's death by now. Do you know whether Wil has changed his mind about wanting to come out? If he has then there's no point my writing to him, is there?'

Still no answer. Her head was throbbing. 'I haven't much time, Nansi. The letter has to be at the harbour sorting office before the afternoon sailing. Tell me, what is Wil saying now?'

The girl put down the pen.

'He is thinking of going to Australia. He thinks you are selling the farm because he hasn't heard from you. Last time he wrote he said he was looking at farming jobs in New South Wales.'

She had never expected Australia. Her plans were collapsing, mere puffs of dust in the thin air.

'Have you written to him since?'

Sounds filtered in from the garden through the open window: monkeys gossiping amongst the fig leaves, a nameless bird repeating its single bright note over and over. Nansi cleared her throat.

'I told him to wait. Mrs Lewis said that if you saw the farm for yourself you would change your mind about selling. She wants you to keep it. She don't want to go back home, miss,

137

she's happy out here. I heard Mr Flynn say to her his friend will take care of the farming, you won't have to do anything. He was going to arrange it all. But then I thought, why don't Wil do it, he would be so much better than any friend of that bugger... Mr Flynn.'

She was twisting her hands in her lap; her face was flushed. 'I'm sorry, miss, didn't mean to say that.'

Margaret smiled to herself. At last she and Nansi had something in common; neither of them cared for Percival Flynn.

'But what makes you think Wil is going to wait? He might decide he has better prospects in Australia.'

'He has his heart set on coming to Africa, I'm sure of it. It's like a new life for all of us isn't it, out here? He says he's been reading books about farming and talking to people who know about this country. He's always asking me to tell him what it's like, you know, the weather, the people. I try to describe it but my English isn't that good and I can't write proper Welsh. I couldn't be doing with school, see. That Miss Roberts, she was always telling me off for mitching. You and Wil was different; model pupils you was. Teacher's pets.'

Margaret stared at the girl. My goodness, was Nansi Davies teasing her? There were other things they had in common – a childhood, memories. Jealousies, too.

'You're wrong about one thing, Nansi – Wil was the star pupil, not me. He was always top of the class. But you are right about him coming to Thorneybrook. I don't want some stranger placed there by Percy Flynn for his own ends. Someone told me the land is very good, that it could become an excellent farm one day. We've just got to hope this letter reaches Wil in time.'

Nansi picked up the pen again. 'I'm a slow writer, miss. You'll have to be patient.'

Margaret smiled. 'That's fine, Nansi. It's a short letter.'

THORNEYBROOK
SUMMER 1921

CHAPTER 15

The child had been there for some while, squatting in the dirt underneath the willow near the cattle trough. Best to pretend he hadn't noticed, pity to scare the little fellow. Wil continued with his task, threading the stiff loop of wire through the hole in each of the fence posts, tightening it off with the wrench, moving on to the next one. The morning was almost over and only half the field finished – back home he and Dad would have been done with this job hours ago. It was this heat, he could feel the sweat gathering at the back of his neck, the rough material of his overalls sticking to his skin. His bottle of water on the ground next to the trough, keeping cool in the shade, alongside the old haversack Mam had given him. He hoped the ants hadn't found a way in like they did yesterday. He had to throw his sandwiches away, crawling with them it was, they were twice the size of the ones back home and with a nip like the devil.

He left his tools and the roll of wire beside the post and walked over to the trough. The child regarded him silently beneath the willow's tangled branches. Wil uncorked the bottle and took a couple of deep draughts; the water was lukewarm, he hadn't realised how thirsty he was, at home you could go a whole morning without needing a drink. He held out the bottle.

'Want some?'

There was no answer. He took a few steps towards the boy and squatted down to study the large flat stone on the ground beside him. Its surface was decorated with curlicues of small pebbles, the gaps between them carefully filled and patterned with plaited grass stems and strips of willow leaf.

'That's nice. Did you make it?'

The boy caught his eye and quickly looked away. He must be about six or seven, certainly old enough to be at school. He was wearing a pair of faded brown shorts and a shirt several sizes too big for him. Wil picked up his bag and brought out the food. No ants. He broke the sandwich in two and held out one half. This time the boy reached up and took the bread in both hands, his skinny arms protruding from the flapping shirtsleeves. They ate in silence; the child must be hungry, poor dab.

He considered his morning's handiwork. The fence was looking good so far, sturdy enough to keep the young stock from straying into the open veld; he'd be able to keep an eye on them in there until they got used to being outside. A pretty black and white bird was perched on the post he'd just finished wiring. It was trying to hook a worm on to one of the wire barbs; every now and then the thing would wriggle and fall off and down it would fly, pick up the worm in its beak, try again. He'd seen it do the same thing yesterday on the fence the other side of the field. He'd lost count of the different birds he'd seen since he arrived on the farm, plumed and crested in vivid colours, quite unlike the palette of blacks, browns and greys back home. He should start learning their names; he could swear he'd seen a bird book in one of the boxes from Bryntowy. There was a stack of them in the front room, waiting for Margaret to unpack when she finally got here.

Colonel Lewis knew a thing or two about birds. Used to know, Wil corrected himself. He missed the old man. He'd always had a kind word for him, asking about school, how things were at Hendre. And he'd been good to Nansi, it seemed, in the weeks before he died. In one of her letters she said he'd thanked her for taking care of him. So he should – under that sharp skin of hers Nans had the softest heart. He took another swig from the bottle. The child had finished eating; he was eyeing Wil expectantly.

'No more food left, I'm sorry.' He shrugged his shoulders, miming empty hands. The boy gave him a shy smile.

'My name is Wil.' He pointed to the boy. 'What do they call you?'

'Sipho, *Nkosi*.'

'Not *Nkosi*. Wil. You call me Wil.'

He wasn't going to use that language, whatever Mr Percival sodding Flynn said. '*Nkosi*' meant lord or master in their language, Nans had written in one of her letters. Mam would have a fit if she knew he was talking like that. It was one of the last things she said to him when they were waiting at Carmarthen for the London train.

'*Gwranda nawr*, Wil, mind you remember where you come from. No lording it over those poor black people. It's their country after all. They're just as good as you, God's creatures, don't you forget that.'

It had been hard persuading her to give up the dream of her son, the office manager. She'd never wanted him to go back to farming, couldn't understand why he'd thrown it all up to come out here. Perhaps these weekly letters he was sending would convince her in the end that he'd made the right decision. *Diolch byth*, Dad didn't need any convincing. 'You go out there and show them what you can do, *bachan*. *Cyfle gwych yw hwn*. Seize the opportunity; there's no future for you here.' Still, it had been tough to leave them, see Dad struggling to his feet to say goodbye, Mam putting on that brave face, like he knew she would in front of his father. A year, he'd said. I'll be back in a year.

'I need some help with the wire Sipho, your fingers are not so stiff as mine.' He pointed to the fence, mimed the task. The boy was on his feet immediately. Together they worked their way down the field, Sipho nimbly threading the wire, Wil pulling it taut then tying it off. The cattle had been cooped up in the shed for days; it would be good to turn them out on to the new grass. Strange to think it was summer over here when at home they'd still be rationing the winter fodder, longing for spring grass.

The sun was lowering over the peaks of the Drakensberg when he heard someone calling from the direction of the farm buildings. A woman was standing at the edge of the field, her arm raised to steady the large metal pail balanced on her head. The boy cast an anxious look at Wil.

'Is that your mother?'

He nodded.

'Then you must go to her. Thank you for your help, Sipho.' He fished in the deep pockets of his overalls and brought out a handful of coins. 'Here, these are for you. Give them to your mother.'

The boy grinned and cupped his hands. Wil tipped the money into them.

'Thank you, *Nkosi*.'

'Wil, remember.'

The boy nodded and ran off across the field towards the waiting figure. Mother and child walked off down the track towards a cluster of huts beyond the thicket of gum trees. Smoke from their cooking fires curled upwards into the dimming light. Wil finished tying off the last post. The air was full of early evening birdsong, the doves loudest – he was beginning to love that lazy murmuring call which filled each day – but also other sounds he didn't yet recognise. The cattle shifted their hooves and made little grunting noises as he walked past their pen towards the workshop. It was one of the first things

142

he built here, fashioned from one of the enormous packing crates belonging to the Lewises. Some of them were already empty when he arrived at Thorneybrook; the two front rooms were stacked with furniture – ugly old stuff, far too big and grand for this poky house. He'd only been inside Bryntowy a few times, mainly at Christmas when the village children sang carols or the old Calennig songs for Nos Galan, New Year's Eve. Margaret used to join them for the singing.

To be honest, he was surprised she was keeping the farm, there was so much to do. Parts of the house were in a worse state than Bessie Evans' shack next to the Stores. At least her place had no holes in the roof. He'd got the wrong end of the stick about Thorneybrook, thinking he was coming to some posh estate like the magazine pictures he'd seen on the ship, *Country Life in the Colony*. He'd no idea he'd be spending his time mending broken windows and floorboards, fixing drainpipes, building temporary sheds to house the first lot of cattle and sheep. He still hadn't found a moment to repair his own accommodation, a small shabby room off the back kitchen with a leaking roof and broken panes of glass in the windows. Come winter the place would be freezing.

He did have help when he needed it, fair play. Moses seemed to know everyone in the area; most mornings he appeared with two or three young men, good strong lads. He dished out instructions in rapid Xhosa and they would disperse to their tasks, slowly; they took too much rest time for Wil's liking, but he enjoyed listening to their chat. He was beginning to pick up a few words of Xhosa. It sounded a bit like Welsh, lilting and musical, they used the same 'll's and 'rh' sounds, and the men seemed pleased when he tried speaking a word or two. He should find someone to teach him properly. The 'kitchen kaffir' people like Flynn and Mary Jamieson used when they spoke to the workers was embarrassing; it was like the way English people used Welsh words, mangling the sounds when

143

it was obvious they weren't really interested in learning the language properly. '*Crachach*', that was the word he'd use for them. Condescending types. The sort of people who turned up at Bryntowy for the shooting and complained if there weren't enough birds.

Thinking of that reminded him he should retrieve the bird book from the box in the front room, see if he could identify the little hangman he'd observed this morning.

He left the tools on a shelf in the workshop and stepped outside. The shed door still bore the faded outline of a shipping stamp: *Union-Castle Freight – Southampton Durban*. He crossed the yard and walked up the short driveway to the back of the house. Tryphena, Moses's wife, was in the kitchen chopping vegetables for next day's stew. She was a large cheerful woman with a pleasant ringing voice and he liked hearing her sing as she worked about the house. Moses was quieter, more self-contained, with a look of Dad sometimes when he was concentrating on a task.

Wil left the kitchen and went through the passage into the hallway. He rarely set foot in this part of the house. The servants' living quarters were outside, in the compound; most of the time he kept to his own room. Away from the summer brightness, the hallway and the rooms leading off it were dark, silent spaces. Inside their ornate frames the gloomy landscapes of the Towy valley regarded him from the walls, gothic fantasies which bore little or no resemblance to the real places he knew.

Something moved in the shadows beyond the hall near the front door. Wil halted. He scanned the darkness ahead, held his breath for a sound. No noise from the kitchen – Tryphena must have gone outside – and in the stillness the house felt oddly clammy, oppressive, as if it too were holding its breath. A footstep, the swish of material against a wall. A figure, growing out of the dark, gliding slowly towards him. Tall and thin, in a long rust-red dress, the colour intensified by the gloom. Her head – he assumed it was a woman – was swathed in a scarf whose elaborate folds obscured her features. His heart was hammering now, like the time Margaret locked him inside the filthy bat-loft for a dare; he imagined blind wings, the sudden swooping attack.

A loud clatter from behind him. The kitchen door at the end of the passage burst open and evening sunlight danced across the walls. Tryphena called out, '*Baas*, the dinner is ready. Come now.'

He turned to her. 'Wait, Tryphena, something's wrong.' When he looked back the hallway was empty. The woman had vanished.

The front door was still locked, nobody lingered in the front rooms, there was no sign of an intruder. The back of his neck prickled. Funny how some places gave you the creeps, like the bat-shed, or the rotting summerhouse at the bottom of Coed Mawr. *Achyfi*, this old house could do with a proper clean, clear out the damp and the ghosts. He left the hall and went back to the kitchen. Tryphena was setting out the cutlery and plates for his evening meal. Normal, everyday activities.

'There was someone in the hall just now, a woman in a long dress. She was wearing a red scarf over her head. Have you seen her?'

Tryphena's expressive face was a blank. 'No person here, *baas*. No woman.' She gestured to him to sit down at the table. 'You must eat.' She ladled a generous helping of meaty stew on to his plate and he realised he was starving. What he'd seen, well it could be the day's heat, or hunger making him imagine things. Best to forget about it. Trick of the light.

'I met Sipho today, Tryphena. He's a clever boy, does he go to school?'

She laughed, showing her strong white teeth. 'Yes, *baas*. Sipho is my grandson. He is good boy. One day he go to the

Mission school near Pieterskloof, when his mother have money to pay for lessons.'

'Where is his father?'

'Father not here, gone away long time, to work in the mines. There is no land for him here.'

As he ate Wil thought about the colliery at home, those long shifts and the men coming up from the coal face, their tired faces lined with dust. It was a heavy price to pay if you had no land.

He glanced at the calendar on the kitchen wall where he'd ringed the date. Margaret and her mother would be here in a few weeks. He'd have to get a move on, fix that leak in the roof above the bathroom, get Moses to finish cutting back the laurel on the driveway, make the place look a bit more promising. Margaret wouldn't mind what it looked like; she wasn't one to make a fuss about a bit of mess, but Mrs Lewis wasn't the sort to rough it, too used to having people like Mam running around for her. She had Nansi for that now; she was having the room next door to Mrs Lewis. It was small but Nans wouldn't mind, anything was better than living in that cramped cottage in Rhydfelin. They'd only managed to exchange a few words at the harbour before Mr Percival Flynn had turned up to drive him to the hostel. So much for his first night in Africa. The following morning Flynn had bundled him on to the early train to Pietermaritzburg, glad to get rid of him probably. *Duw*, he would be glad to see Nans again; what's more it would be a relief to speak his own language.

NATAL
ONE MONTH LATER

CHAPTER 16

Margaret scanned her mother's face yet again, trying to read the signs. She hadn't said a word for hours, not since they stopped briefly near Impendle to let the horses rest and she had muttered something about the cold aching her bones. Even in the midday sunshine she was still swathed in her heavy tweed coat. Judging from the rigid set of her shoulders and the way she clung to the side of the cart as it negotiated the ruts and potholes, she was not enjoying this experience.

The road was worse than Margaret remembered from the time before, especially this last section before the turn off to Thorneybrook. There had been late rains again, Percy informed them, not the torrential downpours of high summer, but enough to make the country roads slippery. At one point they had to abandon the cart and wait by the roadside, their luggage and provisions heaped along the muddy verge, while Moses coaxed the horses across a deep stony fissure which the water had opened up in the middle of the road. Percy had to dismount from his handsome black horse to lend a hand with repacking the cart; when it was ready he made a fuss of assisting Mother back into her seat.

'Not much longer to go, Mrs Lewis. We're on the home straight now, bit of a bumpy ride going down the last hill but then we're on the flat all the way to the house.'

Nansi tucked the rug around Mother's knees again and settled back into her own seat opposite them. Margaret noticed how the girl shrugged off Percy's offer of his arm; she too had felt again that unwelcome pressure of his hand in the small of her back as she climbed back into her own seat.

The countryside had changed so much since her first visit. The tawny winter grass had yielded to a lovely greenness spreading its veins across the veld and the trees were in full leaf, wild flowers jewelling the verges. The sky was patched with large rolling clouds, a paler, less intense blue than in winter. Down on the coast she'd hardly felt any change; the sea breezes were a little warmer perhaps and unfamiliar shrubs bloomed in the gardens along the Berea. She preferred the rawness of the seasons up country, these dramatic alterations to the landscape that accompanied the passage from winter to summer. Like the seasons in Wales, they taught you that nothing ever stayed the same. Her stomach tightened, excitement mingled with unease. This time Wil would be at Thorneybrook; how would it feel to see him again after so much time. So many changes.

The horses were nearing the end of their slow descent towards the Amanzimnyama drift. The river was deeper than last time but they had no trouble with the crossing, even though the water reached the top of the wheel arches. Percy was waiting for them on the other side and she was glad to see his poor horse given a respite from all that showy prancing on the road from Pietermaritzburg. He called out to them as they approached the turning on to the track.

'Not far now, Mrs Lewis. This is Thorneybrook property from here on; the house is just beyond those trees. I'll ride ahead to make sure the servants have tea ready.'

And he was off again in a flurry of hooves and panache. Mother looked relieved; her face lightened for the first time that day.

'I must say a strong cup of tea will be delightful after this awful journey; I've never felt so shaken about. Percival always thinks of everything.'

Margaret caught Nansi's eye. The girl stared at her, unsmiling. Was she, too, thinking of the incident they had witnessed only two days ago? It was impossible to forget, especially since it was all her fault.

They were in the study at Mount Pleasant when he burst in. Margaret was still standing by the bookcase, Precious was on the point of leaving. She ducked out of his way but he had already spotted the book she was carrying. Margaret saw his eyes narrow. He wrenched the book from Precious's hands and shoved her violently against the wall.

'You thought you could steal this from the madam, didn't you? You thought nobody would notice the book was missing.'

Precious was silent, clutching her arms as though his touch had burned a hole in her flesh.

'If you're not off this property by the end of the day I shall call the police.'

She was looking down at the floor, shrunk into herself, invisible.

'Get out!'

Precious fled. They heard her hurried footsteps in the hallway, the sound of the kitchen door closing behind her. Percy strode over to the bookcase and briskly slotted the bird book into its place on the shelf.

'Let this be a lesson to you, Margaret. You are in Africa now, not Wales; you cannot expect these people to have the same values as us.'

She couldn't let him get away with this. 'That was unfair, Percy. Precious wasn't stealing; I said she could borrow the book. We were talking about African birds – she knows a lot about them – and I thought she would like to see the drawings.'

He turned slowly from the bookcase and regarded her with a contemptuous, mocking smile.

'Well that was clearly a mistake on your part. It's tantamount

149

to giving her carte blanche to steal. I'm disappointed in you, Margaret. I hoped you would have acclimatised by now. These people will never respect you if you break the rules; they expect us to be firm with them, show them what civilised society looks like. For goodness sake, you can't treat your own servants as though they were your friends!'

She was painfully aware of Nansi's presence on the other side of the room; she'd come in earlier to find a glove Mother had dropped. She felt her cheeks growing hot. How dare that man assume she would agree with him?

'Where I come from we don't make that kind of distinction, Mr Flynn. I don't see why I should behave any differently here.'

Percy snorted; she was being absurd.

'You'll have to change your ideas, Miss Lewis, if you want to make a success of Thorneybrook. The natives up there will give you short shrift if you don't lay down the law. In fact I shall greatly enjoy watching how you do it.'

He turned on his heel and left the room.

Nansi was standing in the corner nearest the door holding the glove, looking at Margaret. She opened her mouth to say something but then she shook her head and went out.

Margaret remained where she was, her thoughts in turmoil. He had no right to speak to her like that, as if she were a child. And to treat Precious so brutally, with such contempt, was utterly shocking. She wished she had been bolder, stood her ground, but the fact was she hadn't been entirely truthful with him. She wasn't lending Precious *Birds of South Africa*, she was giving her the book. Precious had more right to it than they did. She walked over to the bookshelf, drew out the book and took it with her. The kitchen was deserted, but out in the yard she saw the top half of the shed door was open. She crossed the yard and peered inside. The room was completely empty. Precious, along with her child, had gone.

There was nothing she could do, she had no means of

finding out where they had fled. She went back inside the house and found Nansi at the kitchen sink, washing plates from a pile of crockery on the draining board. She glanced at the book in Margaret's hand.

'Precious wouldn't stay here after what happened. That man's a brute, if you'll excuse my language, miss. Never seen anyone behave like that, not even to an animal. Poor girl, I thought he was going to beat her, probably would have if you hadn't been there. He wouldn't care if I saw, I'm nothing to him, but if he had hit her I'd have given him something he wouldn't forget in a hurry.'

The cart tilted suddenly as the horses made a sharp right hand turn on to the track towards Thorneybrook. Margaret retrieved Nansi's travelling bag from the dusty floor where it had fallen off her lap. The clasp was broken and some of the contents had spilled. The book lay at her feet; Mother had only to look down.

'Thank you, miss. I can manage.' In one deft movement, Nansi took the bag from her and, bending down, scooped up the book and thrust it back inside. Her face was flushed.

'You should have that clasp mended, Nansi, before you lose something valuable.' Mother meant it as a casual reprimand; her gaze was elsewhere. 'I do believe I can see the house at last, beyond that line of trees. Thank goodness!'

Nansi, hugging the bag tightly to her chest this time, gave Margaret a small, fleeting smile. For the time being at least, the book was safe.

CHAPTER 17

As the cart approached the house Margaret saw Percy standing at the foot of the verandah steps; he waved an arm in a proprietorial sort of way as though he were greeting guests come up for the weekend. Her stomach turned. She watched him hand her mother down from the cart and lead her up the steps into the house, apologising profusely for the state of the driveway, the approach to the house. Such nonsense, Margaret thought, looking around her. Everything was vastly improved. All the overhanging laurel had been cut back and the front of the house cleared of weeds and debris. She noticed, too, that someone had cleaned the front windows and repaired the broken shutter. Even the sagging gutters along the roofline were mended. Wil had been busy. She gave Flora a congratulatory pat on the head as she passed. The moss had gone too.

Mother was in the sitting room on her own, her tiny figure dwarfed by the huge stone hearth. She gave a start when Margaret entered; her face looked puffy, reddened. Walking into a strange house, without Father, must be difficult for her, too. Neither of them had imagined this. The heavy curtains were drawn back and leafy sunlight patterned the floorboards, the worn rugs. The room looked much the same as before, only this time smelling of fresh air and polish instead of damp. Her mother gave her head a little shake and straightened her shoulders.

'Well, I must say, they've done some strange things with the furniture, Margaret. It's all a bit of a hotchpotch, isn't it?'

Her voice sounded more bemused than annoyed. She smoothed the back of one of the blue chairs.

'Though I have to admit it's quite a comfort to see these old pieces again after so much has happened. I was beginning to forget what we'd sent out here.' Her eyes swept the room, remembering. 'Ah well, I daresay everything will find its right place once we've got used to the house. Even that ghastly stuffed fox. I always wondered where it went to all those years ago. Used to be one of my husband's favourite possessions, can you believe it, Percival?'

He had just entered the room, apologising for the short absence, some farm business he had to attend to. He drew out a handkerchief and mopped his forehead. His face was flushed and beaded with perspiration; something must have unsettled him. He went over to the tea tray, poured himself a glass of water and gulped it down. He caught her looking at him and immediately turned to her mother, engaging her in a conversation about the room and how it might be improved.

Her spirits revived, Mother happily went off with him to view the rest of the house and to meet Tryphena and the other woman he'd hired to help with the housework. Margaret wasn't included in the tour. They'd got what they wanted; now she was keeping Thorneybrook, she was of no consequence.

She collected up the tea things and put them on the tray. Nansi was elsewhere, probably unpacking Mother's things. She was itching to find Wil and a little disappointed that he hadn't been there to greet them when they arrived. The day his ship berthed she'd been out of town with Mary visiting a friend up the coast; she'd hoped to meet him later that evening, perhaps show him something of the city but Percy had whisked him off to a hostel near the station ready for the early train to Maritzburg. 'William Hughes is here to work; we're not paying him to loiter about in Durban sightseeing. You're too soft with these people, Margaret.'

She took the path along the side of the house towards the farmyard. The rusted ploughshare and all those piles of wood and stone had been removed; the broken wall was neatly repaired.

This was the first time she'd seen the outbuildings properly. They were simple constructions, stout walls of rough stone roofed with thatch and corrugated iron. Three square wooden sheds stood in a line at the far end of the yard; she could hear sounds from inside the nearest one. She hurried towards it, heart thudding. The door was open and there he was, head bent over the worktable, busy as always. She would creep in, surprise him.

He must have heard her – she could never do things quietly – for he suddenly spun round. His face was thinner than she remembered, burnt brown by the sun, but his features – the strong chin, dark eyebrows, the large serious eyes – were unchanged. He didn't return her smile. Wasn't he glad to see her? She hadn't expected this stern look.

'I'm sorry if I startled you, Wil. I wanted to find you, to see how you were… whether there was anything you needed.'

Perhaps she had irritated him, stealing into his workshop without warning. She tried again.

'I expect you're finding the climate very different from Wales. I know I did, at first. It took weeks to get used to the Durban weather, and now we've moved up here I expect it will be different again.'

The words ground to a halt, they were all wrong; it was like talking to a stranger. Wil was unresponsive. Eventually, he got to his feet and they shook hands awkwardly.

'It's good to see you again, Miss Lewis. You're right, this heat does take some getting used to, but I'm not complaining. It's only hot in the day, by the evening there's quite a chill in the air. Thank you for asking, but I don't lack for anything at the moment. The farm's been neglected a long time; there's plenty of work needs doing to get the place straight. I'm drawing up plans for the new pastures.'

Miss Lewis! His voice made her ache for home, for their old easy relationship. She must find a way to bring him back.

'You seem to have done a lot already, Wil. The area around the house is so much better than when I saw it the first time. And the roof's been mended. Thank you.'

He nodded, but his gaze was elsewhere, he had things to do.

She would make one more effort.

'Look, I know things are different from the way they were at home, but I'm still the same person. I'm so pleased you're here, I couldn't manage this place without you. I hope you know that.'

She could feel her cheeks reddening. Wil was still silent; she should go.

'I'll leave you then. I can see you're busy. Perhaps there'll be time later on for a proper chat.'

He had turned back to the worktable and was reaching for his pen and ruler.

She left the yard and made her way back to the house, her limbs feeling as weighty as her heart. She did not want to walk away from him. But she did not want to linger where she wasn't wanted.

Wil was fuming! He listened to Margaret's footsteps receding across the yard and considered going after her. No, not now; it was out of the question. Anger still ploughed through his muscles and rooted him to the chair. He'd been busy putting the finishing touches to the wooden bird table – a welcome gift, to remind her of the one outside the breakfast room at Bryntowy. He was looking forward to seeing her face when she saw it for the first time. Then Flynn had appeared at the door, furious, demanding to see the farm accounts. In seconds he had destroyed all those good feelings.

'Come on, man, I haven't got all day. I want the receipts as well as the figures, I need to check they all match up.'

Flynn was right beside him, his breath smelling of sour tobacco. He was looking at the bird table.

'Good God, Hughes. I'm surprised you've got time to waste on this sort of rubbish. I expected all the fencing to be finished by now; you had those instructions weeks ago. From what I can see you've barely managed one field.'

Wil's fists clenched beneath the work table. At their first meeting on the quayside he recognised Flynn's arrogant behaviour. He was like those colonists he'd observed on the voyage out, issuing orders to the servants from their comfortable deckchairs. In his mind they belonged to the same tribe as the visitors from England who came to shoot duck on the estate, the ones who treated Dad and the other beaters like ignorant peasants.

He wasn't letting someone like Flynn get under his skin; he would bide his time. He reached up to the wooden shelf above the worktable and took down the black ledger he'd bought from the stores at Pieterskloof. The farm accounts were meticulous, he knew that, each purchase neatly itemised in black ink; all the receipts and dockets, arranged in date order, were in an envelope at the back of the ledger. That training at the colliery office was proving useful.

'Everything you need is in here, Mr Flynn, including the accounts for food and wages. You will see that I have brought it up to date.' He made a point of looking directly at Flynn as he handed him the ledger. Wil saw he was nettled; the man would not meet his eyes. His face was pink; the muscles of his mouth twitched. Wil stood his ground. Waited. With an effort Flynn turned his attention to the ledger. He flicked through the first couple of pages, a cursory glance, then he snapped the book shut, tucked it under his arm and went towards the door. Wil watched him hesitate and turn around. People like Flynn couldn't leave without a parting shot.

'By the way, Hughes, I don't remember giving you

permission to destroy the laurel hedge. It's a complete disaster, whatever were you thinking?'

Wil was ready for him.

'I was thinking that you told me the whole place was in a state, and that you expected me to get it under control. That laurel was so thick you could hardly see down the drive. I didn't want Margaret and Mrs Lewis having to hack their way through it to reach the house.'

Flynn's face was now bright red.

'She is Miss Lewis to you; we're not in the backwoods of Wales now. And before you take it upon yourself to make other changes, remember you are on probation here. You weren't my choice for manager, this is entirely her sentimental whim. One more word out of line and I will have you sacked.'

He turned on his heel and left the shed. That brief, sweet moment of triumph vanished and Wil sat there, fuming, struggling to bridle his anger. Flynn was in charge, that was plain, and Margaret must have agreed to this. She had changed. The Margaret he knew would never allow a bully like Flynn to make decisions for her. They were in a different country now; he was an employee, no longer an old friend. He would have to watch his step.

CHAPTER 18

At first glance her bedroom, like the sitting room, looked as it had done when she first saw it those months ago. Except that Semolina was here. The doll was lying on top of the bed, propped against the pillow. She looked different. Someone had repainted her face; it was a shade darker, the eyes were green rather than blue and the grinning mouth a deep magenta. Mrs Hughes' purple felt coat had also gone, replaced by a long-sleeved red dress made of shiny satin. Instead of the hat, the doll's head was bound in the same material.

She lifted Semolina and examined the painted face, the soft slippery material, hoping to find some clue to this transformation. But there was nothing. The change was flawless; no trace of the paler, familiar Semolina remained. She had been rendered far more interesting.

Margaret made to return the doll to her place on the bed when a splash of vivid colour caught her eye. She turned slowly to face the wall, Semolina hanging loose now between her fingers. A confusion of shapes and shades, twisted and distorted and splodged. It was made of red and grey and a dull green. It was a shifting mass of angry strokes and dented canvas. And it dominated the wall opposite her bed. An enormous oil painting.

She approached it tentatively, afraid it might spook. Slowly, the shapes resolved themselves into two figures: in the foreground a man in formal European clothes – dark suit, waistcoat, white collar and cuffs – leaning forward, with one hand outstretched towards a woman half-hidden in shadow. His face, drawn in profile, was creased with frown lines. Delicate pale features – a high forehead, prominent cheekbones and a slender nose above the neat moustache. The light brown hair was cropped short at the sides. His hands gave Margaret a shock: they protruded from the starched cuffs, large and meaty like a butcher's hands. The fingers were stained the brownish red of dried blood. The figure in the background was less distinctly drawn. A slim African woman, swathed in purple from head to toe. Her dark face gazed at the viewer, a blank unreadable expression. Margaret found it difficult to look away.

She had never seen this painting before. It was not the style her parents would approve – too modern, too disturbing, a world away from her mother's serene watercolours or the hunting scenes and family portraits favoured by her father. What it was doing on her bedroom wall was a mystery. She searched the canvas for a name; there was only a black indecipherable squiggle, down at the base of the frame. The painting was an ugly, disturbing presence in this room filled with her childhood, her beloved home – the flowered bedspread, her books, the dressing table. It was too much.

She reached up, unhooked the painting from the wall. It was heavy, filling her arms, weighing her down. It would take too great an effort to hurl it out of the window. Instead, she staggered over to the bed, knelt down and thrust the picture underneath, into the darkness. If she couldn't see it, it wasn't there. She sat on the floor and rested her back against the side of the bed.

Someone had opened the shutters and the late afternoon sunlight bathed the room, warming her skin. She noticed that the old rug had been unrolled across the bare floorboards, its faded pattern of gentle blues and gold softening the room's hard angles. She could hear birdsong, distant voices. Percy Flynn was in the hallway talking to her mother.

'… note of caution about Hughes. He's a little too cocksure, for someone new out here. He hasn't a clue about farming in

South Africa; he can't just stick with what he knows, that's why I wanted you to go with Brian Matthews in the first place.'

'But Margaret insisted on writing…'

'Yes, I'm perfectly aware of her role in this. She went ahead without consulting me and sadly, in my view, she's going to regret she did that. I've gone through most of the farm accounts; he seems to be on top of things, so far, but I don't like his attitude; it won't go down well in this community, certainly not amongst the other farmers. But you're not to worry, my dear Mrs Lewis, I'll get Matthews here when things go pear-shaped. He knows his stuff, spent half his life managing properties like this one…'

The voices faded towards the kitchen. She was trembling with indignation. How dare that man ingratiate himself with Mother, criticise her own decisions, offer to substitute his own manager. Wil would have all her support, she would make that very clear to everyone. When she'd finished unpacking she would find him and make amends for that awkward first meeting.

She got up from the floor. On the bed, the doll smiled up at her, red-mouthed and glassy eyed. Even Semolina wore the face and clothes of a stranger. Once she had finished unpacking she would find Tryphena, ask her who was responsible for these mysteries.

Her diary lay at the bottom of the first suitcase. She opened the top drawer of her dressing table to put it inside. The drawer was empty save for a folded piece of tissue paper. She unwrapped the tail feather of a red kite. Wil's words that long-forgotten spring day – 'Keep this for good luck'. She opened the diary, turned to the back page where she had glued the martial eagle's feather and quickly inserted the kite's feather beside it. She was being ridiculous, she hated superstitions, didn't she? Even so, bound together like this, the two feathers made a kind of talisman. A foolish idea no doubt, but in these strange circumstances, they felt like a protection.

Someone knocked at the door. Percy, perhaps, come to check on her. She thrust the diary into the back of the drawer, bracing herself. Nansi was outside the door, clutching her felt travelling bag. She cast a furtive glance down the hallway, then she opened the bag and brought out the book.

'You said for me to keep this safe, miss. Best you take it now; I don't want Mrs Lewis seeing it. Or Mr Flynn....' Her voice tailed off; no need for further explanation. Margaret took the book from her.

'You're quite right, Nansi, I'll take care of it now, see it doesn't fall into the wrong hands.' The girl gave a wan smile, relieved to be quit of the secret. 'Have you spoken to William Hughes, by the way? I wondered whether he was quite well. He wasn't his usual self when I saw him earlier, he seemed a bit on edge. Perhaps he would tell you if something were bothering him?'

Nansi's face showed no reaction to the last question. 'I haven't seen Wil yet, Mrs Lewis was wanting me to get her settled first. I was hoping to find him this evening if there was time. Or perhaps tomorrow. He said he was keeping some things for me from home. Mam has been knitting and the boys have been making some drawings. My sister Dilys will have sent a letter I know, she likes to tell me what they are all doing, how they are missing me.' She paused with her hand on the doorknob. 'Wil is probably a little bit homesick, I expect, seeing us all again brings it back. I know how that feels.'

The door closed behind her and Margaret stood for a moment, pondering Nansi's words. Surely the girl was glad to escape her large, demanding family; never once had she considered she might be missing home. It was so easy to make wrong assumptions about people, she knew that now. Like Precious, for instance. She wasn't an invisible black servant silently going about her chores, but someone with a life of her own and a child. And with a past that linked the two of them in ways Margaret could never have imagined.

She opened *Birds of South Africa* and checked that the little sketchbook was still inside. Precious and her child could be anywhere now; the book might never reach her hands. Yet what Precious had told her in the graveyard, the day before Percy Flynn threw her out, now bound their lives together. She knew her secret.

CHAPTER 19

That morning in Durban the rain had come suddenly, without warning, drowning the sunshine. The grassy path through the graveyard was slick with mud. The flimsy overcoat she'd flung on at the last moment, when Mother pointed out the black clouds louring above the bay, clung to her body like a second skin; water streaked her face like tears. Yet, even though she was drenched through her body felt warm: African rain was an altogether different experience, not the aching bone-chill of a Welsh storm. The bunch of yellow lilies she'd picked from the garden drooped in a mulch of wet newspaper. They were all spoiled. She'd never be able to arrange them nicely now; she should go back to the house and return the following day with a fresh bouquet. On the other hand, this might be her last opportunity to visit for many months.

She followed the path between a group of simple marble crosses. In the last six months the grass had covered the scars and Father's grave had settled in its place among the community of the dead. It had a headstone now, made of grey marble like its older relative. She and Mother had agreed on a brief inscription. He would not have wanted any fuss.

In Loving Memory of Colonel Arthur Lewis,
1st Battalion, Royal Welch Fusiliers,
late of Bryntowy, Carmarthenshire
Born London, March 1870. Died Durban, July 1920

She bent down to scoop up the dead chrysanthemums from the pot at the base of the headstone. The rain was beginning to ease now; the storm was passing over, heading inland. She crumpled the stems inside the soggy newspaper with the lilies, tidied the stray bits of leaf and faded petals. The sun came out again and water drops sparkled on the dull marble. She got to her feet, wiping her face, and saw she wasn't alone.

A woman dressed in black was standing beside Bancroft's grave with her back towards Margaret, her bright red umbrella oddly out of step with the sombre surroundings. There was something about her still, watchful presence, unmoved by the rain, that made Margaret reluctant to disturb her. A minute or two passed then the woman closed the umbrella, laid it on the ground and in a swift graceful movement crouched down in front of the headstone, pressing her face against the inscription to *Josephine*. She remained like that for some moments. It was only when she got up and began to walk away that Margaret realised who she was.

'Precious?'

Startled, the woman began backing away down the path. Margaret started after her, caught her by the arm. She felt the thin bones beneath the black woollen cardigan.

'Please stop, I didn't mean to chase you off. I didn't know it was you.' Precious was pulling away, squirming under her grip. This was her only chance.

'You knew Mr Bancroft, didn't you? He lived in Mount Pleasant before the Jamiesons. Who is Josephine? That name on his grave.' She pointed to the stone. 'You were looking at it.'

Precious stopped struggling; her body felt suddenly limp, as if all the energy had drained away.

'Please, *Nkosazana*, I do not want trouble.'

Margaret let go of her arm. 'I'm not going to harm you, Precious, I promise. All I want is an answer to my question. I found a book in the house, about birds. Josephine's name was in it; Mr Bancroft gave it to her. And there was also a small notebook with drawings of birds and animals. The person who made these pictures was a good artist. Was it Josephine? Mr Flynn wouldn't tell me.'

Precious slowly raised her eyes and Margaret saw the fear in them. 'I promise not to say anything about this if you answer my question. Was Josephine related to Mr Bancroft? Was she his sister, or a cousin perhaps?'

Precious's voice was barely a whisper. 'No, madam, not relation of Bancroft. She was my mother's sister, Josephine Morobe.'

Margaret stared at her in bewilderment. This made no sense at all. 'Then why is she buried with Mr Bancroft?'

'She got sick when she stay with my grandmother in the country. *Nkosi* Bancroft bring her body down here. It was a secret, he and Simon dig her grave in the night.'

'But why was it a secret? I don't understand.'

'You know why, *Nkosazana*. It is not permitted for people like us to have a friendship with *umlungu*, a white man. She would go to prison.'

'But what about Ernest Bancroft? He must have known he was breaking the law.'

'The law is different for you white people. He wanted Josephine. She was a very special person, you have seen her drawings; the teachers at the mission were always praising her paintings, but there was no money for study so she came to Durban to find work. She found a maid's job at Mount Pleasant and he give her paint and brushes, art books, so she can learn.'

Margaret took a deep breath. *'For Josephine with fondest love'.* The leap was not so difficult to make.

'Mr Bancroft and Josephine, were they lovers?'

Precious hesitated, shrugged her shoulders. 'Perhaps. My grandfather, he named her *Nomhle*, it means 'beautiful'. My family still talk about her.'

'Was it you who wrote her name on his gravestone?'

Footsteps sounded on the path; someone was approaching. A man in a dark suit, carrying a bunch of flowers.

'I do not want people to forget Josephine.' Precious was shivering; she tugged the thin garment tighter around her shoulders.

'When *Nkosi* Bancroft die they put up a great marble stone with his name on it. My grandmother, she never know where her daughter is buried. She also is dead now. Because of this I come to Durban, find work in this same house to stay close to Josephine. Simon show me the grave.'

She grabbed Margaret's hand. 'Please, *Nkosazana*, do not tell any person about this, I cannot lose my job. The child you see…'

The dark-suited man was close to them now. He raised his eyebrows at Margaret and she quickly withdrew her hand from Precious's grasp. He passed on along the path, shaking his head. Precious was clearly unsettled, anxious to be gone, but needing reassurance.

'You must not worry about any of this, Precious. I understand what you have told me. Nobody will know.' Margaret watched her scurry away down the path, head bent, clutching the red umbrella.

She looked back at the graves, her father's and Bancroft's, their stiff marble outlines softened in the sunlight. The people who mattered most to those two men – David, Josephine – had vanished into the earth, unrecorded but not forgotten. She had made Precious reveal her secret, left her worried she could lose her job, her child. It was her responsibility to protect them both.

CHAPTER 20

Moses had lit a small fire in the sitting room. They were glad of it, the house felt cold now that the sun was down. Percy had ridden off after an early supper to stay with the Jamiesons – he had 'some business' to discuss with Mary's father. The oil lamps created a pool of warm light where the women sat, shutting out the rest of the room. Their third night at Thorneybrook.

Neither was inclined to talk. It had been a long day, adjusting to their new surroundings. Margaret settled herself on the floor near the fireplace and began to unpack one of the smaller boxes. Father's book selection was typically eclectic: Gibbon's *Decline and Fall of the Roman Empire;* a hefty tome, *The Gun Dog Breeder's Manual;* Kipling's *Selected Poems.* A dog-eared copy of *The Thirty-Nine Steps.* She opened the first page, creased and smudged by frequent use, and closed her eyes to inhale the scent of pipe tobacco. She was at home in the library at Bryntowy, curled up on the window seat absorbed in her copy of *Moonfleet*, an early birthday present from David. At her feet a young Gwennie snored and twitched in some rabbit-chasing dream. Father was in his old leather chair beside the fire, pipe in hand, lost in Buchan's thriller. A lifetime ago.

'We should make a plan; that's what your father would say.'

Mother's voice startled her. The new surroundings came back into focus and she closed the book with reluctance. Mother was sitting in one of the blue chairs, her notebook open on her lap, reading glasses dangling from the thin silver chain around her neck. She was holding a large sheet of paper.

'I've been looking through this list, it's a copy of the one

Percival made for William Hughes. Goodness me, it seems far too much for one man to complete. I don't imagine old Mr Hughes would have managed half of this at Hendre, even with William's assistance.'

'Surely he'll have help from Moses and the others?' Margaret wasn't sure who these 'others' were, there must be local labourers they could hire. None of this was her concern. She drew another book from the box.

'I expect you're right, he won't have to do everything on his own. I'll have a word with William about it tomorrow. Although…'

Margaret put down the book. There was no mistaking the note of anxiety in her mother's voice.

'Percival seems to think he needs keeping an eye on. I told him we'd been perfectly happy with the Hughes family as tenants; their farm was always in excellent order, your father used to say it was one of the best on the estate. I'm not sure our Mr Flynn was very convinced.'

'Wil knows what he's doing. If you'd seen Thorneybrook before, as I did, you'd be amazed at the difference he's made already. I wouldn't take too much notice of what Percy Flynn says.'

Mother put on her reading glasses again and Margaret returned to *With Kitchener in the Soudan*. The red cover depicted a handsome uniformed soldier in a pith helmet staring into the distance, looking heroic. How Father loved G A Henty's books. After David died, to please him, she'd struggled through *The Treasure of the Incas*, ghastly *Boy's Own* stuff. She flicked through the pages then dropped it back into the box, pulling a face. She reached for the next book.

'You know you won't be able to lead the same life you enjoyed at Bryntowy, Margaret; there'll be no time to bury your nose in books the way you like to. You need to listen to me.'

Her mother was leaning forward in her chair, clutching the notebook.

'According to Percival our financial situation is a little tight; his words. He says we must prepare to make economies, at least until the farm is properly functioning. It means you and I will have to become rather more involved in the day to day running of Thorneybrook than we had expected.'

What was this? Mother liked men to make all the important decisions. 'I don't understand. What do you expect us to do? We don't know anything about farming.'

'Do you remember how your father loved making lists? Well, today I thought I'd take a leaf out of his book and make an aide memoire for myself. Tomorrow morning you and I will start creating a vegetable garden; you remember how much we relied on the one at Bryntowy to supply the kitchen. We shall choose a suitable spot near the house where there's plenty of light and decent soil and I will write to some of my Durban friends for advice about what to grow in this climate.'

In all the years at Bryntowy she had never once heard Mother talk about gardening. She left all that to Mr Phillips and Hywel, the boy from the village. As long as there were fresh flowers on the tables and an ample supply of fruit and vegetables in the kitchen, she was content. This was someone else's idea.

'Is this another of Percy's suggestions?'

Her mother looked affronted.

'Not at all. It's nothing to do with him. Whatever made you think that? I've been mulling this over since we arrived, when I saw the sorry state of the place. Quite frankly, I would never have allowed your father to talk me into coming to South Africa had I known we would be living like this.'

Margaret felt her temper rising; the words escaped before she could control them. 'That is so unfair! You were the one who wanted to stay on in South Africa after he died. You persuaded me to see Thorneybrook even though I wanted to sell it. You wanted me to change my mind. You and Percy Flynn that is. We could have gone home instead, or at least back to Bournemouth; surely you would have preferred to live there with Aunt Rose?'

Mother's voice was irritatingly calm.

'At one time I would have agreed with you, Margaret, but that was before I knew the full truth about our financial situation. I took it for granted we could stay on at Mount Pleasant for a few months and leave the farm to run itself under William Hughes's management. We would find a house of our own in Durban. It seems I was mistaken: we can't afford even to do that. Going back is completely out of the question and there's no point in your being so dramatic about it. We have to make the best of a bad job and set our hands to the plough. As it were.'

She returned to her notebook, the ghost of a smile on her lips. The pen scratched its way across the page; the list grew. A thin tail of hair straggled from her bun where some of the pins had fallen out and there was a determined set to her mouth. Margaret sat back on her heels, winded. How dare Mother call her 'dramatic' when she was just speaking the truth. It was so unjust.

After some while her mother took off her spectacles, closed the notebook and stood up. She stretched her stiff limbs and yawned.

'I'm going to bed, dear. It's been a trying day.' She pointed to the pile of books next to the hearth. 'You can leave those where they are for the moment. I'm not sure this house has room for all the things we've brought out; it's so much smaller than Bryntowy. We should be able to get rid of most of the books and other bits and pieces – Father's old fishing tackle for instance, those Hardy rods must be quite valuable. I can't see either of us taking up the sport. We could sell them in

Pieterskloof or send them down to Durban. I'll ask Percival's advice.'

Margaret readied herself to protest. Wil might like to have those rods; he used to love fishing.

'Before you say anything, Margaret, I see no point in holding on to all our possessions for sentimental reasons. Your father would have agreed with me – they're no use to us now that he's gone.'

Mother's voice was unyielding as rock. 'Our priority is the farm; we have to do everything we can to make it work, even if that means selling what we love. It's the only way. Now don't stay up too late, we have work to do tomorrow.'

Margaret felt her mother's hand gently brush the top of her head as she left the room. The gesture pleased and puzzled; Mother wasn't given to such shows of affection.

She sat on by the fire, watching the shadows creep across the floor. The gilded mantel clock from Bryntowy had been reset; soothed by its familiar steady tick, she felt the tension in her body begin to loosen. Around her the house was settling for the night. She listened to its myriad voices, so new to her: thin scrapings and crackling sounds inside the tin roof; the pop and creak of wooden beams and floorboards; flutterings of small creatures in the rafters. Outside a bird called, long and distantly, and she thought of that vast, empty veld stretching away beyond these walls towards the Drakensberg. How strange to be here, all of them under the same roof, so far from Bryntowy, Hendre, Rhydfelin. She thought of Father and David who would never hear these sounds, never walk through these rooms, ride out together across the grasslands. There was no point trying to make sense of what had happened, she was here now and that was all.

The fire had burnt itself out and the room was rapidly cooling. She rose to draw the curtains. Outside was complete darkness, save for a small, faint light moving in the direction of the house. She pressed her face against the windowpane and stared into the blackness. The light was more distinct now, closer, and she blinkered her face with her hands to see better. Perhaps Wil or Moses were walking the grounds before turning in.

The light was at the window. A stranger's face sprang at her on the other side of the glass. Terrified, she gave an involuntary cry and shrank back. The face did not move away. The eyes glittered, unblinking, almond shaped like the eyes of a cat. Margaret was caught, pinioned inside the glass like an exhibit in a museum of curiosities. Then the light snapped out and the window eerily reflected her own anxious face back to her, framed against the night.

She dragged the curtain across the window and leant against the wall, her heart pounding. The intruder might still be out there, she should call for help. She had no idea where Wil was and apart from Mother and Nansi there was no one else in the house. With shaking hands she lifted one of the oil lamps from the table beside Mother's chair and went out into the hallway. The front door was locked for the night and the iron scraped against the wood as she drew back the bolt and stepped outside. No sound or sight of any lurking intruder. The dense African dark closed around her, the lamp's wan circle of light her only protector.

She picked her way carefully down the steps and ventured to the edge of the laurel avenue. Out here the air felt chill, like the beginning of autumn. Stars glittered icily. In the distance beyond the massing laurel, the gum trees seemed to lean towards her like thin arboreal ghosts. She held the lamp higher, straining to hear a human sound. She was certain the intruder was real, she hadn't imagined those eyes. A twig cracked and a wild, unearthly shriek rose from deep inside the thicket. That was enough. She turned and fled back to the house. The fear surged at her, a mindless, clenching terror. She jammed the bolt into the lock, beyond caring whether it woke the rest of the household. Her hands were trembling so much she nearly dropped the lamp. But nobody stirred, the house remained silent.

She went on through the hall and paused at her mother's door, listening to the reassuring rhythm of her snores. There was bound to be a rational explanation. A nightwatchman in all probability, like the one the Jamiesons employed to patrol their property. Percy must have made a similar arrangement for Thorneybrook; she'd check with Wil in the morning.

She opened the door to her room. Not Semolina lay on the green sprigged counterpane, her mouth a grinning gash. A piece of paper was pinned to her red satin chest. The same handwriting as the first note.

Do not spurn my gifts, Margaret.

The painting was back on the wall.

Two weeks later

Chapter 21

They must have let her sleep late again. Through blurry eyes Margaret saw her mother pass by the window on her way to the kitchen, followed by Nansi carrying a large woven basket. She stopped, looked in and seeing Margaret was awake, called out.

'You'll never guess what we've found. Come and look!'

Margaret pulled on her dressing gown and joined them at the kitchen table poring over a small heap of pale potatoes, clotted with reddish-brown mud. Mother's hands were stained with soil. Dressed in a faded blue woollen dress and a pair of sturdy farm boots, with her hair loosely bound in an old scarf, she could pass for one of Millet's gleaners – a copy of the painting used to hang in Father's study. Her face was glowing.

'Someone's obviously already had a go at growing vegetables. We found some overgrown plots behind the laurel hedge; the place is full of weeds and bramble but there's plenty of room to make a nice sized kitchen garden. If William hadn't pruned and let in the sunlight we would never have known it was there. The soil is good, too. Nansi thinks we could start planting right away.'

Despite another bad night Margaret felt her own spirits lifting; Mother's new enthusiasm was infectious.

'I'll give these potatoes to Tryphena to clean for tonight's supper; fingers crossed they're not full of worms. Could you get dressed and find William for me? I want him to hire some labour for the digging and weeding. We're going to need you as well, dear. I'm sure the exercise will help you sleep better.'

The farmyard was deserted. In their wooden coop beside the sheep pens a dusty hen and her chicks scratched amongst the dirt and a flock of large birds, startled by Margaret's arrival in the yard, took off in a flurry from the roof of the cattle shed. The door of the workshop was open. Wil was still keeping his distance, behaving so formally whenever they met. She longed for the old relationship; he should stop reminding her she was his employer.

She took a tentative step inside. The workbench was swept clean, his tools neatly arranged on the shelves above, others hanging from hooks on the wall. A half-finished bird table stood in the corner beside a tidy stack of garden spades and forks. She went outside again and investigated the other sheds but there was no sign of Wil.

Beyond the farm buildings a rutted track led out into the open veld. A large area of land to the right of the track was enclosed by wire fencing and some young cattle were grazing in there. They lifted their heads as she passed – fine sturdy stock, growing sleek on the spring grass. Wil had chosen well. She would tell him that; it would be something positive, a means of getting them back on the right footing.

The distant peaks of the Drakensberg were shrouded in the early autumn haze; the air was full of birdsong and the buzz of crickets. Sunshine wrapped itself around her like a balm and she forgot her tiredness. The nightmares would pass eventually; there'd been no more ghostly sightings since that evening. No more strange notes left in her bedroom either. The garish painting was gathering cobwebs under her bed.

She spotted Wil near a dip in the field where the ground sloped down to the river, its course outlined by a row of slender pale willow and silvery eucalyptus. She made her way slowly across the uneven ground to join him. He was busy fencing off a tract of marshland; three other men were working with him. She identified the broad figure of Moses hammering a post into the ground. A small boy was standing beside Wil holding a bale of wire; he smiled shyly at her as she came up. Wil tipped back his hat and wiped the sweat from his forehead, his face creased and freckled with mud. To her relief he seemed pleased to see her.

'This is Sipho, my assistant. Say good morning to Miss Lewis. Sipho is the grandson of Moses and Tryphena.'

The boy laid the wire bale carefully on the ground and held out his hand politely. Margaret shook it.

'Hello Sipho, I'm very pleased to meet you. I can see you are a big help to Mr Hughes.'

The boy looked up at Wil enquiringly.

'He calls me Wil. I don't want him to think of me... you know, in that way.'

'Neither do I.' She bent down to the boy. 'My name is Margaret, Sipho. I hope we will be good friends.' She fumbled in her jacket pocket, remembering the little packet saved from an earlier visit to the general stores in Pieterskloof; boiled sweets in an array of different colours.

'Would you like one of these?'

He chose one of the stripy pink sweets and put it into his mouth. A broad grin slowly spread across his face. Wil was eyeing the packet.

'I hope there's enough for all of us.'

She offered him the packet and he took it over to the men. He must have said something funny for there was a sudden burst of laughter. The men turned towards her and waved their thanks. She had done something he approved of at last. In a few minutes he returned and handed the last sweet to Sipho. '*Wakho umama*, for your mother.' The boy tucked it carefully inside the pocket of his shorts.

'I'm impressed you can speak their language. Isn't it very difficult?'

'It's not as hard as you'd think if you speak Welsh; lots of the sounds are similar and if you don't mind making a bit of a hash to start off with, you can get along fine. Sipho's a good teacher, aren't you? We practise a new phrase every day after supper.'

'Perhaps you could teach me some words, Sipho. Though Wil is better at learning than I am; he was always top of the class at our school.'

Wil ruffled the boy's curly hair. 'We have an arrangement; he teaches me Xhosa and I help him with his maths. His mother is happy, she can't afford the weekly school fees. He manages to get to school for a few days here and there, but it's hardly a decent education.'

'Well, perhaps I could help too. Give him some English lessons or... I don't know.' There was nothing else she could offer; unlike Wil she was entirely without talent. Reading was her only real love. 'I brought some of my old books out here; Sipho will be able to start reading them once he's more confident.'

Wil was smiling at her. 'You were always a bit of a bookworm. Remember how you used to hide in the old summerhouse, down by the lake? I could hear your mother shouting for you up at the house but you never answered. Nose always stuck in one of those fancy novels, wasn't it? Or did you just pretend you couldn't hear her?'

She returned the smile. Things were back to normal; Wil was his old familiar self. Sipho slipped away to join his grandfather and the other men and they were free to talk.

'Mother sent me to find you. She and Nansi are making a vegetable garden, like the one at Bryntowy, and she wants you to hire some men to help.' She tried to read his response, his face looked tired and she noticed a scabbing wound across his forearm where the barbed wire must have snagged. 'I'm sorry, I expect it's the last thing you want to be bothered with just now with so many jobs to do. Is it too much for you? Managing the farm, I mean. You've been out of sorts since the day we arrived.'

Wil's face clouded. He picked up the roll of wire and began to uncoil it. Easier to talk when your hands were busy with something.

'No, it's nothing to do with the farm. Flynn was in my workshop that day you arrived, snooping around the place, checking I was doing my work. Do you know, he actually thought I'd been messing with the accounts. Well I soon put him right about that – when he saw everything was in order and up to date he went off with his tail between his legs. But he's the boss round here, not you, am I right? He pays my wages. I can't afford to get on the wrong side of him, can I?'

She wouldn't give him an answer. Stubborn as always, standing there staring at the ground. He noticed there were dark circles round her eyes; she didn't look too good, was she ill? *Dammo*, he'd have to press her harder, get some answers. It was no use to him, being left in the dark about which of them was in charge, she or Flynn. After all, he was only in this country because of her letter; he could have been in Queensland by now, managing a sheep station.

'I've got another question, Margaret.'

She was irritated by his persistence. Wil never gave up easily when he was after an answer.

'I thought Thorneybrook was legally yours now, after Colonel Lewis passed away. You offered me the job, not Flynn, I wouldn't have used up my savings to come here otherwise. Do you have any say in how the money is spent or is it all up to him now? I mean, it's going to be difficult for me to manage the farm properly if I have to go cap in hand to Flynn every time I want to buy stock feed or equipment. You understand that, surely?'

She still wouldn't answer, scuffing the dry earth with the

toe of her boot. This silence was telling him everything: Flynn was in control.

'I'm sorry if I'm speaking out of turn. I can see it's difficult for you. If he's worried about how much money I'm spending then it would be better if he gave me a proper budget for the farm. It's how Dad used to run Hendre, knowing what he had to spend for the year and making sure he didn't waste good money. That's the way Colonel Lewis wanted it; our fathers always had a good understanding.'

Her face was all knotted and frowny now, such a giveaway; he always knew when she was upset. Well, he'd said his bit. It was up to her to choose whose side she was on.

'Mr Flynn doesn't like me for some reason. He'd be glad to get rid of me if you wanted it. And I'd go elsewhere, no question about it, if he was in charge, not you.' *Diawl*, perhaps he shouldn't have gone that far. A bit soon to be looking for another job, but he'd rather try his luck elsewhere than live under that man's thumb.

It was unbearably hot, standing out here in the full sun, wearing a jacket and skirt. Her hands were clammy and she could feel the sweat prickling between her shoulder blades. How stupid to have put on these clothes; she could have chosen something more comfortable like Mother had, that short sleeved blouse and cotton trousers she'd bought in Durban, for instance.

Why did Wil always do this? Pin her down with awkward questions she didn't want to answer? He could be mean sometimes, mocking her when she failed a maths test at school; calling her stupid when she mixed up the Plough with Orion's Belt, out stargazing on Dryslwyn castle. But they weren't children now. Wil was her employee, her manager, and he deserved an answer. He mustn't leave when there was still so much to do at Thorneybrook. Without him, she'd have nobody to protect her from Percy Flynn.

'You've got things wrong. I am in charge, Wil; it's my farm and I will make it clear to Flynn I want you to stay. You'd be surprised to know that my mother accepts we can't live in the old way, having people do everything for us. She's bursting with ideas to improve the farm. You used to say I was spoiled, I didn't know what hard work was, but everything's changed now. It will be good to be too busy to feel sad that we can't ever go home again.'

She'd said too much; the last thing she wanted was his sympathy. 'So when you've finished with the fencing could you come up to the house. We'd all appreciate your advice.'

Wil looked at her thoughtfully. This was more like the old Margaret; she felt things too deeply, that was the way of her, but she was also curious and stubborn and brave. Of course he would stick by her.

'*Dere nawr*, Margaret, stop fretting; you may not be here for ever. We'll do our best to make a success of this place. Your mother's got the right idea. Tell her I'll come over as soon as I can.'

He turned back to his wiring and Margaret set off to relay his message. She waved to Sipho down in the marshlands and received a rare smile from Moses. The sweets must have played a part. The conversation with Wil had lightened her heart, though she was glad she hadn't gone overboard and told him about the other stuff – the doll, the painting, the face at the window. He'd only laugh at her again, say she was imagining things, there'd be a rational explanation. Best to forget about it, then, there was enough to be doing in the real world.

11ᵀᴴ January, Summer 1922

Chapter 22

'Good heavens, I nearly mistook you for the maid. What on earth are you doing up there; you're blacker than an Af! Surely that's her job, not yours.'

Perched on the top step of the ladder, scraping layers of soot and dust from the wall above the stove, she hadn't heard Mary come into the kitchen. On the other side of the room Sipho's mother, Thandi, was on her hands and knees scrubbing the floor. Mary must have seen she was there, but white people often seemed blind or indifferent to servants, she noticed. As far as they were concerned Africans were only visible when they were needed. She looked down at Mary, immaculate as ever in her riding clothes – crisp white shirt, jodhpurs, wide brimmed straw hat, the familiar sardonic smile.

'This is hardly the way to spend the morning of your birthday, Margaret. Come down, I've got something to show you outside.'

Mary turned on her heel and left the kitchen. Margaret heard her brisk footsteps along the newly gravelled path leading to the front of the house. She climbed down the ladder and went to the back door to shake the dust free from her clothes. Their efforts – hers and Thandi's – over many months, were paying off; the kitchen was so much cleaner, better organized, the brass pans and cooking pots gleaming on the shelves next to the stove. Tomorrow's task, a coating of whitewash on the walls, would finish the job.

'*Enkosi kakhulu*, Thandi, thank you.'

Thandi sat back on her heels and grinned up at her. '*Ikhitshi ihlambulukile.*' Margaret hesitated, the phrase was vaguely familiar, Sipho had written it down for her.

'The kitchen is…?'

Thandi made the action of wiping her hands.

'Ah yes, 'clean'.'

There was an answering peal of laughter. '*Ilungile, Nkosazana!*'

Sipho's Xhosa lessons were at last taking effect, though it was several months since they started. Learning any foreign tongue was such a slow process for her. How galling it was to hear Wil, with his deft ear for languages, comfortably chatting with Moses and the other farm workers.

She found Mary on the gravel sweep. She was holding her grey mare by a leading rein attached to the horse's headcollar. Mother called out to her from the verandah steps.

'Look what your kind friend has brought you this morning, all the way from Aviemore'.

Mary was looking very pleased with herself.

'Happy birthday, Margaret. I decided that after a year of living at Thorneybrook you absolutely cannot manage any longer without a horse so I've brought one over for you. Moses collected her saddle and bridle yesterday when he came to Pieterskloof. Petra's as sure footed as a reedbuck – you'll see much more of the country from her back than you will on foot. Besides, I don't want the moths to eat those old riding clothes you wore when you first stayed with us!'

She put the leading rein into Margaret's hand. 'Go on, take her, she's yours now.'

Margaret regarded the mare's placid face. It was a kind gesture, but she had no need of a horse; they'd managed perfectly well without one and she preferred walking.

'But she's your horse, Mary. Don't you need her to pull the trap?'

Mary shook her head. 'Not anymore. Pa's decided to bite the bullet and buy a proper motor car. He's ordered a Ford from Port Elizabeth, some new model designed to cope with this terrain. It's being brought up to Pieterskloof while he's in Scotland so that I have some decent transport here. My little Durban runaround would never cope with these terrible roads. So you see, Petra's going to be redundant once we have the new motor, she'd be far happier trotting around Thorneybrook with you than twiddling her hooves at Aviemore. Come on, lead her off.'

She gave the mare's rump a gentle tap and the animal started to walk towards the yard. Mary followed alongside.

'I've told Hughes to make room for her in one of the sheds while he builds you a proper stable. She's a gentle old thing, used to her creature comforts.'

Wil wouldn't be happy. He had more than enough to do: they'd bought in new livestock recently and the dairy venture was beginning to make a profit. Mother's gardening projects were becoming an added burden: these days she tired more quickly and he was expected to lend a hand. Her latest scheme, following the success of the vegetable garden, was to plant an orchard; the fruit trees had been ordered from a farm near Indlovu. Building a new stable might feel like the last straw for him.

Behind her, Margaret heard Mother's little cough from the verandah, a reminder she was being churlish, she should show some gratitude for Mary's gift. She patted the mare's neck and let the animal nuzzle her hand.

'You're very kind, Mary. I'm sure I'll enjoy riding Petra, once we get used to each other.'

Mary looked satisfied. They led the horse into the yard and tied her to a ring in the wall of the threshing barn, a shady spot beneath the roof overhang. Mary's big bay gelding was tethered nearby. A buzzing cloud of flies lifted off the nearby dung heap. Mary leaned against the barn wall and fanned her face with her hat.

'You know, the more I see of Hughes the more I like your manager. Percy seems to think he's the wrong choice, but he's made a big difference to the place already. He's a man of few words though, isn't he? Couldn't get much out of him when I told him about the new stable. Perhaps he has a problem with speaking English? I guess the country bumpkins where you come from only speak Welsh. That's not much use to anyone is it?'

Margaret bristled. 'Wil speaks perfect English; we went to the same school in the village. He's just naturally quiet, that's all. He's so busy with the farm, I don't think he has any time for extra building work at the moment.'

Mary ignored her. She pointed to a pile of wood lying in a corner of the yard.

'I've told him that's the best place for the stable, facing north so it'll get the sun in winter and be protected from the worst weather. Don't want this old girl to catch cold, do we?' She patted the mare's rump. 'I'm staying the night, I expect you know that.' She laughed, catching Margaret's puzzled expression. 'For your birthday celebration you chump! Percy's coming too; he's been shooting with an old school friend somewhere up in the Berg. He's riding over this afternoon.' She clapped a hand over her mouth in mock consternation. 'Oh dear, I've just realised I've blown your mother's surprise. Please don't let on I told you, she's been planning this for ages.'

Margaret was aghast. Mother should know how she hated surprises. Last year's birthday had passed without fuss; they'd been preoccupied with more important business. She'd hoped no one would notice this one either, until yesterday when Moses brought the mail from Pieterskloof. Among the correspondence was an envelope addressed to her, bearing a stamp from the post office at Rhydfelin. Inside was a card from

184

Miss Roberts with a pencil sketch of Dryslwyn castle and the inscription, *To Margaret, on your 19th birthday, with best wishes from your friend Elen Roberts.* On the back of the card she'd written, *'To thine own self be true.'* So typical of her old teacher to include a quotation; she missed their long conversations about books. She'd barely read anything these past weeks; at night she was so tired she fell asleep the moment her head touched the pillow. No more bad dreams, thank goodness.

She couldn't be true to herself today. She must pretend to be grateful for Mother's thoughtfulness and endure an evening of Percy and Mary talking about things which bored her. Something flashed past the window – a malachite sunbird, its feathers the deepest iridescent green. She was proud she could identify it; Father would have been pleased. She watched the tiny bird alight on a stem of honeysuckle and begin to pluck the nectar from the flower with its long delicate beak.

Percy arrived just before teatime, red-faced and perspiring from his long hot ride across country, and Margaret managed to feign sufficient delighted surprise to satisfy her mother. Chairs were brought on to the verandah and they settled themselves comfortably to admire the view. A month or so ago Wil had felled some of the pine trees which used to hide the grand panorama of grassland and mountains. The house felt brighter, restored to life after its years of solitude and neglect.

How quickly Percy assumed centre stage, she thought, lounging back in his chair with his legs crossed, a cigarette dangling between his long fingers. She'd never seen him smoke at Mount Pleasant; he was careful about his behaviour there. Here, he behaved as though he were the master of the house. He was regaling them with an account of his visit to Allerton, his friend's farm in the high Berg. The rough shooting had been excellent, the wild duck and geese plentiful in the *vleis* and river courses and they'd enjoyed a successful day and night in the mountains tracking eland and mountain reedbuck. Even

Mother was tiring of the monologue – several times Margaret caught her glancing wistfully in the direction of the vegetable garden. She looked quite different now from those terrible days after Father died; she'd put on a little weight and her normally pale skin had the healthy glow of someone who spent a lot of time outdoors.

The conversation moved on to cattle thefts on the Basutoland border. Mary was outraged.

'The government's doing nothing, Pa says. They just assume farmers and the local police will deal with the problem.'

Percy took another long drag of his cigarette. 'There's only so much people can do to protect their stock from those savages. The solution is to send armed patrols across the border to teach them a lesson. You present their chiefs with a heap of dead bodies and they'll soon stop their nonsense.'

Margaret excused herself and went in search of Wil. She hadn't had a chance to thank him for the bird table. He must have brought it round very early that morning while she was asleep, placing it in front of the beech hedge opposite her window where she could watch the birds feeding. He never forgot her birthday.

She found him inside one of the cattle sheds with Nansi. They were talking in Welsh as usual but switched to English when they saw her. Wil had brought Petra and Mary's gelding indoors and they were standing quietly in the gloom, glad to be out of the sun. Percy's black horse was tied to a wooden rail at the far end of the shed. His dark flanks were smeared with dried sweat and dust and he looked exhausted.

Wil noticed her look of distaste. 'I'm going to try giving him a rub down later, get some of that sweat off before he catches cold. He's a nasty bugger, though, won't let me near him without a kick.'

'Can't Percy do that? It's his horse after all.'

'I've been given my orders.'

'Thank you for the bird table – it's a lovely present and you've put it in just the right place. The wood is beautiful.'

He muttered something and turned away. Wil was no good with compliments.

She walked back to the house with Nansi. 'I expect you know about this surprise party.'

The girl nodded. 'Mrs Lewis wanted to make it special for you. A proper Thorneybrook birthday, she called it. You don't look very pleased.'

'I don't really like surprises, or any kind of fuss for that matter. I hate being the centre of attention, do you understand?'

'I'm one of seven children, miss. When there are so many of you nobody can be the centre of attention.'

Was the remark intended as a criticism of her? She couldn't be sure. Nansi was changing, she was more confident and at ease with herself and others in these surroundings. Often, she would be laughing with Mother as they worked or teasing Wil about his untidy appearance. He seemed to like it too, more's the pity.

Mother had really pulled out the stops. All of them – Nansi, Tryphena, Thandi – must have been preparing for days and yet she had noticed nothing. The old mahogany dining table from Bryntowy gleamed with freshly polished silver; the familiar crockery and glassware from home had been unwrapped and places laid for the birthday dinner. On the sideboard a bottle of the red wine Mother had brought up from Durban filled Father's crystal decanter, a retirement present from his regiment. Candles glowed in the branched silver candelabra at the centre of the table. The heavy shutters, normally closed to keep out the day's heat, were open now, to let in the cooler night air. A large pale moth with green veined wings fluttered in, helplessly drawn towards its extinction in the flames. Margaret saw Nansi swiftly trap it in her hands and release it back into the night. She had changed out of her working clothes into a close-fitting emerald green cotton frock, and her curly hair was fastened back with a gold clip – a butterfly emerged from its drab cocoon. Margaret, conscious of her own beige dress with its stiff pleated skirt, felt an envious stab.

Percy, too, seemed to notice the difference in her. 'I must say, Mrs Lewis, your maid has really risen to the occasion. I don't imagine this is the kind of thing she was used to in the Welsh valleys.'

'I don't think we should presume to know what Nansi was or wasn't used to at home, Mr Flynn.' Mother turned to Nansi and smiled. 'That dress is most becoming; the colour is just right for you. Now do sit down everyone, we don't need to be on ceremony.'

Margaret smiled to herself, seeing Flynn so clearly discomfited. She was pleased Nansi and Wil had been invited; Mother had placed them opposite each other at the bottom of the table, nearest the door leading to the kitchen. Reluctantly, she took her own seat at the head of the table – Mother insisted – with Percy on her left, opposite Mary. Mrs Lewis took the chair between Percy and Wil. 'Such a pity your father couldn't be with us, Mary, though I imagine he wouldn't want to exchange the cooler air of the Scottish Highlands for this heat. I had no idea the climate could be so extreme up here, being close to the mountains; for two pins I'd take a dive into the river right this minute!'

She picked up the pretty painted fan Mary had brought her and fanned herself vigorously. Percy glanced at the window.

'There's a storm on its way. I wouldn't be surprised if we get it here some time tomorrow afternoon. I checked your barometer in the hall, Mrs Lewis, the pressure's dropping.' He looked around the table, smirking. 'I don't suppose any of you – with the exception of Mary of course – will have experienced one of our Berg storms. It's quite a thing.'

Wil half rose from the table. 'Perhaps I should see to the animals, they will be...' He was addressing Margaret, but Flynn interrupted.

'I wouldn't worry, Hughes, they're quite used to it. Happens all the time in summer, the sheep and cows just hunker down until the storm passes. It'll probably all be over by teatime tomorrow. Could be some dramatic thunder and lightning before that of course.'

He leered at Nansi, enjoying her fearful expression.

'There's no need to be frightened, girl. I'm sure Hughes here will drop everything and rush to protect you. Assuming, of course, that he's not too terrified himself. I don't imagine you ever have real storms in Carmarthenshire, the climate's far too mild. Out here they certainly separate the men from the boys.'

There was an awkward silence. The man was appalling. Margaret could hardly bear to look at the others. Nansi was gazing at Wil, whose face was flushed and taut with anger. Mary sat very upright and still, an amused smile playing across her lips. Suddenly she jumped to her feet and raised her wine glass.

'That's enough of your teasing, Percy. I think it's time we raised a toast to Margaret. Happy birthday! May there be many anniversaries like this at Thorneybrook.'

They all rose and toasted her. Margaret stole a glance at Wil. He had barely touched his wine. He was trussed up in an ill-fitting dark grey suit with a stiff collar, probably one from his days at the mine office. He looked uncomfortable, unhappy. There was nothing she could say to lighten the mood, Percy had seen to that.

The meal was delicious: delicately flavoured brown trout caught from the river that morning; a shoulder of lamb from their own flock; fresh vegetables from the burgeoning garden. Tryphena and Thandi were summoned to be thanked. Nansi slipped out to the kitchen and returned with a Madeira cake she had made, decorated with red rose petals. Percy decanted a second bottle of wine and refilled his and Mary's glasses.

'What about the birthday girl?'

Margaret shook her head. The wine was making her light headed, giddy. He sat down again, uncomfortably close beside her, and she averted her head from the sickly smell of his cologne. She felt his hand grasp hers under the table. She tried to pull away, but his grip tightened.

'Before Margaret cuts her cake, I should like to give her my birthday present.' He was holding something in his other hand, a small oblong box wrapped in blue velvet. He placed it on the table in front of her, where everyone could see.

'Come on, my dear, open it.'

Her heart was thudding, all eyes were on her. Nansi's hand had flown to her mouth as though anticipating some terrible shock; Wil, opposite her, sat silent and morose. Even Mary looked shaken. Her mouth was open and the wine glass in her hand trembled a little. Flynn gave a loud theatrical sigh and let go of Margaret's hand.

'Well, if you won't open it, I will.'

He lifted the lid and tilted the box towards the rest of the table. A necklace, nestling in its dark blue velvet bed. The polished stones glowed golden-yellow in the candlelight. Margaret heard Mother gasp.

'In South Africa we call these 'tiger's eyes.' Percy was addressing the guests, enjoying his moment. 'They're actually quartz, quite sought-after overseas. I saw a necklace like this in London on my way back to South Africa after my visit to Wales, it was in a jeweller's window in Bond Street. I remember thinking at the time how much it would suit Margaret's colouring. Here, let me help you put it on.'

He took the necklace from the box, held it in both hands and stood up. He moved behind her. She held her breath, knowing what was to come. She dare not spoil the evening, she would have to endure this ordeal. She felt his fingers scrabble at the back of her neck and heard the click of the little clasp as he fastened the necklace.

'There. Perfect. Happy birthday, dear Margaret.'

He was stooping as if he meant to kiss her. She caught Wil's grim expression and swiftly ducked out of the way. There was a brief embarrassed silence, then Mary started to clap, slowly at first, then faster. The others followed suit and the moment was over.

Mother was leaning towards her, admiring the necklace. 'How lovely. Very kind of you, Percival, to give her such a splendid present.'

He beamed at her. 'Your daughter deserves it, Mrs Lewis, for making the brave decision to take on Thorneybrook. I'm very proud of her.' He took a large gulp of his wine. 'I propose another toast. To Thorneybrook, and all who live in her.'

With relief Margaret saw Mother get up from the table and push back her chair. She was looking tired all of a sudden, as though the stuffing had been knocked out of her.

'I really think we've had enough toasts, Percival. It's been a lovely evening but it's well past my bedtime. Goodnight to you all.'

They were free to escape. Wil was the first out. He made his apologies – the horses needed water – and stumbled out into the hot night. Thick darkness pressed in on him, sulphurous and oppressive, and his chest felt tight. He yanked at his necktie, splitting the thin cotton. On the horizon lightning flickered across the Berg; thunder crackled like gunfire somewhere on the Basutoland border. Behind him, Mary laughed.

'Well, at least Percy's good at predicting the weather, he's not quite so accurate when it comes to judging people. Poor Margaret, that was so embarrassing for her.'

She had followed him on to the verandah – the glow from her cigarette as she took a drag gave her face a strange, ethereal look, shadowed by the patch shrouding the dead eye. She exhaled and the smoke hung wraith-like in the heavy air.

'He's still in there trying to make amends. After Mrs Lewis left the dining room I thought Margaret was going to throw that lovely necklace at him, she looked so cross.'

Wil did not respond and so they stood in silence, listening to the storm rumble across the Berg.

'You mustn't take Percy too seriously, Hughes. He enjoys being provocative, stirring things up for the fun of it; he didn't mean to offend you. A low boredom threshold, that's what I think they call it these days. He's always been like that, since we were children.'

'I'm sorry to disagree, Miss Jamieson. I think he knew exactly what he was doing. I don't approve of that kind of "fun" as you call it. Where I come from, we call it rudeness.'

Duw, she deserved that answer for making light of Flynn's behaviour. He'd been within a whisker of punching him and damn the consequences, even if it cost him his job.

A hot light dazzled his eyes and he started back. Mary's cigarette was right next to his face.

'Oh, for goodness sake, man, you sound like one of those old hellfire preachers my father talks about – they have them in Scotland too you know. Are you Welsh always so dour?'

He felt her fingers lightly brush his sleeve.

'I bet underneath you are quite the opposite, William Hughes. I've seen that girl Nansi giving you the eye. A few more months in the African heat and you'll be a changed person. Though of course she might also be!'

She was laughing as she crushed the cigarette stump with her heel and turned back to the house.

He stood for some minutes in the dark until the anger was under control. He shouldn't have let Mary Jamieson see how much he disliked Flynn. Those two were close friends; it wasn't wise to make an enemy of her. '*Gan bwyll*', Dad would say, be careful, boy. No sense rocking the boat. The budget was settled now, thanks to Margaret's intervention; they had enough money to start a small dairy herd. Soon there would be milk as well as beef to sell. By the end of next year they might even be making a small profit. Time then to move on, perhaps. He left the verandah and made his way around the back of the house towards his room, his skin still remembering Mary's touch.

It was after eleven when Margaret entered her bedroom. She had been longing for an excuse to leave the sitting room, mindful that Mother expected her to play the grateful host. Mary and Percy were here for her birthday and would think her rude if she left too early. Tryphena, summoned by Percy, brought them coffee on a tray. Without a by-your-leave he opened the drinks cabinet and poured a large glass of whisky for himself and Mary – one of Father's best malts. The two of them settled themselves comfortably on the sofa and resumed their easy, bantering conversation. Mary kicked off her shoes. After a while they appeared to have completely forgotten Margaret was in the room. She shifted uncomfortably in her chair and the necklace's amber beads winked at her in the lamplight. Percy's gift wasn't innocent, she was certain; the way he'd gripped her hand under the table suggested a darker intention she refused to think about. Now he was leaning against Mary on the sofa, sharing some gossip about people they knew in Maritzburg. She watched him reach over and casually tuck a stray strand of hair behind her ear. His fingers lingered on her neck. They didn't even look up when Margaret rose and left the room.

She went over to the dressing table and with shaking hands unfastened the necklace, opened the bottom drawer and threw it inside. She slammed the drawer and began to pull out the pins holding up her heavy hair; her head was aching from its weight trapped inside the unwieldy bun. She should cut it in a short bob, like Mary's.

Something at the side of the table caught her eye, reflected in the mirror. A small package wrapped in hessian cloth and tied with a piece of scarlet ribbon. A birthday gift she'd overlooked. Her heart fluttered with dread – it might be another offering from Percy, perhaps even more suggestive than the necklace. She untied the ribbon and gingerly unwrapped the package. On the top was a note, in the same familiar handwriting.

For Margaret, birthday greetings.

It was a little portrait this time, drawn in dark, determined charcoal. The likeness was very good: the artist had captured her long bony face, the heavy eyebrows she always tried to hide beneath her fringe. Even the ugly smatter of freckles across her nose. The eyes held her own in a disconcertingly direct, curious gaze: a twin sister demanding a response.

In the bottom left hand corner were the initials *ZGM*.

Margaret caught her breath. So many months had passed, it must be almost a year since the last time. Long enough to forget. Whoever drew this portrait was still observing her in secret, close enough to note her freckles. Perhaps he was watching her this very moment, staring into her own likeness. What was he trying to tell her?

On an impulse she knelt down beside the bed and rummaged underneath it. She drew out the painting and brushed off the dust and cobwebs. Then she hung it back on the wall where she could see it properly. In the light from the bedside lamp the two eloquent figures seemed connected yet disconcertingly apart. The young man's anguish, the distant, enigmatic female figure – there was an important narrative here, intended for her to read. And now, the black spidery marks at the base of the frame made sense. They were the artist's initials. *ZGM*.

Footsteps along the hallway, stopping outside her room. Smothered giggles. Were Percy and Mary planning some trick?

She ran to the dressing table, hastily wrapped the portrait inside its hessian shroud. Readied herself for what might be coming.

The laughter had ceased. Along the hallway she heard the creak of a different door: the guest room where Mary was staying. Mother always complained the hinges needed oiling. More muffled sounds, a burst of suppressed laughter, then silence.

Her room felt unbearably hot. Tryphena must have fastened the shutters against the storm. She went over to the window and flung them open. Lightning still flickered distantly across the Berg and the air was perfumed with the cloying scent of honeysuckle. Was the mystery artist out, watching her? The silent garden, the farm, the vast country beyond their boundaries, gave no clue.

FOUR MONTHS LATER

CHAPTER 23

Wil had left Petra tied to the rickety gate at the edge of the compound while he went in search of Sipho. When they returned he saw the mare's girth had slipped. One of the large woven panniers attached to the saddle had come adrift and the vegetables were strewn amongst the weeds and dusty soil: a clutch of small creamy-skinned potatoes, twists of early purple beetroot, an armful of tender green beans. Sipho rushed to gather them up whilst Wil examined the other pannier; the leather strap attaching it to the saddle was just holding. *Diolch byth*, the contents were still intact, lodged in their nest of straw packing – three of Mrs Lewis's prized mangoes, a small bag of tomatoes, some ripening avocados, and a jar of her strawberry jam.

He should have let Margaret tighten Petra's girth before they left – the mare was hers after all – but he was in too much of a hurry. He hadn't wanted to bring the Cochets all this stuff in the first place, surely the money was enough, but she'd insisted on it, (*'You should always take gifts when you are visiting'*). He wiped the sweat off his face with the back of his hand and checked inside his cotton jacket for her old leather purse containing Sipho's fees for the term. When they had told Thandi their plan last week, her delighted face was a picture, but the way she grabbed his hands and did a clumsy sort of curtsey, well, that made him feel so uncomfortable. At Rhydfelin primary it didn't matter how rich or poor you were, nobody was expected to pay for their children's education.

Sipho helped him make the panniers secure then they unhitched the mare and led her away from the circle of thatched huts into the open veld and headed south, towards the foothills of the Berg. The sun was already high; it would take at least two hours to reach St Martin, by which time they would be glad of shelter from the midday heat. Two small children, a boy and a girl, followed them for a few yards, calling after Sipho in lilting Xhosa. When Wil turned round they stopped and gave him solemn looks, shy in the presence of a white man. He smiled back, called a goodbye – '*Sala kakuhle abantwana*'. They burst into gales of laughter and ran off back to the compound. Sipho was scowling.

'These cousins, Wil, they are always following me. Margaret gave me some picture books and pencils so I can teach them some English words. But they are bad students, always wanting to play, not learn.'

Wil smiled at him. 'Come on Sipho, they're only young. Let them enjoy themselves. There'll be time enough to learn when they're older like you.'

Margaret's lessons were having an effect. He had noticed a new seriousness about Sipho; he enjoyed trying out his English, writing down each unfamiliar word in a little pocket book he carried around with him. If the Colets agreed to accept him as a regular pupil it could be the making of him; at the very least he might find employment as a teaching assistant, or if Margaret put in a word for him someone might take him on as a junior clerk in one of the town businesses. Anything was better than labouring on the roads, or working in the mines up on the Reef like many local men were forced to do. Worse than a prison sentence, that life.

The mission bell was striking noon as they rounded a bend in the track and Wil glimpsed the church's wooden spire jutting from a grove of dark cypress. Beyond the trees the foothills of the Berg rose in a series of rocky terraces, red-veined and blackened by last season's fierce sun. The air was still, a heavy heat-filled silence broken only by the rasping of the cicadas. Something scuttled across their path into the dry grasses and he jumped.

'*Isilwanyana*,' Sipho was grinning at him. 'It's only a lizard, Wil. Not a snake this time.'

Barely a week ago, walking with Moses and Sipho, he'd seen his first puff adder, dozing in the shade of a rock just beyond the cattle shed – a coiled assassin, dark chevrons patterning the dull brownish skin, the perfect camouflage. Moses dealt with it perfunctorily, whacking it over the head with his pitchfork before it could slither away. He tossed the body into the long grass, where for an hour or two a buzz of flies marked its slow disintegration. In Wales it was the sky you kept in your sights, not the ground – looking out for rain clouds or a longed for burst of sunshine, or in spring time the ominous gathering of buzzards. Here, he was learning to keep his head down as he walked, for the ground was full of hidden dangers. It was a relief to turn off the baking track into the shade of the cypress and follow a grassy path through the trees towards a tall iron gate. On the other side of the gate was the mission compound. The focal structure was the church, a simple wooden building painted white, with a porch supported on sturdy pillars entwined with jasmine. He could hear the faint hum of bees amongst the flowers and the sound of children's voices inside a low-roofed square building adjoining the church. Sipho tugged at his arm, his eyes bright with pride.

'That's the schoolroom, Wil. We always sing a hymn before we eat.'

They led Petra past the schoolroom into the shade of some scrawny pine trees and waited. The words of the hymn floated through the open windows: '... pilgrim through this barren land... hold me with thy powerful hand.' Wil caught his breath. They'd sung the hymn, he and Mam, in chapel the Sunday before he left. Sitting through the minister's rambling sermon for her sake, longing to have the goodbyes over and done with, get on the train. A lifetime ago it felt now.

There was a scraping of chairs and then the wide door opened to let out the children; there must be thirty of them at least, boys and girls. One or two looked too old to be still at school. Some of Sipho's friends greeted him as they passed, eyeing Wil and Petra with a mixture of curiosity and diffidence. Two African women emerged from a low thatched-roofed building opposite the schoolroom, carrying baskets of food towards a large pin oak where the children swarmed, chattering and jostling for space in the shade. The younger of the two women, tall and slim, wearing a vivid green patterned dress and an elaborate headscarf of the same colour, clapped her hands; immediately the children quietened and sat down meekly on the stubbled grass. The women began distributing hunks of bread and cheese. An older pupil, a gangly boy in shorts and neat pale shirt, moved among them handing out little glass beakers of water.

Wil heard someone cough and turned to see a stocky middle-aged man in clergyman's clothes approaching from the schoolroom. He looked like one of those elderly bearded Welsh preachers whose portraits lined the walls of the chapel meeting room at Rhydfelin. A pale, domed forehead beneath sparse auburn hair, a thicket of greying beard and the same severe expression behind the round spectacles. Monsieur Cochet shook Wil's hand formally and nodded to Sipho who was jigging impatiently beside Petra, casting longing looks at his classmates beneath the tree.

'You have arrived at a good time, Mr Hughes, Sipho is always hungry! He can see his friends are already eating and wants to join them.' His voice was deep, strongly accented. 'Please come this way, we have prepared some food for you in the mission house. You can leave your horse in the paddock behind the kitchen; it will be cooler there. *Vas manger*, Sipho. Go and eat.'

The boy raced off across the grass to join the others and Wil followed the missionary through a small wooden gate at the back of the thatched building where an elderly black man took charge of Petra and the panniers. Inside the mission house, out of the sun's glare, all was coolness and shadow. The dining room was simply furnished: whitewashed walls, an old oak sideboard, a plain wooden table laid for the midday meal, few signs of comfort. The only ornament in the room was a tall grandfather clock, made of polished wood with delicate carvings of fruit and flowers around its base. Its gentle steady tick from the corner of the room brought to his mind the *parlwr* clock at Hendre.

A tiny woman, bony as a sparrow, stood at the doorway. Monsieur Cochet beckoned to her. 'My sister Madeleine.'

She came forward and took Wil's hand. Like her brother she was dressed formally, in an old-fashioned brown skirt and blouse buttoned at the neck with a plain white collar.

'Sipho has told me about you, Mr Hughes. You have been teaching him mathematics. My brother and I are very pleased to hear this.'

Her English was precise, less accented than Monsieur Cochet's, her eyes were bright, sharp like a blackbird's. You wouldn't mess around if you were in her classroom.

'Sipho and I have a pact, Miss Cochet; I help him with his numbers, he teaches me Xhosa. I think he's the better teacher; I make more mistakes than he does.'

'Sipho is a clever boy, we would like him to attend school more often, but...' Madeleine Cochet shrugged her thin shoulders, '... it is always a question of money. Our mother church in Cape Town is generous but we have many children to educate. And to feed.'

Wil remembered and reached into his jacket for the purse and Margaret's letter.

'Miss Lewis hopes this will be a help to you, and to Sipho of course.'

They had calculated the amount already owed for the boy's lessons; the money from those old books Margaret sold to the dealer in Maritzburg should cover the rest of the term, with a little extra for the school funds. Miss Cochet took the purse over to the sideboard and swiftly counted the money. She read the letter, then took a key from her pocket and unlocked one of the drawers, placing the purse inside. She locked it once more and scribbled something on a piece of paper which she handed to him.

'Your receipt for the fees. We send our regards to Miss Lewis; tell her we are grateful Sipho can continue his education at St Martin.' She pronounced the name in a French way. Monsieur Cochet motioned Wil to join him at the table.

'Sipho will be learning French this term as well as English. We think this will be an advantage to him. Our assistant, Grace, is going to give him some lessons.'

The door opened and the young woman Wil had seen feeding the children came in bearing a tray of food – bread, cheese, slices of chicken, tomatoes. She laid them out on the table and left the room again, returning moments later with a bowl of fruit which she placed next to Wil.

'Please thank Miss Lewis and her mother for their kind gifts; we appreciate them very much. With so many hungry mouths to feed here we can never grow enough vegetables and fruit!'

He was surprised to hear her speak – he was so accustomed now to the polite silence of black servants. He was even more surprised to see her take the chair opposite him and sit down, steepling her long thin fingers and closing her eyes for the mealtime blessing. His hosts were doing likewise so he followed suit, the familiar actions reminding him of chapel going, the weight of prayers. Monsieur Cochet's own prayer was lengthy and Wil stole a glance at the young woman through the gaps in his fingers. Her face was striking – oval shaped, with a smooth wide forehead, prominent cheekbones and a firm chin. Her complexion was lighter than the local people, suggesting she was from another part of Africa. She must have sensed his scrutiny of her face, for she returned it in kind – a solemn, unnerving gaze. Her dark eyes were flecked with green, the colour of her headscarf. Then she dropped her eyes to the table and hid her face behind her hands. Was she praying or laughing at him?

Monsieur Cochet made the sign of the cross and the prayer was finally over. Madeleine Cochet began to hand round the plates of food. As he helped himself to some cheese her brother paused.

'Forgive me, Mr Hughes, for not introducing you to our friend Miss Grace Morobe. She is a teaching assistant at the mission, before that she was one of our best pupils. How long is it now, Grace, that you have been with us?'

The young woman pulled an indignant face.

'Monsieur Cochet, how can you forget? I was nearly three years old when I came to you. Or so you have told me.'

She looked across the table at Wil. 'My teacher is only pretending; he knows exactly when I came here. These two people welcomed me as a little child, and they still treat me like that though I am now twenty and so very, very old!'

She pronounced the 'very's in an exaggerated, teasing French accent. The Cochets continued with their meal as though she had said nothing out of the ordinary. Wil was out of his depth. Since he'd been in this country not once had he observed white people eating with their servants. Even back home, he couldn't recall Mair or Betsan ever sharing a meal with Colonel and Mrs Lewis. Mam would have been amazed.

Thinking of his mother, he was reminded of a question he wanted to ask his hosts.

'The children were singing a hymn when we arrived. "Guide me O Thou Great Redeemer". We often sing it in my chapel in Wales. How do you know it?'

The missionary dabbed at his mouth with his napkin; stray breadcrumbs snagged in his beard.

'Ah, the great William Williams! When we lived in Lyons – before we came to South Africa – we learned many of his hymns. I think our Huguenot church is like your Welsh chapels, we preach the Word made flesh and we sing. It's easy in Africa, the children all love singing.'

The young woman gave a derisive snort. Monsieur Cochet frowned at her. 'Yes, even you, Grace. She is an excellent singer, Mr Hughes, though she pretends to be tone deaf!'

He said something to her in rapid French; she shrugged her shoulders and looked away. Feeling awkward, Wil reached for an apple; he cut it into slow quarters, trying to think of a different topic of conversation.

'Do you sing?'

With a start he realised Grace was addressing him. This was no polite enquiry; he felt its sharpness. It would be more polite to make a light-hearted response.

'Only to the cows when I'm milking. They don't seem to mind.'

'And Margaret? Does she sing? Like all the grand white ladies?'

She was being deliberately provocative for some reason, trying to unsettle him. He would give her a straight answer.

'I don't think so, Miss Morobe. I've never heard Miss Lewis sing. She is a reader; she loves books. Though she hasn't much time for that these days, there's so much to do at Thorneybrook just now.' He was aware that Grace was rising from her seat, but he carried on. 'The farm's been neglected for a long time, and the house needs a lot of work…'

The door slammed. Grace had gone.

They finished the rest of the meal in a polite silence, no one mentioned Grace's abrupt departure. The school bell was ringing for afternoon lessons and Madeleine Cochet rose to shake Wil's hand.

'Please excuse me, Mr Hughes, I have a class. Perhaps next time you visit you will bring Miss Lewis with you. I should like her to see what we are doing at St Martin and to thank her personally for her gifts and her support of Sipho.'

She left the room and he saw her pass the window in the direction of the schoolroom, tucking the folds of her dress tightly around her, a wisp of brown in the sun's glare.

To his surprise Grace was waiting by the front door when he and Monsieur Cochet came out. She walked alongside them as far as the schoolroom. Wil went to shake her hand but she folded her arms and tipped her head to one side, looking down at him. He hadn't expected her to be so tall.

'I think you are finding life here a little difficult; you show that in your face. South Africa is not an easy country for any of us, Mr Hughes. I wonder how it is in your Wales?'

'Oh, it's not so very different, apart from the weather, of course; we have a lot of rain in our part of the world. Farming's much the same everywhere, you just have to adapt to the climate and get on with the job.'

It was the wrong answer of course, he realised that straight away. She gave a deep, rather theatrical sigh, shook her head and abruptly turned her back on them. He heard the schoolroom door close behind her and the children's chatter subside beneath the cool tones of her voice.

The afternoon was slipping away. He should get going, but Mr Cochet insisted on showing him the church first. Like the mission house it was simply furnished, an attractive whitewashed, light-filled space, the benches made of local pinewood with a plain wooden cross suspended from a beam above the altar table. On first impression it appeared similar to chapels at home. And yet, no chapel he'd ever been in displayed such astonishing artwork. The wall on his right was crowded with paintings of birds and animals, in brilliant intense tones. A blue crane standing sentinel in a golden grassland; a pair of sacred ibises, wings arrested in mid-flight against a grey storm-filled sky; delicate gazelle drinking from a river in the green mist of an early morning. On the opposite wall were two enormous canvases: abstract designs, experiments in clashing hues and textures, gouts of paint swooping and swirling across the canvas. He couldn't take his eyes off them.

'These are all Grace Morobe's work.' The missionary was regarding him warily. 'You may think they are unsuitable for a religious house, Mr Hughes, but my sister and I believe in celebrating the skills of all our pupils, however unorthodox they may seem. Grace is an exceptional artist. If she lived in a different country perhaps her talents would be truly celebrated.'

'Even I can tell these paintings are extraordinary, Monsieur Cochet. I've never seen anything like them. Did you or your sister teach her to paint like this?'

The missionary shook his head, smiling.

'Neither of us has that talent, sadly. There are some artists for whom great gifting comes with great pain. Grace Morobe is one of those. She has drawn and painted since she was a little girl, on scraps of paper, stones, leaves, anything that would bear her imprint. If she could not draw she would rage – at herself, her teachers, the other children. To calm her we would buy paints and brushes. One time a missionary from the Cape brought her a book about famous artists from Europe and she taught herself to draw by making copies of their paintings, like these birds and animals. But those ones...' He indicated the abstract paintings. 'I do not know, they come from some dark place in her mind. Hers is a restless spirit, you have seen that already; we can never be sure what she will do next.'

Sipho appeared in the doorway. It was time to go; Petra was outside in the yard waiting for him. The boy made to shake Wil's hand but in a sudden impulse flung his arms around his waist.

'I am very happy to be in school again, Wil. Thank you. But can I continue my lessons with you and Miss Margaret when I am home?'

Wil gently untangled his grasp. 'Of course you can, Sipho. *Sala kakuhle*, my friend, goodbye.'

The empty panniers had been tied in front of the saddle and he checked Petra's girth; he wasn't going to make the same mistake again.

'Please call again, Mr Hughes, to see how your young friend progresses.'

Monsieur Cochet was standing at the door, cleaning his spectacles with a large handkerchief. Wil hesitated. The question was nagging at him, he must ask it before he left.

'I can't help noticing that Grace seems different from the other pupils here. She looks…'

The missionary interrupted. 'Are you referring to the fact that Grace is a Coloured person?'

Iesu mawr, this country seemed to have a definition for every shade of human being! This was another new one. Mr Cochet had put on his spectacles again and his face was stern.

'People like Grace who are of mixed parentage have a particular problem in this country, Mr Hughes: they belong nowhere. Neither to their white nor to their black families. Grace's parents are both dead. Before he died her father entrusted her to our care; at the time her African family wanted nothing to do with her.'

What about her white family, Wil wanted to ask, but Cochet raised his hand.

'You would like answers, but I cannot say more than this. We have done as her father requested: provided Grace with a home and an education, tried to shield her from… certain difficulties concerning her complicated background. But she is stubborn, very inquisitive, I fear she knows too much already. Now you must go, Mr Hughes, it is getting late and you don't have Sipho to guide you home.' His face relaxed into a smile. 'I am pleased to have met a man from Wales, especially one who knows William Williams!'

Wil mounted Petra and turned her towards the gate. Cochet was right, the sun was already low and Moses would be needing his help with the milking. The mare's broad back made for a comfortable ride. Margaret was always urging him to use Petra instead of walking everywhere – it could take a couple of hours just to travel from one end of the farm to the other. They emerged from the cypress grove on to the open veld. Dusk was already settling into the hollows of the foothills and the lowering sun threw long shadows across the grasslands. The air was sweet with the honey fragrance of acacia and lemon-scented grass; in the distance a flight of Egyptian geese arrowed a path towards the river. If it were autumn back home he could be battling with chill drizzle, the start of the long *tywydd garw*, the bitter weather. His parents might not understand, but he knew he was better off in Africa.

CHAPTER 24

Tryphena was sick. Nansi found her collapsed against the wall outside the kitchen door, mopping her sweating face with the end of her apron, her eyes glassy, red-rimmed. In the morning's heat she was shivering. Margaret was weeding in the vegetable garden when she heard Nansi calling for her; together they brought Tryphena inside and lowered her gently on to one of the kitchen chairs. Nansi tried to make her drink some water, but Tryphena pushed the glass aside, rocking back and forth, muttering to herself in Xhosa.

'She needs to see Dr Ormond. I'll find Wil; we'll drive her straight to Pieterskloof.'

Nansi shook her head. 'She won't go, miss. It's not the same out here; when they're sick they want their own people.'

'How do you know that?'

'Thandi told me. They don't trust white doctors; they have their own. Same as Bessie Jones, Cwm Morgan, remember? She used to make medicines out of herbs and stuff; people always went to her first. Cheaper than paying the doctor.'

'Then what do we do? We can't just leave her like this.'

'She needs her family to look after her. Fetch Moses or one of the boys to take her to the compound.'

She went over to the sink and doused a cloth with water. She gently wiped Tryphena's face, talking to her soothingly, 'Rest, you will feel better soon.' The groans quietened. Sick people were in good hands with Nansi, she always knew what to do. There was no point in Margaret hovering here, getting in the way.

She left the kitchen and ran over to the yard. Moses might be out in the fields with Wil. She'd barely seen him since his visit to the mission weeks ago. They'd decided to buy in more grazing stock and hired two extra boys from the compound to mind them; these days the yard was constantly busy. As she opened the gate Musa, one of the new farm hands, was coming out of the milking shed with a barrowload of dung. In her halting Xhosa and clumsy mime she managed to convey the urgency; he left the barrow and followed her to the kitchen.

Thandi had arrived and was helping Nansi lift Tryphena to her feet. Her eyes were closed, her body limp and heavy. This was madness; Tryphena needed a doctor not some local herbalist, she should really insist they took her to Pieterskloof. Thandi issued some rapid instructions then Musa took hold of Tryphena in his strong arms, lifted her out of the chair and hoisted her on to his back. She was breathing heavily, barely conscious now. With Thandi on one side and Nansi on the other, supporting Tryphena against the boy's back, they left the house and followed the worn footpath towards the huts. Margaret trailed behind the little cortege, carrying Tryphena's faded pink cardigan, feeling useless.

In all the time they had been at Thorneybrook she'd never once been inside the African compound. Beyond the stockade fence some scrawny chickens grubbed about in the dirt; a small brown goat tethered to a rope stared at them through pale slitted eyes. The round huts – she counted five of them – surrounded an area of scuffed beaten earth; in the middle were the blackened remains of a fire. She noticed how the conical roofs were neatly thatched, with smooth mud walls dark as chestnut and low narrow doorways. One of the huts was painted a bright turquoise blue. Other than the goat and the chickens the place was empty. The men left early for work on neighbouring farms and most of the women were out in the fields or tending their vegetables in a scrawny patch of land beyond the *kraal*.

Thandi disappeared into the blue hut. Minutes later she

209

reappeared and beckoned them over. With Nansi's help, Musa eased Tryphena off his back; her eyes were now open and she was able to move her legs a little. They walked, half-carried her inside the hut. Margaret had to dip her head to avoid striking the wooden lintel. The interior smelled pleasantly of woodsmoke, dried grasses and some pungent herb she didn't recognise. Through the dim light from the little window opposite the doorway she saw a small wooden table with two chairs, a narrow mattress on the floor covered with a patterned blanket, cooking utensils on a low makeshift shelf, a large three-legged iron pot on the floor. She watched Musa and the two women gently lower Tryphena on to the mattress and cover her with the blanket; she was whispering to Thandi who knelt beside her. The younger woman nodded and looked up at Margaret.

'Tryphena is feeling a little better, *Nkosazana*. She say she is very grateful to you, but you must leave now. *Udokotela*, our doctor, is coming soon.'

Nansi gave Margaret a meaningful look.

'We should go now, miss; we're in the way here. Thandi will tell us if she needs anything.'

Margaret backed out of the hut, shielding her eyes as she stepped from the gloom into the sunshine. A woman was approaching. As she neared the hut she became aware of Margaret's presence. She stopped dead, looking terribly anxious, her body poised for flight. In that moment Margaret understood who she was.

'Precious? What are you doing here?'

She was thinner than Margaret remembered. Her face had a hollowed out, pinched look, and her dress, made of some flimsy cotton fabric, hung loosely about her body. Margaret took a step forward, wanting to reach for her hand, but the woman started back.

'I'm sorry *Nkosazana*, I did not expect you to be here. I will go now.'

'No, you mustn't go, I am so glad to see you. Where have you been since you left Mount Pleasant? I came to find you that day, but you'd gone.'

Precious's gaze shifted beyond her, to the doorway of the hut. Margaret turned and saw Nansi standing there.

'You knew Precious was here, didn't you? Why didn't you tell me?'

Nansi did not reply. Her expression was sullen and unresponsive, a Bryntowy look. How stupid she'd been to think the two of them had forged a friendship, a shared understanding.

'Nansi, I demand you tell me what is going on.'

'I wanted to before, only Wil said we shouldn't.'

'Wil! What has Wil to do with this?'

Nansi was twisting a lock of hair at the side of her neck.

'We were afraid, me and Wil, that if you knew Precious was here you would tell Mr Flynn and then he would drive her away, like he did before.'

'What makes you think I would tell Mr Flynn?' Indignation churned inside her. They had no right to make assumptions about her relationship with that man. She could see Nansi was hesitating. Was it so difficult to give an honest answer?

'The night of your birthday, when he gave you that necklace, we thought it meant you were going to marry him. I told Wil about what he had done to Precious and he thought she should stay in the compound until we could find somewhere else for her to live. She's got nobody to look after her.'

'It is true, *Nkosazana*.' Precious spoke so quietly she could barely hear the words. 'My family are gone from this place long time ago.'

'And your child? Is he with you?'

Precious shook her head and hugged her thin arms across her chest. 'No, he is not with me.'

'Her child is dead,' Nansi said quietly.

'He was always sick, *Nkosazana*, you saw how he was at Mount Pleasant. I give him food but he would not eat it.'

'Where did you go, when you… when Mr Flynn told you to leave Mount Pleasant? What did you do?'

'I try to find other work, cleaning house, weeding garden. It was very difficult, especially with the boy. Nobody to look after him. So I decide to come back here, to find my family. I told you before, *Nkosazana*, about my grandmother. She is buried near here.' She gestured vaguely, out towards the veld. 'I walk a long way, all the road to Maritzburg. I have no money, I beg for food. A white man stop, he is going on to Pieterskloof; he give me lift on the back of his truck. Then I walk again.' She stopped to catch her breath, her thin body trembling with the effort of speech.

'She was lying on the roadside by the drift. Wil found her and brought her back here. She was very ill, far worse than she is now. Thandi has been looking after her.'

'When was this?'

'About three weeks ago. I'm sorry, we should have told you. Precious said you were kind to her in Durban, you would understand. It was only because of Flynn that we kept quiet.'

She did understand, more acutely than they realised. She could see how it must have looked that evening, Flynn's necklace claiming her, the fumbled attempt at a sealing kiss. She reached for Precious's hand and held on to it this time.

'You mustn't worry about Mr Flynn. This is my farm and I wish you to stay. We will all take care of you and when you feel better there is work for you here if you wish it. My mother is not so strong these days, she will be glad of your help.'

Precious managed a faint smile. 'Thank you, I will be better very soon.' She gently disengaged herself from Margaret's grasp and made her way slowly into the hut.

Margaret turned to Nansi. 'I don't want you to tell Mrs Lewis about what happened in Durban. I'll make up a reason why Precious has come here. Mother was always fond of her.'

On the way back to the house Nansi trailed behind her. There was a new awkwardness between them that Margaret had to put right; it was unbearable to think she and Wil had misread the situation between herself and Flynn. She waited for Nansi to catch up.

'You need to understand there's no question of a marriage. You know my opinion of Percival Flynn; I thought I'd made that clear ages ago. Perhaps you could explain that to Wil. He of all people should know me better; we've never kept secrets from each other.'

She chose those last words carefully. Nansi needed to know her relationship with Wil was unbreakable. The girl gave a brief nod and they parted at the kitchen door. Margaret went around the side of the house towards the vegetable garden to resume her weeding. Unusually, her bedroom window was wide open; the breeze was lifting, she should close it. Stretching to reach the catch, she noticed a scrap of red cloth snagged on the rough wood of the casement. The material was soft to the touch, satiny.

She peered into the room; all looked much as she had left it earlier. Yet, for the rest of the day, busy with her tasks, she felt uneasy. The intruder had returned.

MIDWINTER

CHAPTER 25

Mr Nel was full of apologies. The blood pressure pills for Mrs Lewis hadn't arrived with the weekly order. He'd checked the original list again, yes there was an entry for the pills, he wouldn't have forgotten an important item like that. He'd get a message to the dispensary in Durban, insist they send up a new supply by the end of the week. Mrs Lewis could get by until then, couldn't she?

Margaret sighed; of course Mother would 'get by'; she was tougher than she looked, though the truth was she couldn't manage more than an hour in the garden these days without complaining of a headache or being short of breath. No point in saying that to Mr Nel, standing behind the counter wringing his hands. Perhaps they should take Dr Ormond's advice after all, move Mother to a flat in Durban or somewhere down on the coast; this high altitude was proving to be bad for her health.

Outside the chemist's Margaret turned up the collar of her jacket, feeling the snap of winter on her skin. Frost silvered the wooden planks of the walkway; the roadside potholes lay hidden under a glaze of ice. Her second winter in South Africa, she knew the signs: by noon all would have melted in the thirsty sun.

Pieterskloof was busier than usual for a Wednesday: vehicles, mostly horse drawn, lining both sides of the main road in front of the shops; the usual sprawl of local Africans outside Naidoo's General Stores. A dark suited elderly man doffed his hat as she passed, Mrs Beverly waved at her from the pavement opposite. She was a 'local' now, one of them. She had chosen this life, for the time being at least.

She should hurry. Wil was sure to be at the post office by now, finished with his own chores and anxious to get back to Thorneybrook with the weekly provisions. In her handbag was the manager's mysterious note, delivered to her last week by Moses: *For collection only by Miss Margaret Lewis. Strictly in person.*

The small package was waiting for her on the post office counter, wrapped in plain brown paper and tied with a piece of string. No postmark, no address, just her name in large printed letters. The manager Mr du Plessis, a stooping sallow-skinned man with a straggling goatee beard, frowned at her over his reading glasses.

'This is most irregular, *juffrou*.' He spoke with a heavy Afrikaans accent, the 'r's rolling out, thick as treacle. 'It was outside the door, on top of the mailbag. Someone must have put it there in the night.' He pushed a thick black ledger across the counter in her direction and pointed a nail-bitten finger at her name halfway down the page. 'Sign there, *asseblief*.'

Margaret did as instructed, picked up the package and left. The trap was parked by the roadside opposite the post office and she could see Wil sitting in it, absorbed in his copy of the *Natal Witness*. With his old hat tipped backwards off his forehead, his dusty hair, sunburned face and arms, he looked like all the other white farmers in this country. Such a different life they were leading now. She clambered in beside him. He folded the newspaper and put it at his feet, casting a rueful glance at the package in her hands.

'Well that's a disappointment. I thought it was going to be a huge parcel, those new tools for the workshop I asked you to order from Durban. It's not as if it's your birthday.' He gave her a sharp look. 'Or could it be another special gift from your admirer?'

She knew she was blushing. Wil should know better; that necklace business was a long time ago. Percy had kept a distance since then, thank goodness. He rarely stayed the night and when he called the visits were brief and business-like. They often coincided with times when she knew Mary was at Aviemore. She always made sure Precious was out of the house when he called; they dare not risk an accidental meeting.

She started to unwrap the parcel with a creeping sense of dread. Wil was wrong; this wasn't Percy's style. He would have presented the gift to her in person, preferably with other people watching. She peeled off the last of the paper wrapping. A slim book, bound in cream cloth, the spine a deep mossy green. Elegant gilt lettering above a delicate design of wispy bell-shaped flowers: *Poems by Emily Dickinson.* She opened it, expecting to find an inscription or a message on the fly leaf. The page was blank. She knew Wil was watching, gauging her reaction; she wouldn't let him jump to the wrong conclusion again.

'This isn't from Percival Flynn if that's what you're thinking. I've never heard of this writer, Emily Dickinson; there's no message inside it.' She held it out to him. 'Take a look at it yourself if you don't believe me.'

Wil took the book from her. *Mawredd*, she was so prickly, he'd obviously touched a nerve. There was nothing on the first page apart from the printing details at the bottom.

'It was published in Boston in 1896. She must be an American poet. A pity we can't ask Miss Roberts, I bet you she's heard of her.'

He flicked through the pages to the end, held the book upside down and shook it. A piece of paper fluttered on to his lap. Margaret seized it. A single sentence, written in emerald green ink.

'He said you were a reader.'

Wil leaned across. 'Is that all? Nothing else?'

She snatched the book from his hands and started leafing through the pages. Why would someone give her this book? She'd never been keen on poetry despite Miss Roberts's efforts to get her interested in Milton and Wordsworth. Too long and dreary. At least these poems were shorter – that was some relief – but the punctuation was bewildering: fragmented lines, peppered with full stops, dashes, exclamation marks. A thought came to her. Olive Schreiner's novel had a similar quirky style. Could this be a gift from Mary? Emily Dickinson might well be another of those strange women writers she admired. If so, why the mysterious note? In irritation, she tore it into pieces, snapped the book shut and tossed it behind her into the back of the trap.

'I've no idea who sent it to me and I'm not interested in reading it. My mother enjoys poetry, she can have it.'

She stole a glance at Wil, waiting for him to tell her she was being silly. But he was lost in thought, gazing into the distance.

'Come on Wil, we need to get home. I'm getting cold sitting here.'

He straightened up, pulled down the brim of his hat and picked up the reins, clicking the mare into action.

'*Dere Petra fach, amser mynd*. Time to go, old girl.'

They travelled the first mile or so in companionable silence. Wil always enjoyed this part of the journey to Thorneybrook: the tawny grasslands sweeping down to the river, the smoky outline of the mountains as they breasted the first ridge. Glancing across at Margaret, he saw she'd retrieved the book and was absorbed in one of the poems, her body swaying with the movement of the trap. She couldn't resist words on a page, whatever she said about not liking poetry. He controlled the urge to make a joke; she'd only be cross with him for disturbing her. From the corner of his eye he saw her shift her gaze from the book and take a deep breath.

'You know, Wil, some of these poems are extraordinary. Not really my cup of tea, but just listen to this one:

> *Before I got my eye put out,*
> *I liked as well to see*
> *As other creatures, that have eyes,*
> *And know no other way.*

> *But were it told to me, to-day,*
> *That I might have the sky*
> *For mine, I tell you that my heart*
> *Would split, for size of me.*

'Doesn't it make you think of Mary? I'm beginning to think the book came from her.'

He shook his head. 'Not likely. I think Mary Jamieson's too plain speaking for that kind of weird stuff.'

He was probably right. Mary seldom mentioned her damaged eye, even when the skin around it looked so obviously inflamed. There were no books of poetry on the shelves at Aviemore, nor at Mount Pleasant for that matter. *He said you were a reader.* Was 'he' a reference to Percy after all? Had Mary sent the book to her at his suggestion? She pictured the two of them, the night of her birthday, whispering together on the sofa. The bedroom door closing behind them. What did they want from her?

Wil relaxed the reins; Petra knew the way home. He needed to think clearly. The note had been vexing him ever since they left Pieterskloof. They were his words, his answer to that blunt question, did Margaret sing. These poems were just the kind of strange thing Grace Morobe would read. It would be just like her to send them to Margaret on a whim. Damn, he should have told her straightaway about meeting Grace at the mission; he'd been so busy with the farm he'd forgotten all about it.

He brought Petra to a halt on the grass verge.

'Let me see the book again.'

He hunted through the pages, scanning the short poems until he found what he was looking for. Her name, written in tiny, meticulous letters below the last poem in the collection. *Grace Morobe.* He planted the open book on Margaret's lap, triumphant.

'I think this is the person who sent it to you.'

He watched her eyes dart across the pages and stop. She turned towards him and he saw the colour had drained from her face.

'How do you know about Josephine and Ernest Bancroft? Did Nansi tell you?'

Her finger was pointing, not at Grace's name, but at something written on the opposite page. *To my dearest Josephine from ELB. July 1900.*

He shrugged his shoulders; the names meant nothing. He felt her hand clutch at his arm.

'Look, Wil, you have to help me. I can't make sense of any of this. I've been handed a mystery I'm supposed to solve and it's driving me mad. There are clues – names, paintings, now poems – and I don't understand how to connect them. And I know this will sound ridiculous, but it feels as though it's all my fault.'

Her mood had changed so rapidly he was at a loss to know what to say. He'd never seen her upset like this, not even after David died. He wanted to put an arm around her, comfort her out of her terrors, but he knew she wouldn't want that. Better to listen, let her do the talking; the 'mystery' was probably a lot simpler to solve than she thought.

She didn't need his encouragement to talk; it all came pouring out of her. Ghostly faces at the window, messages on gravestones, names he'd never heard of. If she weren't so agitated he'd make a joke, say it was like something out of *Terrifying Tales at Midnight*.

'Do you see now, Wil, why I'm so upset? I can't bear being tricked, made to seem like a fool.'

Only once before he'd seen her in tears, when they found the bucket of drowned kittens below Hendre bridge. Perhaps he should tell her about his own encounter with the 'ghost' in the red dress, get her to see none of this was real. He found a grubby handkerchief in his pocket and silently handed it to her.

Margaret mopped at her face. It was a relief to tell him everything, however melodramatic it sounded. Wil would help her unravel it all, or at least be straight with her if she was imagining things. She passed the soggy material back to him and they were quiet for a while, staring at nothing in particular, hearing the creak of Petra's harness, the distant call of birds.

Wil stole another look at her. The wiry brown hair had sprung loose from the thick plait and her cheeks were grimed with dust. What if she decided to throw in the towel because of this nonsense? Sell the farm and go home, just when they were getting the place straight? He wasn't ready to look for another job. Damn Grace Morobe and her stupid prank; she had no idea what harm it would do. He should tell Margaret what he knew before something else happened. He lifted the book gently from her lap and showed her the last page.

'Have you ever heard of Grace Morobe?'

She shook her head. 'I don't know that name.'

'I met her at the mission the day I went to pay Sipho's school fees. She wanted to know whether you liked singing and I said you preferred books; that you were a reader. Grace wrote that note and put it inside this book. I guess she thought you liked poetry. I could have put her straight about that.'

Margaret stared at the page, chewing at her nails.

'Do you think this Grace Morobe is connected in some way to Ernest Bancroft? He's the man who left me Thorneybrook; I'm not sure you knew that. The farm should have been David's, not mine.'

He didn't know; it wasn't his place to ask. None of her family talked about her dead brother, they kept their feelings to themselves, people like them. Stiff upper lip and all that.

'Perhaps you should ask Grace yourself. I have a feeling that's what she wants.'

The sound of hoofbeats interrupted the conversation. Two riders were approaching fast along the road, loose stones skittering from beneath their horses' hooves. Margaret buried the book inside the wrapping and shoved it under her seat, just in time. Percival Flynn pulled up his sweating horse beside the trap. His companion halted a short distance away.

'We were on our way to find you. Mrs Lewis was wondering where you'd got to. Nothing wrong with the old pony I hope?' He was addressing Margaret, ignoring Wil.

'We're quite alright, thank you. Just having a chat and enjoying the view.'

Flynn looked nonplussed.

'Beats me what there is to stop and look at here, you can't see the mountains at all, just grass.' He turned his pale gaze on Wil. 'I'm surprised you think you have time for a 'chat', Hughes. I've been inspecting the farm in your absence, seems like your boys are having an easy time of it. I caught two of them lazing about in the yard, gave them a piece of my mind.' He twisted round in the saddle and beckoned the other man over.

'Let me introduce you to a friend of mine, Brian Matthews. He's something of an expert on farming in these parts.'

Flynn's companion was a burly man with a shock of thick black hair and a stubby moustache. He raised his hat to Margaret, nodded curtly at Wil.

'I was just telling Miss Lewis here that those Afs of hers will be running circles round her if she's not careful.'

The man gave a mirthless laugh through cracked, tobacco

stained teeth. 'You got to be tough with the natives, miss. Show them who's boss from the start.'

'Brian's come up with me to take a look at your place and suggest some improvements. He manages a big dairy farm in Zululand at the moment, but he's just the kind of person you could do with at Thorneybrook, Margaret. Someone who understands the country, not an outsider.'

Margaret was indignant. 'If you're implying Mr Hughes is not up to the job, Percy, then you couldn't be more wrong. He's an excellent manager and our workers respect him, as I do. We don't need any advice on how to run the farm, thank you. I mean no disrespect to you of course, Mr Matthews.'

The man gave a sullen nod; she had made her feelings clear. He turned in his saddle for Flynn's response and his expression suggested contempt. It was a humiliation of sorts, satisfying but dangerous. Flynn face was flushed with anger. He yanked his horse around and roughly kicked it on, bringing it close to the trap so that the top of his right boot was on a level with her eyes.

'We shall see, Margaret. I suggest you both abandon your little chat and get back to Thorneybrook as fast as you can. You don't want to cause your mother any further anxiety do you? Given her poor health, that is.' He threw Wil a look of disdain. 'I'm going to take Matthews cross country, get his advice about the river lands. I hear you're making quite a mess of them, Hughes. We'll see you back at the house, Margaret.'

The two men turned off the road and set their horses to a fast gallop, disappearing over the rise in swirls of thick grey dust. Wil's face was shuttered, the thin lines of his mouth tightly drawn. She knew better than to talk to him right now. He directed Petra gently back on to the road and they travelled the rest of the way in gloomy, preoccupied silence.

Chapter 26

She was standing in the corridor outside his room, fully dressed. Beyond his window shutters the dawn was only a glimmer, the first birds just beginning to stir. In the dim light her face looked pale, the skin beneath her eyes smudged with grey.

'I couldn't sleep. I've been counting the hours until I knew you'd be up. I want to show you something, come!'

The state of her bedroom in the sleepy light of the oil lamp made him smile, it was so like her old room at Bryntowy. She hadn't changed her childhood habits; he imagined Mam and Betsan in the doorway, shaking their heads at the mess, '*Wel, wel, edrychwch ar y llanast yma!*' Papers and books strewn across the floor, clothing draped any old-how over the chairs, the bed. She took no notice, stepping carelessly across the debris to open a drawer in her dressing table. She handed him a brown leather notebook, open at the last page where she'd glued some scrawny bird feathers. There was also a little card and another piece of paper – birthday greetings, a welcome, what did she want him to do with these?

'There's more, look over there.'

She was pointing at two pictures on the wall above the bed. The smaller one was a drawing of Margaret. He was no judge of art but he could see it was a good likeness; the artist had captured her strong nose and chin, the unruly mass of brown hair framing her face, and that direct, slightly puzzled expression in her eyes. The large painting was a shocker. *Achyfi!* He'd never seen such ugly, clashing colours, and the paint all smeared across the canvas like the artist had a knife not a brush. That poor man stretching his arms towards the woman, he looked in agony.

'What do you think?'

Duw, it was hard to stop staring. There was something about the woman's face, those cold eyes ignoring the man and looking straight at you. Made the hairs on the back of your neck stand up. And there was someone else in the picture – he could see it better now he'd moved closer. A child, right at the back of the painting, so faint you could easily miss it.

Margaret was fidgeting at his side. 'Don't just look at the pictures, Wil, look at the initials at the bottom of them!'

It took him a little while to decipher them. When he turned around she was pacing the room, back and forth, hugging her chest.

'All night I kept thinking, I don't know anybody called Grace Morobe. Precious never mentioned her, I didn't see her name in any of the books at Mount Pleasant, I heard nothing about her from Percy or Mary. Then I remembered I had seen the name before, on the back of that birthday card I just showed you. You see, I thought 'Grace' was some kind of greeting, like 'Peace' or 'Welcome', not someone's name. You said Grace Morobe was an artist, well, could these be her initials, *ZGM*? Though I don't know what the *Z* stands for.'

He recalled the huge abstract canvases on the walls of the mission church. This painting made the same violent assault on his senses. You couldn't resist them, even though you wanted to turn them to the wall.

'Monsieur Cochet showed me some of Grace's artworks. They were very peculiar, gave me the shivers, I can tell you. You see, I thought Grace was their servant to begin with, but when they spoke to her like she was their equal I was really confused. She was quite rude to them.'

'What does she look like?'

He scratched his head, trying to recall Grace's features, the way she moved, the greenness of her dress.

'Tall, with a thin bony face, strange eyes, scary like.' Damn it, he was no good at describing people; animals were much easier.

'She's not a properly dark African, her skin's lighter than Tryphena's, sort of golden like Mam's honey. Monsieur Cochet said she was a Coloured person if that means anything.'

'Does she live at the mission?'

'Her mother's family didn't want her because she's mixed race so her father asked the Cochets to take her. They probably didn't want her either. I don't blame them, she's a handful that one.'

Margaret strode over to the bed and fished out the book of poems from underneath her pillow.

'I read them all last night, that's why I couldn't sleep. The last poem of all, the one above Grace's name, makes me think she wanted me to see a link. Here, you read it.' She thrust the book into his hands. He hesitated, glancing at the little clock on the bedside table – a quarter to six; he'd be late for milking.

'Come on Wil, it won't take long. Just pretend you're in one of Miss Roberts's lessons where you have to tell her what the poem's about or she won't let you out to play.'

He rolled his eyes at her and looked at the poem, *Bequest*. At least there were only two verses.

You left me, sweet, two legacies, -
A legacy of love
A Heavenly Father would content,
Had He the offer of;

You left me boundaries of pain
Capacious as the sea,
Between eternity and time,
Your consciousness and me.

Nefi wen! Daffodils and skylarks he could understand but not this kind of stuff. He glanced up and saw Margaret watching him, her eyes gleaming.

'You do see it now, don't you? I have to admit it took me a while.'

He shook his head. 'Sorry, not a clue. Better with numbers I am; you should know that.'

She snatched the book back. 'It isn't what Emily Dickinson meant but I think the poem is telling us something about Grace Morobe. *'Two legacies'*, *'You left me boundaries of Pain'*, *'Between eternity and time.'* If her parents are dead and she's been rejected by the rest of her family, then she's a nobody. Isn't that dreadful?'

She sat down on the bed, overcome by the thought of such misery and annoyed with Wil for not understanding. The truth was plain as could be, it was in the poem and in the painting. The man reaches out for the woman but she is lost to him. When she dies he buries her in his own grave. Nobody would know she was there. Thank goodness for Precious and her determination not to forget Josephine.

Wil stared at the painting, at the faint childish figure in the background, set apart from the other two, forgotten. Monsieur Cochet had suggested more or less the same thing. Grace Morobe was nothing, just an embarrassing blot in someone else's history.

'Did you know there's a third person in the picture? You have to search for her, I think that's deliberate, she's supposed to be a secret.'

Margaret left the bed and peered intently at the canvas; she was breathing rapidly, her body tense with concentration. Daylight was spilling through the shutters and he heard the back door to the kitchen open, the clatter of pans. She barely noticed him leaving the room.

Precious was outside in the yard, scrubbing a dirty pot with cold water from a bucket. She'd put on some weight in the time since she'd been with them and she'd lost the haunted look, but the moment she heard Margaret's question she dropped the pot and tried to run away. Margaret caught her by the arm and repeated the question.

'Did your Aunt Josephine have a child?'

Precious was straining to pull away but Margaret hung on.

'I'm not going to tell anyone, I promise. I just need to know the truth.' She felt the arm slacken. Precious's voice was a whisper.

'It was a secret, *Nkosazana*. Only *Nkosi* Bancroft know about the baby. He sent Josephine up here to stay in Thorneybrook. My grandmother look after her until she have the baby, but afterwards she got sick, so sick. He was here to visit her many times, my mother see him crying for her. But she died when he was back in Durban.'

'What happened to the baby? Did she die too?'

Precious was twisting the hem of her apron, casting terrified glances towards the gate leading out of the yard.

'No, *Nkosazana*, she is still alive. Please, I must go before…'

A sudden noise behind them. Margaret turned to see Flynn striding towards them from the kitchen. His face suffused with anger.

'What the hell is going on, Margaret? I gave this girl her marching orders a long time ago in Durban. What is she doing up here? Did you invite her?'

Margaret bristled. How dare he intimidate her, throw his weight around like this. In her house. 'I don't think this is any of your business. Precious is my employee now. I'd thank you to leave her alone.'

He lifted his arm and for a mad moment she thought he was going to strike her. She held her ground and he drew back, wiped a hand across his mouth.

'You are meddling in things you know nothing about, you have no idea of the damage you could do to yourself and your mother! I tell you, Margaret, that girl is bad news, get rid of her. If you don't, then I will.'

Precious seemed frozen to the spot, rigid with fear. Margaret saw Flynn clench his fist and move towards the girl.

'Is everything in order, Miss Margaret? We heard shouting. It woke Mrs Lewis too.'

Nansi was still wearing her nightclothes underneath her winter coat. Her curly hair was loose about her shoulders. She ignored Flynn and held Margaret's gaze. 'I'll make Mr Flynn's breakfast, shall I? Since he has to leave so early.'

Flynn unclenched his fist and backed towards the door, looking flustered. 'Your maid is mistaken, Margaret. I've a business meeting with Hughes this morning; there are some bills I want to go through with him.'

Margaret returned Nansi's gaze, nodded. 'Thank you Nansi, breakfast as soon as you can, please.' She turned to Flynn. 'The bills can wait for another time. Precious, would you find Moses and ask him to saddle Mr Flynn's horse. He will be leaving in ten minutes.'

Precious was out of the yard almost before she finished the sentence.

Percy sneered. 'As you wish. I've made some notes based on Brian Matthews's recommendations – I'll leave them on the hall table. Make sure Hughes reads them, won't you.'

Nansi was inside the kitchen, bashing pans about; he wasn't going to get much of a breakfast. Margaret smiled at the thought of this added irritation. Suddenly his hand was cupping her chin, the pale eyes inches from her own.

'Good to see you've found something to smile about, my dear girl, considering the circumstances. You're looking very tired; the farm's proving too much for you, I fear. I don't like to see you worn down like this.'

She wrenched her chin away and his hand dropped to her shoulder. She attempted to shrug it off but he pressed harder, into the bone. Up close his skin was blotched and raw, patched with years of sunburn. She could smell his stale morning breath.

'I wish you would trust me, Margaret, let me take the burden from you. You know I only want what is best for you. When your father was very ill, in fact just a day or two before he died as I recall, I made him a promise I would take care of you, keep your affairs in order. My only wish is to save you the worry of all this...'

Her shoulder was hurting. 'You misunderstand, Percy, I don't need taking care of. I'm not a child and my "affairs" as you call them are in good order.' The thought suddenly came to her. 'Unless there's something else you know that you're not telling me. Something about the history of Thorneybrook?'

Flynn lifted his hand from her shoulder and his eyes darted anxiously towards the yard gate through which Precious had fled. She took a deep breath.

'Who is Grace Morobe?'

He recoiled as if she'd struck him.

'How do you know about her?'

'I'm not going to tell you until you explain who she is and why she's trying to get in touch with me.'

'What do you mean, get in touch with you?'

'Notes she's sent me, pictures, other things...' She must be careful not to say too much. She'd called his bluff, she was certain, though she had no idea where this was going. His answer, when it came, was not what she expected.

'Grace Morobe is dead, Margaret. Whoever has been trying to contact you is playing a dangerous game and means to harm you in some way. You need my help, even if you don't want it. I'm the only one who knows how to deal with this.'

Nansi was at the door again. 'Your breakfast is ready, Mr

Flynn. In the dining room.' She waited until he moved, and Margaret felt her quiet protection.

Minutes later, standing in the hallway by the front door, she watched Flynn emerge from the dining room. Mother had appeared from her room; she looked rather bewildered by his unexpected early departure. He pulled on his coat and hat and bade them a hasty goodbye. As he started down the steps he paused.

'I forgot to give you Mary's greetings, Margaret. She's going down to Durban shortly and will be staying at Mount Pleasant for a week or so. She was hoping you might both join her for a few days, the coast's lovely at this time of year. I'm sure Mrs Lewis would enjoy a change of scenery.'

Mother's smiling answer, how kind, they would love to pay a visit, that is if she could persuade Margaret to leave the farm for more than one day. Another handshake, doffing of the hat and he was gone, thank God. They heard him whipping his horse into a gallop down the driveway.

Where was Flynn going now? Not to Aviemore, since Mary was away. Not to Maritzburg either. He had something else to do. Margaret's heart was beating fast. She'd been so intent on finding out the truth from him and protecting Precious she hadn't thought about the consequences for Grace. They must warn her. She must find Wil immediately; he would know what to do.

CHAPTER 27

They rested the horses near a mountain river where the water slid thinly around boulders and clumps of reed. On the horizon above the escarpment black clouds were massing and the strong breeze which had accompanied them up the valley had now dropped. It was very still. Margaret counted seven vultures circling lazily high above a tangle of thorn bush.

She cupped her palms in the stream, took a thirsty gulp of water and splashed the rest over her cheeks. Something practical to keep the anxiety at bay. Wil was crouched over the map Monsieur Cochet had drawn for them.

'We have to follow the river for about half a mile to where it joins another stream. There's a track from there up to the *kraal*.'

There was no point dwelling on it, she thought. It wasn't their fault they'd arrived too late. Wil said he couldn't leave the cow to struggle on, her calf half in, half out of her, flailing to be born. It had taken all his strength and Moses's to haul on the rope trussing its skinny legs and pull it out into the daylight, and then there was all the mess to clear up, the usual farm chores; it was mid-afternoon by then, too late to travel to St Martin. By the time they got there the following morning Grace had gone.

At least she had the facts clear in her mind now. They all made sense. Grace was the child of Josephine and Ernest Bancroft; after Josephine died he had entrusted his daughter to the Cochets because he knew they would keep their promise to look after her; they were good, godly people. And he paid them well for the little girl's keep, Madeleine Cochet had been surprisingly open about that. Margaret liked the missionary's shrewd, no nonsense attitude, her neat black-clad composure. It was she who had spotted Flynn riding along the track towards the mission two days earlier; it gave them just enough time to find Grace and send her running for cover into these mountains.

'I still don't understand why Flynn told Margaret that Grace was dead?'

Wil had that exasperated look on his face she knew of old; like her, he hated any kind of muddle. Monsieur Cochet was understanding.

'A good question, Mr Hughes. Mr Flynn wants you to believe that Grace died as a child. He has guessed this is not true despite our best efforts to hide her. Her father made us promise never to tell anyone she was living with us at the mission. He placed certain papers in our keeping, for Grace to have when she turned eighteen. You see, Mr Hughes, he was convinced South Africa would be a different place by then, that she would have the same legal rights as a white person to claim her inheritance. Sadly, South Africa has not become the country Grace's father hoped for; there is still no equality between the races. About three years ago, Mr Flynn turned up at St Martin. He said he was Mr Bancroft's lawyer and that he knew Grace was with us, that there were important documents in her possession which he could advise her about. We, that is, my sister, didn't trust him.' He looked warily at Miss Cochet sitting in the chair opposite him. 'Tell them, Madeleine.'

'There was a woman with him, I had seen her once before, at the library in Pieterskloof; she has a damaged eye, wears a cover… how do you say it? *Bien*, a patch. He was the one asking the questions, but she was always watching me, my brother, the pupils. I remember she had a bag of sweets in her pocket; she came with me to the schoolroom and handed them out to the children, even when I told her they only have sweets on feast days. She tried to question them – who was their teacher, who else lived at the mission.'

'I still don't understand why you pretended Grace was dead.'

'Mr Hughes, we made a solemn promise to her father we would keep Grace safe. We told Mr Flynn she had died of yellow fever when she was four years old, the year after she came to us. Indeed, some of our children had died of the disease that year. He and the woman wanted to see where she was buried so I showed them; fortunately, there are no names on any of the gravestones.'

Spoken without the shadow of a blush, Margaret thought, admiringly.

'Did they believe you?' Wil's questions were persistent.

'The woman did, yes. I heard her say to him, "Let's go, there's nothing more we can ask; there's no other evidence." They never returned. But this time, when I saw him riding down the track towards the mission.' Miss Cochet paused, shook her head. 'I was afraid. I fear he will not give up looking for her now he knows you have met her.'

'Does Grace know about the papers her father left? When I met her here she told me she was twenty so she's been of age for a while.'

A pause. An uneasy glance between the siblings. Monsieur Cochet cleared his throat.

'That is correct. We intended to give the documents to Grace at the appropriate time, but the visit of Mr Flynn and the woman troubled us. My sister and I decided it was wiser to keep them locked away for the time being. Grace was happy here, we did not want to unsettle her. After a while, when there were no further visits, we judged it safe to hand over the documents. However, my sister discovered…'

'The box containing the papers was missing from the bureau.' Miss Cochet interrupted him. 'I always keep it locked.

We think Grace stole the key and removed the box. She has never spoken to us about this and we decided it was better not to question her. She is a strange young woman, unpredictable. You have seen this for yourself I think, Mr Hughes; she can go a whole week without talking; sometimes she disappears for days on end.'

'But she always returns for the children's sake, if not for ours.' Monsieur Cochet seemed anxious to defend Grace. 'There is a place a few miles from here up in the mountains where she sometimes goes when she wants solitude. I will draw you a map where to find her. Miss Lewis, it is time you two met each other.'

They remounted and followed the river. Wil led the way on Monsieur Cochet's sturdy black cob, while Margaret followed on Petra, picking her way carefully over the stony ground between spiny clumps of acacia. The valley tightened around them. They entered a narrow gorge sandwiched between steep rock-strewn slopes and the light darkened, the air became thick, oppressive. A grey bird with a vivid orange neckband – a Cape longclaw – suddenly flew out of the scrub just in front of them, causing Petra to stumble. Margaret quickly regained control, but the incident unsettled her. The stillness of the mountains, their implacable, watchful silence – she longed to turn back to the lower ground, to regain perspective, recover a human scale in this landscape. Wil turned in his saddle and called out to her, pointing towards a long curving ridge on their left; there was a track they could take leading to the summit. Not far now.

The col was clearly visible from the ridge, a shallow saucer of ground nestling in the foothills where once a community had lived. The hut was the only habitation remaining from the former *kraal*: a mud-walled rondavel, the thatched roof in tatters, the door half hanging off its hinges. A gaping hole in the wall where a window might have been. Outside the entrance a stone water jar and beside it a pair of scuffed leather sandals, placed neatly side by side. A long piece of green material hung limply from a pole driven into the rough ground to the right of the hut.

They dismounted and Margaret held the horses' reins while Wil went forward. He halted at the threshold and called out. 'Grace? It's William Hughes, Monsieur Cochet told us where to find you. Margaret is with me.'

They heard a small scraping noise from inside, the sound of a chair being pushed back, then someone appeared in the entrance. Margaret held her breath. The woman was taller than Precious, her bearing more erect. Wil's description was right, her skin was the rich colour of honey. She had braided her hair tightly so that it fitted her scalp like a cap, setting off her face's strong, angular features. The hem of her red dress was torn and a smear of dried blood stained her leg just above the ankle.

'Is he with you?' She was looking at Wil. He shook his head.

'No. Monsieur Cochet is at the mission.'

She gave an impatient hiss. 'Not him! The other one. Did he come with you?'

'No, he has gone away. Before we arrived. The Cochets would not tell him anything, even though he demanded to search the whole place. They're not afraid of him, neither should you be. He's just a bully.'

'But a bully has power, doesn't he?' Grace had turned her attention to Margaret. She recognised those almond-shaped eyes with their curious, appraising expression.

'When he put the necklace around your throat and tied you up with it, I saw what he wanted. He thinks you will marry him, Margaret. Will you?'

It was Grace she had seen outside the sitting room that night. She'd been there again, months later, the night of her birthday. What gave this woman the right to invade her life?

A sudden gust of wind set the long green scarf fluttering atop its pole. Grace's question hung between them, unanswered. And for the first time in their long relationship Wil's face was unreadable. He would not help her.

'What I think about Mr Flynn has nothing to do with you, Grace, or anyone else for that matter. But I have a question for you. Since you refer to the necklace, I'd like to know why you were intruding in my house. Not just once but many times. It was you I saw, wasn't it, outside the window?'

Her head was throbbing. She felt her gaze being dragged upwards, beyond Grace, the hut, the grass circle. The three of them were like actors performing for the gods. These monstrous dragon peaks, they shut out the sky; a stifling, impenetrable barrier squeezing the air from her lungs. She longed for the soothing green hills of Carmarthenshire.

'Why did you create all this mystery, Grace? Leaving me those messages, the paintings, those weird poems? Was it some kind of guessing game; did you expect me to work out the answer on my own?'

Grace uttered a peal of wild laughter. 'But you were not on your own, you had Dr Watson to help you. Like Sherlock Holmes!'

'Margaret is much better at solving clues than I am; she's read all the stories.' Wil's deep, familiar voice was a balm, like cool water, and she loved him for it. 'Go on, Margaret, tell Grace what you know.'

'I found out about Josephine when I was in Durban, staying at Mount Pleasant. Her cousin Precious told me about her relationship with Ernest Bancroft and then I worked out that your father must…'

Grace's smile vanished. 'You are so happy to think you have "worked out" who I am. You white people who like to play the games, you have no idea about people like me. You think you know everything, but you understand nothing.'

She turned her back on them and disappeared into the hut.

Margaret sensed Wil move towards her and shook her head; she didn't want his sympathy. Grace was right, she was too pleased with her own cleverness. Her head felt light, buzzing with noise. The too bright sky, the oppressive mountains, Grace's bitter words. She dropped the reins and let them trail along the ground behind the horses as they moved in search of grass. She needed to get out of this vile circle, find cover in the trees down near the water. She would hide in the summerhouse, lock the door behind her, be safe. She turned and stumbled away from the hut back towards the ridge.

Then Wil was at her side, his loud voice echoing in her ears – 'You look done in, better sit down for a bit' – and she felt the hard earth smack into her side as she hit the ground.

She must have reached the river at last, she could hear its gentle trickling music. She opened her eyes. Grace was bending over her, pouring water from an earthenware jar into a small cracked cup. Cooling drops splashed her face. 'Drink this Margaret, you will be better soon' – and indeed she did feel better; it was the heat after all. Wil was still here, thank goodness. She felt the solidness of him, the weight of his arms supporting her back.

He helped her to her feet and she staggered into the hut, grateful for the dim light and a wobbly old stool to sit on. So foolish of her to faint like that. Grace was kneeling on the far side of the room, beyond a small ring of dead ashes where a fire had once burned. Margaret saw her lift a plank of wood and take something out of a hole in the ground. She came over and dropped it into Margaret's lap. A small wooden box with a glossy painted lid, birds entwined with flowers.

'Here it is. Mr Percival Flynn's Holy Grail.'

CHAPTER 28

'I came to Thorneybrook many times. Nobody was living in the house, it was long before you and your mother came. I used to walk in the empty rooms and think about my parents, what my life would be like if they were still alive. I was never afraid because I was born there. It is my house. Sometimes I slept over when it was too dark to go back to the mission. I always liked the small room off the hallway – the one nearest the trees. You can hear the birds in the early morning. That is why I decided it would be your room.'

They were sitting on the grass outside the hut. It was easier to read the small print, the carefully constructed legal language, in daylight than to peer at it in the gloom. The empty painted box lay on the ground beside Margaret, Ernest Bancroft's will spread in front of her. Grace squatted a few feet away from them, with her back towards the mountains. She had snapped off two pieces of *rooigras* and her long busy fingers plaited them together as she talked.

'One day two people came to Thorneybrook, Percival Flynn and a woman. I could hear them outside, laughing. Then they came into the house and went to the big room. They were in there for a long time. Later, he started to show her the other rooms so I hid in one of the sheds until I heard their horses going away. They had no right to be in my house.'

Margaret refolded the stiff parchment along its creases. The letter Bancroft had written to Grace was already back inside its blue envelope. Wil was deep in thought. This news might change Margaret's life. His and Nansi's too. As for Grace's account, well he always suspected there was something going on between Flynn and Mary Jamieson. He remembered her touch on his arm that evening on the verandah after Margaret's birthday. Flynn was bad news, but he wouldn't trust that woman either.

'You should take these documents to a lawyer, Grace, before Flynn gets hold of them.'

'Mr Harding, my father's lawyer, knows he altered his will, it says so in this letter. My father gave Harding a copy of the codicil. Margaret, you must do it, it's better you speak to him, he will not believe me.' The grass plait finished, she took Margaret's hand, and deftly tied the fragile bracelet around her wrist.

'There, we are sisters now. Family.'

Margaret regarded the strong intelligent face, the brown eyes with their curious green flecks, the intricately braided hair. '*I bequeath my estate Thorneybrook, in the province of Natal, to my daughter Zenzile Grace Morobe and to the oldest child of Colonel Arthur Lewis of Bryntowy, Carmarthenshire.*' Would David have been happy to share his inheritance with a stranger, someone who was illegitimate, of mixed race, and a woman? What would Father have done?

She already knew the answer. She'd seen him read Flynn's note that afternoon in the drawing room. They knew about Grace all along and they'd decided to destroy the codicil. Margaret was never to know of Grace's existence. Her head throbbed with a deeper pain.

'You can't go back to St Martin, Grace. It's too dangerous. Flynn won't believe the Cochets, he's bound to return. You can't keep running away every time he appears.'

Grace stood up, brushing the dust from her long skirts. Margaret put the papers back into the box and closed the lid. Her mind was made up.

'You must stay with us at Thorneybrook while we try to sort things out. Your cousin Precious will be pleased and I know

Nansi will understand when Wil explains everything; she dislikes Flynn almost as much as I do.'

Grace looked down at her. The sun at her back cast her long shadow across the wide circle of grass.

'And what about your mother? What will she do when you tell her who I am?'

'She will listen to me.' There was something else she wanted to say, if she could find the right words, but Grace was already on her way back to the hut and the moment had gone.

Chapter 29

What she had wanted to say – coaxing Petra down the steep track behind the others on Monsieur Cochet's horse, Grace clutching her precious box – was impossible to put into words. To possess such a letter from your father, something so precious you could turn to whenever you felt low or alone. Ernest Bancroft had called Grace his *beloved daughter,* knowing he would never see her again. Only once had Father called her his 'dearest girl', just before he died. David was the one he truly loved. She could imagine Mr Jamieson saying those words, hugging his daughter close in the sunlit stableyard. She couldn't forgive Mary's semblance of friendship while all the time she was plotting with Flynn. She should have known better than to trust her.

The Cochets understood their decision to move Grace without needing to be told the detail. Until a lawyer had certified the documents and confirmed that Grace and Margaret were the legal owners of Thorneybrook, it was safer they should not know the whole truth. Only Wil saw them exchange a look of relief: it was time for someone else to take charge of Grace. She would be missed of course, the children would be sad and Sipho would have to have his French lessons with Mlle Cochet instead. Grace would always have a home at the mission if her circumstances changed.

In the late afternoon Wil rode back to Thorneybrook. He would return with the trap the following morning to bring the two women back to the farm and to remove from St Martin all trace of Grace's existence. The Cochets should not be compromised if Flynn turned up again in search of her. He would tell Mrs Lewis that Margaret had decided to spend the night at the mission to give Sipho some extra English lessons. She wouldn't doubt Wil's word.

'*Pa amser yw hyn*? What time do you call this?'

Nansi was waiting for him at the end of the long drive, a lonely figure in the dusk beneath the spectral trees.

'I thought you were only going for the morning, not the whole day! I've had to do the milking as well as darning and sorting out Mrs Lewis's laundry, then she sent me off to look for you. *Uffern*, Wil, you could have told me Margaret wasn't coming back with you.'

'*Mae'n flin 'da fi*, Nans. Sorry, it was a last-minute decision.'

She tossed her head and turned her back on him, all in a huff.

'*Aros funud*, wait, let me explain.' Nansi was scurrying up the drive, loudly berating him. He put Petra into a trot alongside her.

'Please stop, Nans. Give me a chance.'

She slowed a little, to catch her breath. 'Sick of waiting I am. These days you spend all your time with her, don't think I haven't noticed. I thought we had an understanding. You were coming out here to join me, see what the country was like, make a decision if we was going to settle down, buy our own place. Damned if I know what's going on in your head any more William Hughes – you going to marry her? Well if you are you'd better get in before Percival Flynn jumps. He's as good as asked her already!'

She was nearly at the laurel gate when he flung himself off Petra and grabbed her arm.

'*Paid â bod mor ffôl*, don't be so stupid. Why don't you just ask me what I've been doing instead of accusing me like this? I've not changed. I still want us to make a life out here together; neither of us wants to go back home to nothing, do we? You've got to trust me. Margaret does; she trusts you too. She said I had to tell you what's going on, that you'd understand.'

He put a hand up to her cheek, tucked an angry curl behind her ear and pulled her close. '*Dere nawr, cariad*; you've got it all wrong.'

He felt her shoulders relax into him, the slowing thud of her heart. A sleepy crow called from the branches above them, scutterings and rustlings amongst the fallen leaves. He closed his eyes and for a brief moment allowed himself the dream of Hendre, what might have been had they stayed put in the Towy valley. Then he opened his eyes and looked about him, inhaled the warm African soil. He and Nansi had more than Wales in common now; grander visions altogether.

Two weeks later

Chapter 30

'You haven't changed anything in here; why not?'
'Because I didn't need to, this is exactly how I would have arranged the room myself, you just saved me the trouble. Apart from Not Semolina, that is; I don't understand why you had to change her – paint her face and dress her in those clothes.'

Grace was sitting on the floor in front of the bookshelf, selecting books at random, deciding whether they interested her enough to read. It took so long for her to answer Margaret wondered whether she had heard her question.

'I wanted her to feel comfortable in her new country. That old doll was so dull in her horrible coat and thick stockings, she looked hot and cross. Like you do sometimes. I used to watch you walking around the farm in those heavy English clothes with your face all red and your hair sticking out. Africa doesn't suit you.'

'You've never explained why you spent so much time spying on me. Why didn't you just introduce yourself?'

'You mean you would have asked me in for a cup of tea?' Grace raised her eyebrows cynically. 'I don't think so. English ladies like to keep their distance with servants. I wanted to know what kind of person you were first before I revealed my identity.'

'Is that why you put the painting in my room? For me to work out they were your father and mother? It was Wil, not me, who realised the figure in the background was you.'

'You are both such very clever sleuths! I watched you through the window that night after I hung the picture in your wall; you stared at it for a long time and then you took it down and threw it under the bed. That was so funny, I did not expect you to do that.'

'I thought it would give me bad dreams. I like it better now. And what is so important about Emily Dickinson? Why did you send me her poems?'

'Madeleine Cochet gave me the book last year, after I had been ill for many months. She's a clever woman; she understands me better than her brother. William said you liked reading so I decided to send you the poems. Emily is like the two of us, she doesn't belong anywhere, she is trying to find who she really is.'

'The poem on the last page, was it about you and your parents? I noticed you had written your name underneath it.'

Grace shrugged her shoulders. 'I could choose any of the poems – they all say the same thing. You are on your own, nobody cares. I don't belong anywhere.'

'But you do. This is your house, as you say. You were born here. You have your father's letter and the will to prove it.'

Grace ignored her. She returned her attention to *The Story of an African Farm* which she'd been reading for some time.

'My God, that Mary Jamieson underlines everything! She must be a suffragette. Madeleine told me about them; they say women have no power, men have everything. But this character Lyndall, she's a white South African woman, she is free to run away, to make mistakes, fall in love. My mother tried to live like that and look what happened to her.'

'Your father loved her, though. He encouraged her to draw and paint, he took great risks to be with her. Some people might say he was brave.'

'Pah! He hid her away, sent her up here to give birth to me, then gave me away to the missionaries. Worse, he actually paid them to keep me. There's nothing brave about that. He was a coward and a hypocrite, wanting to hold on to his secret African mistress just like all the other white men.'

'I don't think that's fair, Grace. He did acknowledge you as his daughter and leave you an inheritance. You only have to read what he wrote to know that.'

Margaret went over to the chest of drawers and took out the little wooden box. The letter was inside. She could almost recite them by heart, having read them so often in the long nights.

You were our hearts' desire, your mother's and mine. We named you Grace because that is what you are for both of us - a gift and a promise. Your mother gave you your other name, Zenzile, which means 'she will do it for herself'. She gave you her courage and, I hope, her artistic talents. My prayer is that you will grow up in a free South Africa which nourishes all its peoples, where you will thrive as a woman and our beloved daughter always...

'Those aren't the words of a hypocrite, Grace. I think you owe it to both your parents to take your inheritance and do something with it.'

'You mean run this place with you?' Grace hugged her knees, rocking with laughter. 'I don't know the first thing about farming! I couldn't even grow mealies in the mission garden; they always died!'

'Well, we have Wil. He's the expert. Moses and the others, they're good workers, they know what to do. And look at me, I didn't know how to do anything when I first came here. Where I grew up, all they taught me to do was embroider tablecloths and organise tea parties. I wish I had half your talent.'

There was a gentle knock on the door and Nansi poked her head inside the room. 'Your mother's in the house, miss,

I thought you would have heard her arrive. She's in the sitting room with Miss Jamieson, I've given them tea.' She frowned at Grace. 'You need to make yourself scarce before they catch sight of you.'

Grace sighed and pushed herself up from the floor. 'Banished to my lowly hut. I'm making a drawing of Precious. She's very patient, sits still for hours if I ask her.' She paused at the door. 'When shall we tell your mother about me? I'll go mad if I have to stay cooped up much longer.'

'It won't be long now, I promise.'

First, she would need to get rid of Mary.

Chapter 31

It was quite a touching scene. The two of them on the sofa, Mary's neat head nestled into Mother's shoulder, the hat and gloves carelessly strewn across the Turkey rug, the tea cooling in the china cups. Through the open window the chirruping of doves, the sweet fragrance of the Philadelphus billowing from the cream jug on the table. Mother frowned at her over the top of Mary's head and put a finger to her lips. Margaret backed away.

'I'm sorry, I didn't mean to disturb you. Nansi said you were both in here.' Her chest felt tight, she was unaccountably on the edge of tears. Mary stirred and lifted her head from Mother's shoulder. She leaned back against the plump sofa cushions and wiped her cheeks. The black eyepatch had slipped off and dangled comically from its elastic below her right ear. For a moment she looked very young, a child almost. She yanked at the patch and refastened it across her eye with trembling fingers. Her face was very pale.

'Don't go, Margaret, I'm feeling better. I don't know what came over me just now, it was the shock I suppose, telling someone. You've been very understanding, Mrs Lewis.' She gave a wan smile. 'I don't normally blub like this.'

'What's happened?'

'Mary's had some news from her father. It's rather thrown her as you can see. Drink your tea, dear, it will make you feel better. Hand her the cup and saucer would you, Margaret.'

Tea – the solution to every problem. What was Mary's real reason for coming here? She wasn't especially close to Mother, something was up. She watched Mary dutifully swallow the tea and settle herself once more amongst the cushions with a little sigh. She regarded Margaret with a mournful expression.

'Pa's getting married again. Someone he's only recently met in Scotland. They were introduced on the golf links at St Andrews, apparently they hit it off straight away, if that isn't too awful a pun.' She sniffed loudly, constructed a brittle smile. 'It's not as if it's the end of the world; I'm nearly twenty-four, not a child.'

'When will they be coming home?'

'That's the thing, Miss Fraser doesn't want to move out here. Pa's so besotted with this woman he's decided to sell Aviemore and clear most of his interests in South Africa. I'm provided for of course, he set up a trust fund for me after Mummy died. He can't touch that.' She shrugged her shoulders, feigning nonchalance. 'Hey ho, I'll just have to get used to being abandoned.'

Margaret couldn't think of anything to say; she stared blankly at the tea tray with its silver pot and jug, the little beaded cover on the sugar bowl to keep out the flies. Mother was gazing wistfully at the window; there were probably more important things on her mind – dead-heading the roses, hoeing the onion patch. Margaret pictured Mr Jamieson, still young looking and full of practical energy. He deserved some happiness after all those years without a wife.

'How long will you be staying at Aviemore?'

Mary's face quickly brightened.

'Ah yes, you've reminded me why I called by. It wasn't really to tell you about Pa, that just came out because dear Mrs Lewis was kind enough to listen to my woes. I'm driving down to Durban on Friday, thought you might like to come with me and stay at Mount Pleasant. I'd welcome your company. It would stop me brooding about Pa and his dreadful girlfriend. He's not renewing the lease on the house, of course, so this may be one of the last times I'll be staying there. Mrs Lewis, would you be happy to part with Margaret for a few days?'

She sensed another trick; this was not the original invitation Percy Flynn issued that morning he left Thorneybrook. He and Mary wanted her to come alone. She tried to catch her mother's eye.

'I doubt whether I can be spared, don't you need me at home?'

'Nonsense, Margaret. I'm sure a change of scenery and some sea air will do you a world of good, so kind of you to suggest it, Mary.'

Her duty done, Mother said her goodbyes and escaped to the garden. Mary jumped up from the sofa and recovered her discarded hat and gloves.

'Excellent! That's settled then, I'll pick you up early on Friday. Percy will be so thrilled when I tell him you're coming with me. He said you looked a little peaky when he was here last time, a bit irritable, not your usual sunny self. Is William Hughes pulling his weight? You can't always trust the Welsh, Percy says. Nation of slackers.' She came up close, making a pretence of putting on her gloves, and adjusted her tone to a confidential whisper. 'My old friend has a really soft spot for you, Margaret, in fact, I think you've stolen his heart. If Percy weren't like a brother to me, I might well be jealous!'

She leaned forward and, to Margaret's horror, planted a swift kiss on her cheek. 'There, you have my blessing.' She put on her hat and pulled the wide brim over the eyepatch. 'See you on Friday!'

Margaret stood at the doorway and watched the car disappear from sight along the laurel drive. Her cheek stung from the poisonous kiss. What darker plan were they hatching?

'Thank goodness! I thought she'd never go.'

Mother appeared around the side of the house pushing a wheelbarrow full of weeds and flower heads. 'There's something not quite right about that young woman. I can't put my finger on it, but I really don't trust her.'

She rested the wheelbarrow beside the statue of Flora and looked up at Margaret. 'I rather hoped you would be more insistent in refusing her offer to stay in Durban, but I know I can't decide these things for you. She's a sly one, Mary Jamieson, cleverer than she looks; don't be taken in by those crocodile tears. I think it's a jolly good thing her father is marrying again – it's not much fun being on your own when you get old. And since we're talking about trust, when were you planning to tell me about the other young woman you're hiding?'

CHAPTER 32

Wil leaned forward and turned up the paraffin lamp, a quiet movement only Margaret noticed, the others being too absorbed to notice the dusk stealing through the windows. Warm light spilled across the dining table, picking out the painted birds on Grace's box, the auburn glints in Nansi's hair; it fingered the anxious lines on her mother's face as she addressed Grace.

'I'm asking you to see it from my husband's point of view. And mine too of course. I admit he did tell me about the codicil. The whole thing seemed preposterous to us you see, the whim of a dying man. Percival Flynn told us it would never hold water in court – he was very careful to explain that in this country natives and Coloured people have no legal rights to white owned land. In any case, he said, you were probably dead so that settled the matter for us.'

Grace regarded her solemnly from the opposite side of the table then her gaze shifted back to the small sketch pad in front of her. They all knew what she was doing – making a portrait of Mother – but nobody said anything. After all Grace was the reason for this gathering; she was a powerful presence in the room. Her charcoal pencil covered the paper in swift decisive strokes. Margaret shifted in her chair. This was unfair. Her mother wasn't on trial, this wasn't a court room where they hired an artist to make sketches of the accused for the morning papers. Her parents had behaved badly, there was no question about that, but their readiness to accept Flynn's story was understandable. He alone was at fault. He had hoodwinked them and robbed Grace of her legacy.

She studied her mother's face. Ill health had hollowed it a

little but the fine bone structure, the strong clear eyes, gave her a steely beauty Margaret hadn't noticed before. She had surprised them all. She had listened carefully to Margaret's account and afterwards received Grace with astonishing warmth, with no trace of rancour that this stranger was challenging what most white people considered their rightful due, their property. She had even praised Precious for her courage in keeping faith with Josephine Morobe. Margaret was ashamed – yet again she had misjudged those closest to her.

Mother turned to Wil, sitting beside her. Her voice was low and subdued. 'Inheriting Thorneybrook was a godsend to us, William. It solved our financial problems. We had no choice but to accept; there was Margaret's future to think of as well as our own, the farm would be her property one day, though of course we didn't know it would happen so soon. I don't expect you to understand our decision. It must have felt as though we didn't care what would happen to your parents or the other tenants, all the people who depended on the estate for their livelihoods. But it wasn't like that, I assure you; leaving Bryntowy was one of the hardest things I've ever done. I loved that place.'

Wil shifted uncomfortably in his chair. Nansi said he should change out of his work shirt into the smart one with the stiff collar, being as how they were all meeting in the dining room. He hadn't set foot in there since Margaret's birthday dinner. Mrs Lewis shouldn't confess all this stuff to him. They'd all survived, including his parents. Water under the bridge it was now. Nansi, sitting beside Grace, reached across and took Mrs Lewis's hand.

'Don't be worrying yourself, it wasn't that bad what you did. I'd never have left Rhydfelin if you hadn't asked me to come with you. I'd be still stuck there living with my mam and the little ones. I'd have been lucky to get a job in the village stores. There's prospects in South Africa for working people like me and Wil, a chance for us to get on. We've started to make plans already…'

She broke off, catching his frown. Nans had said too much, now wasn't the time to bring up that subject, he'd told her they should wait for the right moment. Margaret was quite shocked, he could see it in her face. Thank goodness, at least Mrs Lewis was smiling.

'Well that's one good thing Margaret and I have achieved. I'm so pleased you two are not regretting your decision to come to South Africa. I honestly don't know how we would have managed otherwise. Isn't that right, Margaret?'

She couldn't answer. There was a hard lump at the base of her throat, her body felt winded as though someone had punched her in the stomach. Nansi and Wil, making plans? Why hadn't he told her?

'My husband was very fond of you, Nansi, we both appreciated how you took care of him in those last days. I was so sure South Africa would improve his health and help him get over the war, losing David so young.'

She was brave, Margaret thought, facing everyone around the table, answering for the mistakes of the past. Dealing alone with her loss of son, husband. Emily Dickinson understood that kind of grief.

> They say that 'time assuages,'
>   Time never did assuage;
> An actual suffering strengthens,
>   As sinews do, with age.

When she copied those lines into her diary, she'd been thinking only of herself, her own despair at losing Bryntowy, not about the loss of David or Father. She barely gave any thought to how her mother might be feeling, how she too might be struggling with grief and homesickness and regret.

Mother just got on with things, she never let you see inside. Yet, when Margaret told her Grace was alive, her first words were, 'I always knew that one day there would be a reckoning.'

A screech of charcoal pencil on paper broke the stillness in the room. Mother burst out laughing. 'That portrait of me had better be a kind one, Grace. Good artists should flatter the elderly, not highlight their wrinkles.'

Grace shot back. 'Good artists must be honest, Fay; if they lie we should never call them good.'

Margaret caught the look of alarm on Nansi's face. Nobody, apart from close friends, called Mrs Lewis by her first name; it just wasn't done. Mother didn't bat an eyelid. 'I concede, Grace, you have a point. I don't believe Rembrandt ever hid his age.'

Grace was still sketching. 'If you look at paintings by Kokoschka or Kollwitz the old people are more interesting because they don't hide what they really look like. That's why I like drawing you, Fay.'

Mother leaned forward. 'How do you know about these European artists? They're very avant garde I've heard. I didn't think people...'

'People like me, you mean. I read about them in a book Monsieur Cochet gave me; he's quite enlightened for a missionary. There, it is finished.'

Grace thrust the sketch across the table. Mother put on her reading glasses and studied it. 'Oh dear, you have been very honest, I look like a pickled prune. In future I must try to stay out of the sun.' She put down the sketch and regarded Grace. 'I'm very interested in that startling painting of yours, the one Margaret hid under her bed for a while until she was brave enough to hang it on the wall. Don't look so affronted dear, even I have to visit your room occasionally. Now Grace, the style of that painting is what they call Expressionist, am I right? A long time ago I won a place to study art at the Slade but my father refused to allow me to take it up, said it was a waste of money. I try to read what I can about modern art but I'm very ignorant. I would enjoy hearing your views.'

Grace shrugged her shoulders, pulled a face. 'I don't have "views", I just know what I like. My mother was an artist they say, maybe I am like her. You have some talent, Fay, I like one of your pictures, the boy with the sad face. I hung it in the hallway because the light is better there. But your landscapes are not so good, too sentimental, just cows and pretty hills. I only put them there to fill the space.'

Margaret could see Wil's shoulders shaking; Nansi had a hand over her mouth. Mother drew herself up, looking aggrieved. 'Well I hope one day you will visit Wales and see those hills for yourself, young lady, then you'll understand why I painted them that way.'

Margaret was growing anxious. Those two could settle their artistic differences another time, there were more pressing issues.

'We need to decide what to do about claiming Grace's inheritance.'

'Margaret's right; we can't just sit on this.'

'You don't need to remind me, William, I have given it some thought already. Grace must stay here; she needs to keep out of sight until the business is sorted. Margaret is going to Durban on Friday with Mary Jamieson; she can take the papers with her to the lawyers' office.'

Wil frowned. 'I'm not sure that's a good idea.' He hesitated for a moment, casting an anxious look towards Margaret. 'I'm sorry to tell you this, Mrs Lewis, but we don't think Mary Jamieson can be trusted.'

'Oh, have no fear on my account, William. As I told Margaret the other day, I rumbled Miss Jamieson a long time ago. I think we should all be wary of her. No, Margaret must find a reason to go into town on her own without Mary, she's always been good at inventing stories. The lawyer's office is in Smith Street, I called there with your father once or twice. He seems a decent man, James Harding. He came to the funeral I recall. Though why he's allowed Percival Flynn to handle our affairs is a mystery to me; we've all been taken in by that man.'

'Not all of us.' Nansi's voice was so quiet, only Margaret and Wil heard.

CHAPTER 33

My God, Durban weather could be trying even at this time of year, before the real heat came. In high summer, Mary said, the only way to cope with the heat was to lie in a cold bath. Margaret sloshed more water over her face from the china basin the maid had brought to her room. Lindiwe was new, a more confident personality than Precious, with a broad smile and girth to match. Margaret could hear her in the early mornings cackling loudly at one of Simon's jokes as they swept the leaf fall from the verandah. Durban could be a windy city too. Yesterday the palm trees in the neighbouring garden bent double in the damp gale blowing up the Berea. Today in contrast, a dull grey line separated the horizon from the paler wash of cloud and the leaves of the jacaranda trees along Fraser Lane hung limp and lifeless, sedated in the heavy subtropical air. Even the monkeys were stilled, thank goodness. She'd forgotten how invasive those little thieves were with their shrill chatterings, their bony grasping fingers.

She patted her face with the towel, puzzling how to leave Mount Pleasant unseen and make her way into town. She had the address of the law firm – 2 Kings Buildings, Smith Street – it shouldn't be difficult to find. The papers were in an envelope inside her handbag, covered by a silk scarf Mother had provided. Margaret regretted the decision to keep Grace at Thorneybrook; it would surely strengthen their case if Bancroft's joint heirs presented themselves to Mr Harding in person. But Mother and Wil were adamant: you could never be sure with Grace, she was so blunt she could easily say the wrong thing and offend a staid Durban attorney. Margaret was better off going alone this time.

She wished she had travelled by train, slow though it was, rather than be Mary's hapless passenger on the long journey down to the city. She'd driven her father's Ford at reckless speed along the dirt roads, enveloping them both in gritty dust clouds and showers of small stones. Overtaking a straggle of goats on a blind bend, they narrowly missed an oxcart coming the other way; later she ignored the sign at the Mandla bridge to slow down and the car almost toppled into the river, swollen by the early summer rains. Mary talked incessantly, at such a rate it was hard to follow her train of thought, the subjects changed so quickly. She did seem genuinely distressed by her father's impending marriage: she often used the word 'betrayal' and complained he didn't care about her feelings. On their first evening at Mount Pleasant Margaret heard her on the telephone, pouring out her grief to one of her friends. Perhaps Mother had been unfair. Perhaps they had all misjudged her.

The following morning Mary received a phone call from Bridie McAllister. They needed a fourth at tennis, someone had let her down last minute, would you be a sweetheart and help out? Margaret can always sit on the terrace and watch the match, we know how much she dislikes playing. Seizing the opportunity, Margaret complained of a headache brought on by the heat – 'Best you go on your own, Mary, I'll feel much better after a rest.' From her bedroom window she watched the car turn out of the drive and head east towards Sheldon Avenue.

Half an hour later, the cab driver deposited her in Smith Street outside Kings Buildings, an imposing red-brick edifice overlooking the busy thoroughfare. It was midday; from the grand rotunda of the central Post Office amidst the palm trees she heard the clock chime the hours. Smith Street's hot pavements were clammy with people: Indian hawkers calling from handcarts spilling with ripened bananas, mangos, yams and watermelon; panama-hatted businessmen in white linen suits strolling to lunch at the Durban Club; a group of ladies in smart dresses and white gloves, their dyed hair stiffly lacquered, gossiping their way to tea at one of the new department stores. She dared not step off the pavement on to the road for fear of being run over in the chaos of horse cabs, bicycles and rickshaws.

Clutching her handbag with its precious contents, she pushed open the heavy outer door in the centre of the building. A grand foyer, refreshingly cool after the sweaty mayhem of the street. The polished marble floors and walls suggested order and propriety, a certain kind of Britishness. On the left-hand wall nearest the door a row of brass plaques bore the names of the legal firms who occupied the building. The offices of Harding & Robbins, Lawyers were on the first floor along a corridor at the top of the wide gleaming staircase. She was in luck, said the secretary at the reception desk – a brusque middle-aged woman with carefully dyed hair and prim lipsticked mouth – Mr Harding was unengaged at present, though it was customary for clients to make an appointment first. She was ushered into a stuffy mahogany-panelled office, the blinds drawn against the midday heat. The wooden blades of a huge ceiling fan valiantly struggled to beat back the heavy, muggy air.

Mr Harding, a pleasant-looking man with oiled, greying hair and the amiable look of a well-fed seal, listened carefully as she told him the whole story, his hands neatly folded on top of the large desk. When she produced Bancroft's will and the letter, he raised his eyebrows and his plump cheeks reddened a little. He read the details slowly, without comment. From a drawer in his desk he produced a large magnifying glass and examined the signature at the bottom of the will. Margaret could feel the sweat pooling behind her knees. The lawyer put down his magnifying glass and ran his fingers through his sleek hair.

'Miss Lewis, you say this woman, Grace Morobe, is presently staying with your mother at Thorneybrook farm?' He pronounced each word distinctly in an English manner, with only the slightest trace of a South African accent.

'That's correct. We thought it best for me to see you on my own. I can arrange for Grace to travel down to Durban if you would like to meet her, to satisfy yourself she is… authentic.'

The lawyer folded his pudgy hands in front of him and smiled across the desk. 'That will not be necessary, Miss Lewis. I am well acquainted with the circumstances. Two months before he died Mr Bancroft came to see me. He knew he was seriously ill and needed to rest but he was a very stubborn man, always did things his own way. He had made up his mind to add a codicil to his existing will, he didn't want my advice about the wisdom of making such a change. I gave it to him anyway. I said he could provide for the child in other ways – money, a good education. From what you have told me of Miss Morobe's circumstances it seems he did as I suggested, in that regard at least. As for this codicil, it has no legal standing whatsoever. South African law is clear on this point: as the illegitimate product of his liaison with a native woman, Miss Morobe cannot inherit his property.'

'But he left it to both of us; surely as the joint owner I can insist on sharing the farm with Grace even if the law won't recognise her right to own it with me?'

Harding's whole demeanour altered. He was no longer smiling.

'Miss Lewis, you're being naïve. If you decide to choose that route you will become a laughing stock amongst the farming community and your Durban friends will refuse to have anything to do with you. Not everyone, perhaps, would shun you; there are some people like the missionaries you talk of, who would be sympathetic, but mark my words, the mood is changing. Attitudes towards the other races are hardening.

Since the war ended the Boers are flexing their muscles all over the country. Who knows, if they get their way, one day everyone in South Africa will be living in their own separate areas. You and Grace Morobe will be forced apart whether you like it or not.'

He folded the will carefully, placed the letter on top of it and handed them to her. 'There is one other matter. My hopelessly optimistic friend Ernest Bancroft never bothered to have his new will witnessed. He must have believed his word alone would be sufficient.' He paused and gave her a long look. 'Unless, of course, he always knew in his heart that the will would have no legal standing, in which case this bit of paper is just a worthless token, a means of salving his conscience about the woman and her child.'

He left his desk and waited politely by the door while she gathered up her things. Her hands were shaking as she fumbled with the handbag clasp. Above her head the fan feebly batted the leaden air. The sympathetic expression on Harding's face as she walked to the door – an adult's to a rather petulant child – made her blood boil. She would not let him see her disappointment; there was one other question she must ask.

'Percival Flynn knew about the codicil, Mr Harding. Did you tell him?'

The lawyer looked genuinely puzzled.

'No, of course not. I have to admit I never gave the business a second thought after Ernest Bancroft died; however, as my junior partner, Mr Flynn expressed an interest in taking on your father's legal affairs. In view of his distant connection with your family, it seemed appropriate. Ernest had given me a copy of the codicil, that is true, but I don't remember what I did with it; as I said before, the whole idea was preposterous. I have no idea how Flynn discovered its existence, he never mentioned it to me.'

He held out his hand in farewell. 'It has been good to meet

you at last, Miss Lewis; you have a strong resemblance to your father. I enjoyed my brief encounters with him in the short time he was in Durban; his sudden passing must have been deeply distressing for you and your mother. Do give her my very best wishes when you return up country. I imagine you'll be glad to escape this Durban heat!'

The door gave a decisive click as he shut it behind her. That was the end of the business as far as Mr Harding was concerned. She stood for a moment in the outer office, collecting her thoughts. There must be another way of proving Grace's inheritance; she couldn't just give up like this. The stony-faced secretary was busy at her typewriter; she didn't bother to look up when Margaret left.

She had almost reached the foyer when she heard a door open on the first floor and the clatter of heavy footsteps racing down the stairs behind her. Percival Flynn came to a halt on the step above, panting heavily, his grey striped tie askew.

'Forgive me for giving you a fright, I heard your voice outside Harding's office. What on earth are you doing here, Margaret, I thought you were playing tennis with Mary and her friends this morning?' His expression softened and a little smirk crept across his face. He leaned towards her. 'Were you looking for me, perhaps? I'm very flattered if that's the case. Allow me to take you somewhere nice for lunch.'

What an idiot she'd been, to come here without first checking Percy's whereabouts this morning. This was his place of work, there was every likelihood she would run into him. Her head felt fuggy, the clammy cotton blouse was sticking to her back and he was grinning at her in that smugly repellent way. He might have guessed her reason for coming here, she wouldn't be surprised by that; he was probably waiting to hear the lie come squirming out of her mouth. Well she would take the initiative.

'As it happens, I was looking for you, Percy. Mr Harding's

secretary thought you were out so I asked to see Mr Harding instead. I gather you knew Mr Bancroft had made a codicil to his will. Mr Harding was most interested to read it.' Flynn's expression froze. His eyes narrowed. He looked down at her handbag and put his hand out to take it from her. She jerked the bag away and clutched it to her chest.

'I'm surprised, shocked actually, that you didn't think to tell me you'd found a copy of the codicil when you visited us at Bryntowy. You even advised my father to say nothing about it to me after you'd destroyed it. For your information, Grace Morobe and I have decided to honour the dying wish of her father, Ernest Bancroft. Thorneybrook belongs to both of us now and there is nothing you can do about it.'

Amazed at her own boldness, she left him open-mouthed upon the staircase, and stepped victorious into the choking heat of the city.

CHAPTER 34

Mary was sprawled in the hammock slung between the lilac trees, still wearing her tennis clothes. Ice chinked at the bottom of her tall glass as she waved it in Margaret's direction.

'Ah there you are! We guessed you must have gone out to stretch your legs. You look much better, the walk must have done you good. Wish I'd stayed home – playing tennis in this weather's a bloody nightmare, I nearly dissolved. Come and join me when you've put your things away, I'll call Simon to pour you a drink.'

Margaret went up to her room and buried the documents in her suitcase, locking it afterwards as a precaution – she couldn't be sure what Mary might do when Percy told her what had happened that morning. Vague plans of mounting a legal challenge in the courts had swirled damply inside her head as the cab rattled its way up Berea Road from the city, but by the time she had walked the short distance to the gates of Mount Pleasant they had all evaporated. In reality, the sweetness of her parting shot to Percy amounted to nothing. James Harding had pronounced what deep down she most feared, there was no legitimacy to Grace's claim. They were defeated before they had even begun. And now she would have to endure another week in Mary's restless company, dreading a visit from Percy to compound her misery. Perhaps he would stay away, he must have a pretty thick skin not to realise by now how much she disliked him.

Two gin and sodas later, lolling on the shady rug amongst soft cushions and the scent of hibiscus, she was feeling more generous. She could get used to this idle life, the chatter of servants behind high white walls, the drowsy insect hum, the African sunshine seeping through her body. Behind her the hammock strings creaked as Mary lowered herself to the ground.

'Just popping to the kitchen to give instructions for dinner. I've invited some friends round this evening – don't look so worried Margaret, it's not a formal affair, far too hot for dressing up. Stay here, enjoy your zizz. I'll get Simon to bring you another gin.'

She listened to Mary's footsteps crunch across the gravel path towards the house and closed her eyes.

The kite's wing was softer than she remembered. It shaded her face from the light and she felt the tender, downy filaments brush across her skin. A faint rusty scent of dried blood, earthy must. Wil was right to take it down from that cruel hook in the cowshed door and let her care for it; the bird could rest now, gather its strength, nestled against her warm face. She heard a muffled burst of giggles somewhere behind her. The kite took off suddenly and piercing light filled the space. A man's voice called out.

'Oh well done, Percy. Sleeping Beauty awakes. She'll need a kiss from you now!'

She opened her eyes to find Flynn's face inches from her own, the mottled skin sheened with perspiration, fleshy pink mouth hovering above her forehead. She struggled to a sitting position and pushed him away. Laughter erupted all around her. Percy was now squatting on the grass beside the rug, laughing and waving the feather duster at her. Mary strode over to him and snatched it out of his hand.

'That's enough, Percy. You've gone too far.'

She had changed into a pearly linen sleeveless dress and loosened her hair; the scarlet patch was like a vivid slash across her eye. She turned and looked down at Margaret, unsmiling.

'It was time to wake you – you've been asleep for ages and dinner's almost ready. You'd better go and change.' Margaret felt a little intimidated, the difference in their ages suddenly apparent.

Mary had invited five people to dinner: Bridie McAllister with her husband Jock, a brawny Englishman with a quiff of thick bottle brush hair; a dull faced lanky chap called Henry and his wife Susan, tall, blonde with an aristocratic nose and vacant eyes. And, to Margaret's horror, Percival Flynn, who smiled, told jokes, poured wine, as though their morning encounter had never happened.

They ate out on the verandah in the glow of candles lit by Simon after the swift fall of dusk. The dull headache which followed the gins and the long sleep in the sun beat at Margaret's temples. She was trapped in a maze of brittle, vapid conversation. Wine and then more wine. She had never drunk so much in her life, it stunned her senses. Faces swam in and out of focus, wreathed in cigarette smoke, so many jokes she didn't understand, gossip about people she'd never heard of. Across the table, amidst the laughter, Percy's blue eyes, whenever she caught them resting on her, were like steel.

Jock McAllister lurched from his seat and walked unsteadily to the gramophone which Mary had summoned from the drawing room. He placed a record on the turntable, cranked up the handle. The singer's voice crackled reedily, like someone under water.

'Up you get young lady.' Margaret felt herself being yanked from her chair and pressed tightly to McAllister's chest. He crooned drunkenly into her ear: 'Now I ain't got nobody, and nobody cares for me. That's why I'm sad and lonely, won't someone take a chance with me.' His shirt clung to her skin and she tried to turn her head away from the stench of sweat and stale wine.

'Come on Maggie, don't be shy, move to the music! I bet

you're a wild young thing back in the old country!' Without warning he gripped her waist and clumsily jerked her body backwards over his left leg so that her head was lolling inches from the ground. Gales of laughter from the table; Bridie calling, 'Jock, let the poor girl alone, dance with your wife instead!' He swung her upright again and she managed to free herself from his grasp. She made her way queasily back to her chair and sat down. Her head was swimming.

In a corner of the verandah Mary and Percy were dancing slowly together, his head bent over hers, Mary leaning into him. Like that time at Thorneybrook, the evening of her birthday. He whispered something to her and Mary looked round; she waved a braceleted arm, scarlet beads complementing her eyepatch.

'Margaret dear, Percy wants to dance with you but he's too shy to ask you after the duster joke. He thinks he's offended you.' She turned back to him and gave him a playful shove. 'Go on Percy, I'm sure she'll forgive you.'

Margaret shook her head; she could barely stand, let alone dance. She reached across the table for the water jug and with shaking hands tried to fill her glass.

'Allow me.' Percy hurried over, snatched the jug from her and filled her glass. He placed it gently in her hand and she drank, grateful for the coolness of the water. She was aware of him taking the empty seat next to her. 'It's fine, we needn't dance; have some more water, you'll start feeling better soon.' He refilled her glass from the jug and reached across the table for the wine decanter. She felt his other hand brush against her knee. She took another sip of water. The hand moved up to her thigh and rested there. She dared not move away. Jock and Bridie were approaching the table arm in arm and the tedious conversation resumed.

The guests left around midnight, Mary walking with them to the end of the drive for final goodbyes. Little lamps hung like glow-worms from the trees along the path. Margaret's limbs felt leaden. She allowed Percy to take her arm at his suggestion – 'Let's walk a little, you've been sitting too long' – and he steered her away from the lighted path towards the trees at the bottom of the garden.

'You were very quiet this evening, cat caught your tongue? Odd that, you had plenty to say this morning.'

She did not reply. Dark shrubs jostled and crowded around them as they entered the dense thicket bordering the perimeter fence, his hand a heavy weight at the back of her neck, pressing her downwards. Her heart was a trapped bird, beating at the bone cage. Night creatures scattered, terrified, from out of the dry leaves as she fell; the backs of her legs scraped the hard stubbly bark of some tree, her arm chafed from his clutching, she heard the bodice of her dress rip open. Then the dry heat of his mouth clamped her own. Nobody would hear her cry.

Somehow, she found a will to resist. She wrenched her mouth away from his and kicked out, straining against the weight of him pinning her to the ground. He groaned and she felt his body shift away, just enough for her to roll out from under him. She pushed herself up onto her knees. He loomed over her out of the darkness and she felt a sudden, smarting pain as he struck her, hard, across the side of her face. But then, thank God, he was gone and she was on her feet and stumbling away, back up the garden. Disorientated, blinded by the darkness, the blood already stiffening against her skin and her right cheek stinging with pain, she careened into someone on the path. She recoiled, turned to run.

'Miss Margaret? Let me help you find your way.' Simon's warm, solid presence; she could have kissed his hand. She followed him around the side of the house, through the kitchen and into the empty hall where he left her. A small oil lamp on the table at the foot of the stairs cast a flickering light on the portrait of Ernest Bancroft. His face looked melancholy, defeated.

She picked up the lamp and forced her wounded body up the stairs, clinging to the banister rail for support until she reached the landing. Mary was standing outside her bedroom door wearing a plaid dressing gown over her nightdress. Her damaged face was ghostlike in the lamplight. Instinctively, Margaret's left hand fluttered to the front of her own dress and gathered the thin material, feeling it pucker against her skin, the holes where two of the buttons had torn off. Wordless, Mary turned away and went back into her room.

No sleep. A long waiting for the dawn, the early birdsong and the monkey taunts. Her whole body ached, she'd become an old woman overnight. The side of her face was still smarting from Flynn's blow. After she had roused herself enough to wash and put on clean clothes, she found a note pushed under her door. *I can't bear this any more, we need to talk. Come to the study. M*

She was standing in front of the bookshelves, still dressed in her nightclothes. No eyepatch, the reddened blankness like a birthmark on the ghostly skin. She too had not slept. Margaret took the chair nearest the window and rested her elbows on the faded velvet arms, trying not to be sick.

'You said we needed to talk.' It was an effort to speak.

Mary stirred slightly; she looked distracted as if her thoughts were far away. Her hand moved towards the empty eye socket, fingers itching to stroke, then dropped back again to her side.

'You don't have to say anything if you don't want to. This is all my fault not yours. Forgive me if you can, it was so terribly wrong of me to leave you alone with him; it was meant to be a lovely evening.'

Margaret opened her mouth to say what had to be said. Yes it was a dreadful, unforgiveable thing, you had no right to play games with me, you have no idea who I am, what I feel about anything. But words carried no weight, they were mere bubbles of sound. The bruises on her arms and legs, her face, were bone deep, beyond expression. Mary was shaking her head'.

'What happened last night goes back a long time. Two years ago Percy told me he had found a document at the law office which named you, not your father, as Ernest Bancroft's heir. He was absolutely obsessed with this discovery, couldn't stop talking about it. He knew I'd be interested because of my connection with this house which had once belonged to Bancroft. He was determined to bring you this information himself. I thought he was mad, a letter would have sufficed, but he loved the drama of it, being the one to break the news. Percy adores power.' Mary's face flushed. 'I'm sorry, I don't need to tell you that.'

It was easier to keep looking at the floor, to concentrate on the mazy patterns in the Turkey rug.

'It became a kind of game from then on, you see. He and I used to joke that he would make you fall in love with him; we thought you'd be a naïve little country girl. Percy would charm his way into your family and then you'd marry him. He has very little money of his own, despite the impression he gives; Thorneybrook land is valuable, there's money to be made out of it if you know the right people. And Percy does.'

The vine tendrils were strangling the flowers, twisting them back on themselves in a vicious repeating pattern. They forced the fragile petals towards the centre, the single heartless O. With difficulty, Margaret tore her gaze away from the rug. 'What made you go along with his plans? Why didn't you stop him?'

Mary gave a deep sigh. 'Because I was bored, I expect. Perhaps you're surprised by that. You have no idea how excruciating it can be to play golf and bridge with the same old people day in day out, listening to their dull nonsense. Percy and I are kindred spirits, we're restless, impatient people.'

'Then why didn't you marry each other?' Percy would never be short of money then.

Mary gave a small, twisted smile. 'I'm not exactly marriage material am I? Not with this face. Besides you should never marry your best friend; we'd end up hating each other or worse. You were a far more interesting proposition.'

'I don't understand.' Margaret was thinking of herself and Wil, how impossible that they should ever grow to hate each other.

'You aren't the person we fabricated; you won't let yourself be moulded. Percy was more attracted to you than he realised, I could see that from his expression whenever you came into a room. But you weren't interested, you saw through him, he could foresee his careful plans slipping away. I think that's why he decided to… to behave as he did, last night. I'm so dreadfully sorry, I had no idea this would happen. I'm sure he didn't mean to hurt you.'

Margaret was silent. This was too much to bear; even now, she was trying to defend him. Mary's voice was barely a whisper.

'There's something else I should have told you. I found some documents in the back of a locked drawer in the bureau. Mount Pleasant is full of secrets; I was always snooping around the house when Pa was out, it was fun, another game. I gave them to Percy, I didn't think there would be any harm in it.'

'What documents?'

'A marriage licence, between Ernest Bancroft and someone called Josephine, I remember thinking she must be English until I read her surname, Morobe. She was a native, an Af; what can he have been thinking of?' Her nose wrinkled in distaste.

'What was the other document?' Margaret's heart was pounding.

'A birth certificate. They named the child Grace and some

African name or other; her parents' signatures were on the certificate, Ernest and Josephine Morobe Bancroft. You should have seen Percy's face when I produced them.'

She could imagine it. Disbelief, disgust. Followed by a swift calculation.

'What did he do with them?'

'He said he would take them to his office for safekeeping; he would make enquiries, try to find the child. I even went with him once to the mission school near Pieterskloof – he had an idea the odd missionary couple there knew about her. They told us she had died of yellow fever; the mother too. Percy said we should forget all about them, they never existed. After that he travelled to Wales to visit you.'

'But the certificates are proof Grace is the legitimate heir to Thorneybrook; her parents were married. Any law court would recognise she has legal rights now.' The ache had vanished, her head was clear, there was still hope. Mary stared at her, shaking her head.

'This is South Africa, Margaret. You know natives can't inherit white property. It's unthinkable! In any case, Percy got rid of the documents; he told me so. Why should any of this matter now these people are dead?'

She read the answer in Margaret's face.

'My God, they're still alive. You know where they are, don't you?'

Margaret nodded. 'Josephine died a long time ago but Grace is with my mother at Thorneybrook and she has other documents which prove the farm belongs to her. Percy knows she's alive and he hasn't given up trying to find her and destroy any evidence of her existence. Can't you see he's been lying to you all along?'

Mary flopped down on the nearest chair and covered her face with her hands. Margaret was exhausted, beyond feeling. Convincing Mary of the truth about Flynn was a hollow triumph. The reality was that she and Grace had nothing to fight with. The original codicil was unwitnessed, invalid. She would return to Thorneybrook empty-handed.

Outside in the garden the monkeys were screeching with laughter. Mary lifted her face from her hands.

'Who would believe this, Margaret? It's like one of those old plays we read at school where the ghost turns up at the last minute and takes revenge. It serves him right – you shouldn't try to bury the past, it will always uncover itself.' Her expression hardened. 'I shouldn't have indulged him; he's abominable. I tell you, Margaret, Olive Schreiner was right, don't ever trust a man, they are full of lies, every one of them. Even the ones you think are true.'

Margaret remembered that happy embrace in the stable yard at Aviemore, the doting father and daughter. Mary's bitterness grew from other, older roots. Not all men were like Percy Flynn. She thought of Ernest Bancroft, of her own father, of patient Mr Hughes helping her find the eggs still warm under the broody hen. David's laughing, open face. And Wil, of course. In the old days she trusted Wil with her life.

'Where do you think Percy is now?' There was an urgency in Mary's tone.

'I don't know. I can't remember what happened after he…' Her voice tailed away, strangled among vines. The house was beginning to stir. She heard footsteps passing the door from the verandah, a clatter of china. Lindiwe was cleaning up last night's disorder. Mary scrambled to her feet.

'My God, I've just had a terrible thought. He's on his way to Thorneybrook, I'm sure of it. I've no idea what kind of mood he's in or what he's planning to do, but we have to get to Grace before he does.'

CHAPTER 35

'Hold the rope tighter, she'll drown if you let go!' *Y diawl*, you'd think she was a townie, brought up in Swansea not Rhydfelin. 'Come on, Nans, put your weight into it! Pull!'

There was a long sucking noise and slowly the calf emerged out of the ooze, first the head, comically festooned with weed, globs of dirt snagged on the tiny horn buds. The shoulders followed as the mud yielded to the rope's pressure; the body should come quickly now. *Dammo*, the animal was straining against the rope instead of going with it, the pebbly eyes rolling in panic.

'Keep it steady, I'm going in; see if I can lift her from behind.'

He lowered himself slowly into the torrent, in seconds the water was up to his waist. His feet prodded the river bed searching for stones to give his boots firmer traction against the current. The bottom half of the animal was still trapped in the hole where the bank used to be before the landslide ripped the roots out of it. A few yards upstream he could hear the mother moaning for her calf. If she went in too he'd have to let her swim her way out of danger. God knows she could end up miles from here, smashed by rocks, vulture food. He inched towards the calf, battling the strong undertow tugging at his legs, pulling him into the faster, deeper water. His hands made contact with the animal's bony flanks, half submerged in the mud. She had stopped struggling now. Nans was still holding fast, good girl; he could see her on the bank above him, sturdy legs braced, keeping the tension on the rope. She was soaked to the skin like him, her springy hair plastered flat against her cheeks. She caught his glance, mouthed some words against the noise of the water. He pushed his arms deeper into the mud, feeling its oily slickness running through his fingers.

Diawch erioed, this was going to be hard. His hands touched the calf's back legs, felt the long slender bones. Wrapping his arms around the animal like a wrestler, he took a deep breath and heaved upwards, his whole body straining against the resistance of mud and churning water. Two more goes and she lifted free. He held on to the animal, quieted and buoyant now in the weight of water, and they steered her upstream to the drift where the river ran shallow.

'Loosen the rope, let her find her feet.' The dainty hooves scrabbled for purchase on the stones, water streaming from her neck and sides. 'Now pull her up gently, not too fast. That's it, *da iawn* Nans. Well done'.

He thought he knew all about floods, didn't he? The Towy regularly broke its banks in spring, transforming into a vast lake brim-full of scudding clouds, broken branches, bits of houses, sometimes a bloated sheep carcass turning slowly in the current on its way to the sea. These African storms were something else. Dry as dust the land was two days ago, yesterday four inches of rain in an hour and the little Umzimyama was a raging tide of destruction. Next year they must build stronger fences, plant more willows along the banks. They couldn't afford to lose any more stock.

The calf looked a sturdy little creature now they'd cleaned the mud off and checked her over; she'd be a good milker one day. He wouldn't have gone to all that trouble for a male.

They left the calf with her mother and battled their way home through the rain, the glistering, claggy red soil sticking to their boots. Thunder rumbled ominously over the mountains. As he came into the yard Wil saw Flynn's sweat-lathered horse tied to the post; he hadn't even bothered to unsaddle the poor devil. Why was that man here again? Margaret was still in Durban, not due back until the end of the week, Mrs Lewis said. They could hear someone shouting, somewhere up by the house. Nansi threw him an anxious look, gathered her skirts up and raced away, leaving him to see to the horse. Minutes later she was back again, her voice urgent with worry. '*Brysia* Wil, hurry. Something bad's just happened.' He shut the stable door and quickly followed her to the kitchen. Across the Drakensberg came another volley of thunderclaps; the sky behind him was darkening.

Flynn was sitting at the kitchen table, ashen faced and trembling, holding his right arm over a basin. The water was full of blood. Beyond the door to the hallway Wil could hear a muffled howling like an animal in pain.

'Where's Mrs Lewis? That's not her we can hear, is it?'

Nansi, busy at the sink, shook her head. 'No it's not. Last I saw of her she was in the vegetable garden.' She glanced at Flynn with disgust. 'I'll take care of him. It's only a cut, I've seen worse. The bleeding's stopped now; I'll find a cloth to bandage his arm.' She pointed towards the hallway. 'You go and help in there.'

The cries were coming from Margaret's room. He pushed open the door. The usual mess of flung clothes, open drawers, stuff all over the floor. But he was treading on broken glass and smashed wood and there was Grace on her knees by the window, rocking herself back and forth, tears streaming down her face.

'Are you hurt?' He couldn't see any blood on her clothes, but her face was streaked with a darker stain than tears. He made a space in the debris and knelt beside her. 'Hold still, let me have a look at your head.' He tore off a piece of his shirt, dabbed at the sticky patch on her hairline, wiped away a trickle of blood. The wound wasn't deep, she might have caught the edge of something hard as she fell. The side of that wooden chest perhaps. He looked around the room, at the dreadful mess.

'I've just seen Mr Flynn in the kitchen; Nansi's dealing with his arm. What happened here, Grace?'

She wiped her cheeks with the back of her hand. 'He

deserved it. I was finishing this sketch for Fay.' He saw the crumpled piece of paper on the floor beside her. 'I didn't hear him arrive. He came rushing in, shouting I'd ruined his life, I shouldn't have been born, people like me were the worst kind of mongrel. I just laughed, he was being ridiculous.'

'What did he do then?'

'He started pulling open drawers, hunting through Margaret's clothes, throwing everything out. I don't know what he was looking for. Then he saw my paintings on the wall and… well, you can see what he did.'

Now Wil understood. The debris he'd mistaken for Margaret's discarded belongings were shreds of canvas, slashed and ripped to pieces.

'Then I got really mad; he had no right to ruin my work, those paintings were my gift to Margaret. I tried to stop him, take the knife from him. That's when he cut my head. I thought he was going to kill me.'

'So you grabbed the knife to protect yourself and it caught his arm. That's what happened isn't it?'

She gave him a blank, exhausted look. 'If you say so.'

He left her and went back into the kitchen. Flynn was still sitting at the table, his arm now bandaged with a rough piece of sheeting. Nansi was behind him at the sink washing her hands. He spoke to her in Welsh: Everything's fine, she's not badly hurt, just shaken up. See what you can do to help, I'll deal with him. She nodded and he watched her go towards the door, so wonderfully calm and practical. There was no one to touch Nans, she was the one for him.

Flynn raised his head and gave Wil a look of utter contempt.

'Do me the courtesy to speak English, Hughes. I don't understand your peasant language.'

Wil's fists were up before he could stop himself.

'That's it. Get out of here, now, before I make you regret what you said.'

278

Flynn lurched to his feet, upending the chair and sending it crashing against the stone flags. Wil saw his eyes flicker to the outer door, chancing an exit. He'd seen him off, the man looked proper scared, no need for a fight then. He felt Nansi's quiet strength beside him. She hadn't left the room after all.

'Your horse is waiting for you at the back door, Mr Flynn. Moses has fed and watered him. Even peasants know how to respect dumb animals.' Not a tremor in her voice. Well said, my girl.

The room was darkening, rain began to lash at the window panes. Flynn stood his ground, he wasn't finished yet. Wil's fists curled again. *Iesu mawr*, he'd have to punch him one after all. But then he saw that Flynn's gaze was directed beyond them. Mrs Lewis was standing in the doorway, her arm around Grace. That severe look of hers would scare the living daylights.

'This is our house, Mr Flynn, and you are trespassing. You'd better do as Mr Hughes suggests and get off the premises immediately before I send someone for the police. We want nothing more to do with you.'

Flynn opened his mouth to protest, shut it again. His bullish demeanour collapsed, the energy drained from him. Nobody would argue with Mrs Lewis when she made up her mind. Cradling the bandaged arm with his good hand, he stumbled out of the kitchen. Moments later they heard the horse give a shrill high whinny as Flynn kicked it into a gallop. The hoofbeats faded into the drumming rain.

The room was dark indeed. The wind was up, shaking the limp pallid leaves of the gum trees outside the kitchen door. A sudden flash of lightning lit up the window where Nansi was standing.

'My God, Wil, all of you, look out there. It's like the end of the world!'

CHAPTER 36

The engine was struggling, making loud hiccoughing noises like it had swallowed too much air. Margaret grabbed the side of the motor car with both hands to steady herself against the shuddering vibration. Beside her Mary was gripping the steering wheel and frowning, her features taut with the effort of willing the vehicle onwards through sheer mental force. Her tiny feet bounced on the pedals. They crossed another flooded culvert where the road was almost submerged by the flume of dirt brown water pouring from the hills.

Earlier in the day, when they stopped at Maritzburg to fill up with petrol, the garage owner warned them not to continue; everywhere the rivers were in spate, he said, even the bridge over the Tugela had gone, the worst summer storms in years. The old Zulu by the petrol pump, shaking the dead flies from his rag after cleaning the windscreen, muttered something to Mary, gesticulating at the dark clouds pluming in the west.

'He says the rivers are like angry snakes; they lie still but when the rain comes they wake up and their bodies thrash and heave and lash things to pieces.' She laughed and gave Margaret's arm a quick squeeze.

'Don't worry old thing, we'll be safe as houses in this bus. Pa knows a thing or two about motor cars even if he hasn't a clue about women!'

Margaret climbed back into the car and watched Mary crank the engine into life. She seemed more cheerful now they were away from Durban and on the open road; driving gave her something specific to focus on.

That stop at Maritzburg seemed hours ago now and she was getting anxious. Something must be wrong with the engine, despite Mary's confidence in the car. What if they broke down and had to stay the night somewhere while they had the car fixed or searched for another lift? She should have told Mother to keep Grace hidden while she was away, just in case. Flynn might be at Thorneybrook already. Suppose he'd driven up instead of riding, borrowed a motor car from that awful Brian Matthews or another of his cronies? She shuddered, reliving the rough hands on her shoulders slamming her into the earth, the cold punishing eyes, the nauseating smell of lilac.

The sky was thickening, dark rain clouds massing above and around them. She felt the first fat drops spatter her face; beads of water were already darkening her grey travelling skirt. The real storm would begin any moment – arrows of cold slicing rain followed by the full force of the deluge which drowned your sight and choked off your breath. They should halt and pull up the hood for protection. Mary was muttering under her breath, clinging like grim death to the steering wheel as they bounced over another pothole; nothing was going to make her stop. The hiccoughs turned into a long, high pitched whine as the motor car inched its way up the steep rise, the final one before the Umzimnyama drift.

They halted at the top with the engine running. Below them the valley was a grey smudge, all familiar landmarks dissolved in floodwater. Mary turned to her, should they go on? Margaret nodded agreement: they had no alternative, it was too risky to turn back now. Mary pulled on the throttle and the car started to move forward. In moments, without warning, they were sliding helplessly sideways on a road which was now a cataract, churning with sand and rubble. Mary battled to correct the skid, standing on the brake pedal and wrenching the steering wheel round, but nothing could stop the terrible downhill pitch. Margaret wiped at her rain-blinded face, searching for the white painted pole on the riverbank which marked the beginning of the ford. Was it that white blob in the distance poking out above the churning waves? But that was the middle of the river. The whole valley was the river. The noise of the water, louder even than the engine scream, pummelled her ears.

They were now slithering helplessly towards the torrent. Boulders rolled and crashed against each other, smashed gum trees swept past, their thick trunks roiling and turning like drowned bodies. Then the heavy motor car slammed into the water. For a moment it seemed to settle as the wheels found purchase on the stony bed. The car rocked gently in the current. The engine sputtered but it stayed alive.

'Come on now, that's it, nice and steady. We'll get through old girl, you can do it.'

Mary's voice was soothing; she talked to the machine like a tired old horse, coaxing it out of trouble. Margaret felt a peculiar sense of calm. How extraordinary, she wasn't afraid any more, they would just let the river sweep them along, the motor car would become a barge and she and Mary would be like the Lady of Shalott floating serenely past Camelot.

There was an enormous ear-shattering bang. The vehicle bucked and twisted and suddenly the water was everywhere, spurting through a jagged hole in the chassis under their feet. The car began to tip. Mary was calling to her. 'Get out, get out, swim for the bank!' Her eyepatch had slipped off and the bruising around the white dead eye was a livid purple. Margaret hesitated. She felt Mary grab her hand and squeeze it. Glimpsed a ghost of the old mocking smile.

'Don't worry, my friend. You're a survivor. Go!'

For a moment Margaret clung to the small cold hand. She heard herself screaming, 'You must come too, you must!' But Mary was shaking her head. The water had reached her chest and then Margaret saw why she couldn't move. The force of the current had driven Mary's seat forwards, pinning her tight against the steering wheel. The car's shattered remains began to move forward into the main current. Margaret let go of Mary's hand and clambered on top of her seat, feeling the car plunge and dip beneath her like some powerful sea creature. It was letting the river take it. Mary was completely motionless now, the water was lapping at her chin. Her eye closed. Margaret took a deep breath and jumped.

CHAPTER 37

They must be so strong, those talons, to lift you hundreds of feet like this, wing you over the treetops, drop you gently on to the soft hillside. A red kite could easily take a rabbit, but not a drowned body heavy with river water. A martial eagle then. The tips are rough, but the bird's claws feel warm and firm, slowly stroking her skin awake.

'Lift her some more, Wil. She'll breathe easier sitting up. See, her colour's better today.'

Margaret opened her eyes to feel the slide of strong hands under her shoulders, moving down to the small of her back, gently raising her up. Behind her someone was plumping the pillows; a downy feather escaped from the casing and hovered in front of her eyes in the uplift of air. She stretched out a hand and it dropped softly into her palm.

'Don't move.' The voice came from the corner of the room, near the window. She heard a pencil scratching across paper. 'That's it, you can relax now. I've finished.' She leaned back into the pillows, aware suddenly of a dull aching in her head, a sharper pain across her chest. A chair scraped on the floor, there was a rustle of skirts, Grace's long olive brown face peering gravely into hers. Her head was bound in yellow cloth, like sunshine. 'I will bring you the picture later. Nansi says you have to rest. That's correct isn't it?'

Nansi's low voice behind her, its soothing Welsh lilt. 'Yes, she needs the peace now; the doctor thinks it will be a while before she mends.'

The wings enfolded her once again. She buried her face in the bird's warm body, the smell of must and earth and wind, and it flew her back to sleep.

There was more to mend than broken ribs and a lungful of flood water. 'Time will heal', she heard Monsieur Cochet say to Mother on his way out of the sitting room where she lay on the blue sofa propped up with cushions. The fox examined her from inside his dusty case, the slanting glass eyes giving nothing away. She understood that Mary was dead. After the floodwaters receded they found pieces of the motor car washed up on the bank two miles downriver. Wil didn't tell her they'd also found the bloated body of Percy's horse lying in the mud a few yards away. Someone had hacked at the stomach to cut off the girth and remove the saddle; they'd even slashed the poor creature's mouth for the bit. There was no sign of Percy, though they'd scoured the riverbanks all the way to Jakob's Drift.

On a day in early April, when the veld grasses were beginning to turn autumnal gold, Mary's father paid a brief visit. He was thinner, greyer, bespectacled. The strong African light hurt his eyes, he said. They didn't talk about Mary, it had all been said months ago at her funeral. Aviemore was sold at last, he'd come up to make the final arrangements. The Arundel Castle was sailing at the end of the week and he was returning to Scotland for good.

'Who has bought your farm?' Mother asked.

He waved a weary, dismissive hand. 'Oh, that lawyer friend of Mary's, Percival Flynn; you might remember him, Margaret, he used to stay with us from time to time. Queer sort of a chap, don't know what she saw in him, too full of himself for my liking. Never looked you quite in the eye. Someone told me he's been made senior partner now that Harding's decided to retire; he'll be earning a packet no doubt. Deals in property on the side apparently. He's hired a manager for the place, they're planning to turn it into a golf resort. In ten years' time you won't recognise the old farm, it'll be swarming with rich Jews from Jo'burg.'

Margaret caught her mother's eye and winced.

Grace entered the room as he was taking his leave. She brushed past him, flopped into the chair beside Margaret and lit a cigarette. Jamieson raised his eyebrows, looked enquiringly at Mother.

'Grace Morobe – a relative of my late husband.' She held out her hand and gave him one of those polite, dismissive smiles she'd perfected in Bryntowy days. 'So kind of you to call, Mr Jamieson. Do give my love to bonny Scotland; I haven't been there for a long time.'

Time. There was too much of it, that was the problem. Her ribs had mended but the cough persisted and made her retch, her mouth tasted of mud and dank river water. The headache was still there too, just behind her left eye, troubling her dreams. She took to lying in the sitting room most days with the shutters drawn against the light and a small fire burning in the grate. Whatever happened outside seemed to matter less and less; it was an effort to think about the farm. Wil would appear with a bill for her to sign or to ask her opinion about some new idea he wanted to try out. She watched him searching for some topic to engage her interest: Sipho came top of the class in English, he wanted you to know; they brought the last of the harvest in yesterday; Nansi's been making plum jam. She tried to listen but his words wouldn't stick, they floated away like gossamer. She was dimly aware of him getting up from the chair and quietly stealing away for fear of waking her.

Autumn dragged itself into winter.

Someone was tapping on the window. She closed her book, pushed the rug aside and went to open the shutters. Winter sunshine dazzled her eyes at first, but then she saw Wil standing outside with Petra and the trap.

'Put something warm on, we're going for a drive.'

Reluctantly she dragged herself away from the fire into the chill hallway to find her overcoat and hat.

They drove towards the Berg, well beyond the farm boundary, and crossed the Umzimnyama, reduced to a safe winter trickle once more. The smoke from several firebreaks drifted in a brown pall across the hillsides and the air was scented with burning *rooigras* and the dry red soil of the high veld. The peaks of the Drakensberg closed in around them. Today, their remote indifference suited her mood.

Wil halted Petra on the brow of a hill from where they could just make out the farm buildings below them through the smoke haze. They left the trap and walked a little way into the veld to a small rocky outcrop. Here they sat for a while, contemplating the view.

It had been Nansi's suggestion to bring her to this place.

'Best you take her on your own, *cariad*, away from the farm, just the two of you. That way you can talk like you used to at Bryntowy. She'll be understanding you better.' She had kissed him then, the sweet-salty taste of her.

He picked up a stone from a hollow in the rock and flung it. They heard it thud into the grass beside a rusted jerrycan someone had abandoned on the side of the road.

'Do you remember those competitions we used to have, who could hit the chimney pot on Bessie Jones's roof? You kept the score in that little notebook you always carried in your pocket. You used to tie it up with baler twine to stop the pages falling out.'

She was frowning, hugging her knees against the cold. He tried again.

'And that day Bessie rushed out of the house with her stick and we had to scarper into the woods?' She wasn't biting, probably didn't remember silly occasions like that anymore. Better to come out with it straight.

'I've been offered a job, manager of a big dairy farm in the Transvaal. It's a good opportunity for us to settle somewhere, put down roots.'

She turned then and looked directly at him. Grey serious eyes, so large now in that thin pale face.

'Us? You and me?'

He used to love that catch in her voice when she was excited, it always made him feel everything was possible. His heart lurched for pity – this time she had the wrong end of the stick. He would have to spell it out.

'No, Margaret,' he said gently. 'I was talking about Nansi and me. We're thinking of getting married. You won't mind will you, if we move on?'

There, he'd said it. No going back now. He ventured a glance at her face, trying to read the expression. The old Margaret would have laughed at him or thrown something at him, he never had to guess her reactions. This new silence of hers was unnerving. He watched her get stiffly to her feet and pull the old coat tightly around her. She put a hand up to her mouth to stifle a cough and stood for a moment, gazing into the distance, down to the grove of pine trees surrounding Thorneybrook. Then she bent down and picked up a stone, weighed it for a moment in her palm. Leaning back, she flung it, sure as an arrow. It struck the can with such force that the thing spun round and keeled over into the road. She turned and looked down at him, a faint, wry smile on her lips.

'You forgot, Wil Hughes, my score was always the highest.'

From now on then, there would be only the three of them – herself, Mother and Grace. She pondered this bleak fact as Wil drove them back to the farm, a secret look of contentment stealing over his face when he thought she wasn't looking. She saw it all now. How foolish she'd been to think the two of them would continue their lives at Thorneybrook as if nothing had changed. They weren't children any more. She should have understood a long time ago that his future was with Nansi, not her.

They turned in at the farm gate and drove up to the house. Wil helped her out of the trap and she held on to his arm a moment longer. 'I'm glad you told me; you'll make a good future here, the two of you, much better than if you'd stayed in Wales, I'm sure of it.' Her eyes were blurry and she turned her head away, embarrassed. Wil patted her hand, smiled his old lop-sided smile, and said nothing. It was better like that.

CHAPTER 38

The decisions formed slowly, as the days passed. With Wil and Nansi gone, she owed it to Grace to stay on; they couldn't prove Thorneybrook was hers but there was nothing to stop them living here and farming the land together. They would simply ignore the grumblings of the white farmers and the pinched-faced gossipy women in the town. Moses would take over from Wil as farm manager and Precious would take Nansi's place; she'd like that. They would prevail. Despite all that had happened, she was making plans again and it felt good. She would not let herself think about the new owner of Aviemore – Percival Flynn had no claim on her now.

The three of them were in the sitting room one Sunday afternoon. Margaret was lying on the sofa in a half doze, Mother was in her chair knitting something large and shapeless to keep out the cold. She'd grown thinner of late, she tired more easily – just old age, she said, unconvincingly. Grace was sitting on the floor in her usual place, leaning against Mother's chair as close to the fire as she could get – this house is so cold, Fay, too many chilly spirits hovering about the place. She had taken off her scarf and the firelight gilded her braided head, a golden-brown aureole of flame.

Margaret leaned over and scooped up the pages of the letter which had slipped from her lap as she slept. The monthly missive from Elen Roberts full of the comings and goings at Rhydfelin, a list of the recent books she'd enjoyed. Margaret hardly read anything these days; her appetite for books, like so much else, had diminished since the accident. Miss Roberts had attached a newspaper cutting to the last page of the letter:

a grainy photograph of a large woman in a feathered hat standing in front of a suffragist banner. Underneath she had written, 'Another Margaret to inspire you. Went to hear Lady Rhondda address a women's march in Swansea last month. Came away feeling quite fired up and wishing you had been there to hear her.'

Mary would have liked Elen Roberts, she thought wearily, closing her eyes again. She listened to the crackle of logs in the grate, the familiar creakings as the house stretched its dry timbers, Grace sighing as she turned another page of her book. Wales was a lifetime ago.

'Margaret, stop this sleeping. You too, Fay, put down your knitting and listen to this poem.

> *'Could I but ride indefinite*
> *As doth the Meadow Bee*
> *And visit only where I liked*
> *And No one visit me'*

Grace's voice was lovely, bringing richness and depth to the simple rhythms and imagery. Margaret felt a sharp tap on her leg. 'I said wake up, this is important.'

With an effort Margaret raised herself to a sitting position. Mother's needles were stilled, the woollen garment heaped on her lap. She, too, was listening to Grace, now standing with her back to the hearth, holding the book in front of her a little theatrically, like an actor at a poetry reading. The yellow beading on her long green skirt glittered in the firelight.

> *'And flirt all Day with Buttercups*
> *And marry whom I may*
> *And dwell a little everywhere*
> *Or better, run away!'*

Grace stopped reading and regarded the two of them solemnly.

'Emily Dickinson is right, you know. I must run away, like the bee. I don't want to live like this, not being able to choose where I go, what I do. I don't like this old house; it's full of things that belong to your world, there's nothing of me here. It was always your dream, Margaret, not mine, that we should be together in Thorneybrook, but do you see, I am like a prisoner here. My father's dream was also wrong, there will be no freedom in this country for people like me. One day the Boers will come and throw me off the farm and you won't be able to stop them.'

Margaret felt her heart contract. All the plans she'd been making made no sense without Grace. Her words had collapsed them in a moment, exposed them for what they were: ignorant dreams, made in the dark. The room was heavy with disappointment.

'None of us can be entirely sure about our future.' Mother shifted in her chair and regarded Margaret. 'I made a promise to your father before he died, that I'd honour his wish for us to move to Thorneybrook, knowing that your first thought would be to sell the place and go back to Wales. That's why I was so ready to go along with Percival Flynn, even though I had an inkling he might have another motive for persuading you to keep the farm. I was immensely relieved when you came back to Durban after you'd broken your arm and said you'd decided to stay on. And we have made a go of the place, haven't we? We can feel proud of our efforts. I had no idea the two of us could work so hard! More importantly, we've honoured Grace and that was your doing, not mine. I'm ashamed of the way I used to think. However, Grace is probably correct, we were both foolish to imagine she could ever truly own Thorneybrook.'

She glanced about her at the shadowy room, the lumpy old furniture, the mothy fox. Mementoes of a different country, another era. 'The truth is I'm tired, Margaret. I want to go home. We don't belong out here.'

She gathered up her knitting, stowed it away in the old carpet bag beside her chair, and got stiffly to her feet. Her breath exhaled in soft puffy gasps. She looked over at Grace, who was stooping to put another log on the fire.

'Of course you must go away, my dear. This country is too small for someone like you, you need to stretch your wings and fly. I will miss you, though; there'll be nobody to tell me what a terrible painter I am.'

Grace looked up and shook her head. 'That is nonsense, Fay. You have some talent but your life has been too comfortable; you have to suffer a little. That's why you'll never be a real artist.'

Mother was smiling. Grace's bluntness, they would miss that too, perhaps.

'Where will you go when you leave South Africa?'

'To Paris, of course. Where else would I live?'

The Towy Valley,
Carmarthenshire
Spring 1924

Chapter 39

A scatter of loose stones, fingers straining to catch hold of the slippery grass, everywhere the smell of wet earth. Right foot sliding, jab into the soil with the left, that's the way, find a foothold. See that yellow gorse bush over to the right, make a grab for the bottom branch, watch out for the prickles. Got it. Now pull up, pull up. The lovely buttery scent of crushed gorseflower. And there's the sheep track, remember how it winds to the left below the battlements. Nearly there. Must have been all that rain, months of it they said in the post office, half the path washed away.

She brushed aside a heap of old curranty sheep droppings and settled herself in the shallow dip below the castle wall, her back propped against the weathered stone, sheltered from the mild spring breeze. This was always the best place to see things clearly. Their favourite view, hers and Wil's, when they were children. Where they used to play the siege game.

'Imagine you were on sentry duty and you looked down and saw 11,000 English soldiers camped by the river, and they were setting up one of those massive catapult things, you know to hurl the stones at the walls.'

'Trebuchets.'

'Trust you to remember the proper name. What's the first thing you'd do?'

'Sound the alarm, wake everyone up.'

'Nope.'

'Pour a pitcher of boiling oil over them.'

'Nope, wouldn't work.'

'Start shooting them with poisoned arrows. The Welsh were the best bowmen.'

'That's in the jungle, not here.'

'I give up. What's the answer, clever stick?'

'Run, of course. Fast as you can. No point being on the losing side, is there? Leave everything behind you, just save yourself.'

In the end they had left everything they brought out with them. Mother wanted to be free of all the old Bryntowy stuff, none of it would fit where she was going. Mr Du Toit, the new owner of Thorneybrook, was happy to buy the lot; he'd taken a particular liking to the stuffed fox. Moses and Tryphena would be staying on – they were good workers, he said; the place had been well managed.

The sale of Thorneybrook provided more money than they had expected – enough to settle their debts, pay for the passage home, enough even to begin a new life. Before they left for Durban to board the Union-Castle liner, Margaret took the diary, Not Semolina, and *The Story of an African Farm* and buried them in a corner of the kitchen garden beneath one of Mother's apple trees. The two tail feathers were already in her suitcase, carefully wrapped together in tissue paper. Going with her, for luck.

She took the envelope out of her pocket and opened it. A little draught of air lifted the flimsy sheet of paper in her hand. It was only a short letter, written in a hurry, the words jostling each other on the page.

Chère Margaret,

Comment ça va? Bien, j'espère. You see I am French now, Madeleine Cochet would be pleased. Precious is also learning French, the family she works for are paying for her lessons. She is happy to be here with me I suppose, she tells me Josephine would like this city.

Paris is like the melting pot of the world! So many wonderful painters, film makers, poets, theatre people. Have you heard of Josephine Baker, 'La Revue Nègre'? She is all the rage, they love black people here.

I share a studio in Montparnasse with other artists – the building looks like a beehive, but we live like rats not bees, nobody has money. We talk about art all day and I am learning so much. Next month I am showing one of my paintings at the Salon des Indépendants, my new friend Germaine says this could be important for me.

Tell Fay I no longer paint in the same way as before, I am now a 'surréaliste'. She will appreciate this, I think she understands that art must be always changing. Hélas, no more delicate birds and flowers. You, my sister, would not like my paintings at all!

You must visit me in Paris, I will show you around the city. But maybe I will move to New York soon. Give your mother une grande baisse from me! I miss you sometimes.

Zenzile

Margaret put the letter away. She would readdress it to the nursing home in Bournemouth, something else to make Mother smile. She was happier these days; the drier climate of the south coast was better for her heart than this patch of damp west Wales and Aunt Rose's house was just around the corner. Grace's little sketch of Margaret which they had repaired now hung next to the portrait of David where she could see them from her chair. The photograph of Father in uniform stood on the bedside table, jostling for space with her art books. She seemed content.

Something white was fluttering near the gate at the bottom of the hill. Elen's scarf, reminding her. She'd lost all track of time, they would be late for the meeting with the architect and the man from the county council. The plans for the new library and the school extension were waiting in the car; after the meeting they were catching the train to Cardiff where Elen was addressing a meeting of the National Union of Women Teachers. Her voice floated up the hillside, '*Dere,* Margaret, come on. You haven't time to be dithering about up there, we've got work to do!' No mistaking a teacher's call to duty.

Rough, rasping sounds, like an old man clearing his throat. Halfway down the hill, Margaret halted and looked up, shielding her eyes from the watery sunlight. A pair of ravens, nesting on the last fragment of the fortress, shored against collapse by concrete and iron staves screwed into the stones. She watched them for a moment, flying in graceful circles, catching the updraft. Over the castle, across the Towy's ancient meanders, always in sight of each other. Together, apart, at ease in this bountiful spring.

~

Born in St David's, Pembrokeshire, and raised in Laugharne, Carmarthenshire, Siân has lived much of her life outside Wales. An Edinburgh graduate, she taught Anglo Saxon and Medieval Literature to university students in South Africa, worked as an assistant editor on The Lancet, and ran English and Drama departments in several well-known London secondary schools. She returned to Carmarthenshire ten years ago to teach, write and relish life in the beautiful Tywi valley. 'Unleaving' is her first novel.